THE STAR OF WHATEVER

A Humorous Fantasy Novel

THE WESTERN LANDS AND ALL THAT REALLY MATTERS

BOOK II

ANDREW EINSPRUCH

Cover design by Maria Spada of Maria Spada Design.

Editing by Vanessa of Red Dot Scribble.

Proofreading by Abigail of Bothersome Words.

Layout by Andrew Einspruch of Wild Pure Heart.

ISBN: 978-0-980627-23-7

DEDICATION

To Billie and Tamsin

Everything of greatest value that I've learned, I've learned from you.

A LOT FOR SOMEONE WHO
IS DEAD

Princess Eloise Hydra Gumball III, Future Ruler and Heir to the Western Lands and All That Really Matters, sprinted into the Purple Haze, becoming the first person ever to go in twice.

As the deadly fog swallowed her whole, filling her head with buzzing, the rest of the world ceased to exist.

Eloise opened her eyes and saw lavender mist everywhere. She could recall running into the Purple Haze and up a hillock of skeletal remains. She also remembered being airborne after a sudden fall off a precipice, landing scarily far below on a pile of bones, which hurt like Çalaht's ingrown toenails when she smacked into them, but shifted enough to keep her fall from being fatal.

The next thing Eloise noticed in the Purple Haze was the dead body of her fraternal twin sister, Johanna Umgotteswillen Gumball. Except it seemed to be breathing rather a lot for someone who was dead.

Eloise clambered across the piled skulls, femurs, vertebrae and disjointed fingers to get to her sister. "Jo! Jo!" She turned her sister over, the bones beneath her clattering and scraping with the movement. "Jo, can you hear me?"

"El?" Johanna reached up and touched her head, groggy. "My head hurts."

"You probably landed badly."

Johanna sat up. Then she saw what she was sitting on and scrambled to get off them. "What is this?"

"This is the inside of the Purple Haze. And that's what happens here."

Johanna recoiled at the sight of the bones. "Why?"

"I don't know."

"We've got to get out of here, El. Which way is out?"

"I fell, so I'm not quite sure yet. But I think 'out' involves a lot of 'up.'"

"That buzzing! Do you hear a buzzing?" Johanna slumped to her knees and pressed her hands to the sides of her head.

"Yes. I hear it."

"It's awful. Just awful," said Johanna. "I'd rather listen to you sing than hear that buzz."

So, her sense of humor was still there. That was a good sign.

The two of them sat for a few minutes, looking around, taking in what they could see through the fog.

"I think there's a pretty obvious question we should be asking," said Eloise.

"Like, how are we going to get out of here?"

"More basic."

Johanna reached over and laced her fingers through Eloise's. "Why aren't we dead?"

Eloise nodded.

They sat for a long time, Johanna recovering from being fogged and Eloise from the exertion of saving Gouache, and thinking about that very question.

❧ 2 ❧

DISAPPEARED

everal hours earlier...)

(S Hector de Pferd and his fellow horse, the Nameless One, found a comfortable spot off to the side of the main square of Castle Blotch at Stained Rock, the seat of the Half Kingdom. From there, they could watch the comings and goings. Hector positioned himself so he could see the main castle door, while the Nameless One found a spot where he could observe the activity through the servants' entrance.

Hector expected that he would have a lot of time to think about the many holes in their plan. Horse Guards (like him), and horses in general, get used to waiting. People didn't understand how good they had to be at it. They waited all the time—for parades to start, for business to conclude, for carts to be unloaded, for the purveyors of war to be organized and dispatched. Waiting became second nature, and a horse either got drowsy with it or, if they were smart, they got sharp with it and used it as a chance to learn something. Horses could fade into the background; people often forgot they were there. Sometimes that meant they heard things that were supposed to be private. That was why all Horse Guards and Guard Horses received spycraft training.

Their plan, such as it was, was a disaster waiting to unravel. The likelihood that Princess Johanna would consent to putting the downer down in her mouth was minuscule. The chances of her keeping the vile-tasting stuff in her mouth were even smaller, even if she was, as Eloise described it, "prattled to the gills" (a turn of phrase that fish found offensive). They were hoping to get Johanna *compos mentis* enough to realize that marrying her uncle was a spectacularly bad idea, but there were too many unknowns, and way too many things that could go wrong.

However, it was the only plan they had, so Hector and the Nameless One watched Princess Eloise, her champion, Jerome Abernatheen de Chipmunk, and the guard, Lorch Lacksneck, enter the castle to attend an audience with King Doncaster. Then he and the Nameless One found their spots and began their wait.

Activity at the castle seemed normal enough. There were no unexpected sounds from within, and traffic outside was as expected, and so it remained as shadows crept across the courtyard.

In the early afternoon, the door opened and Princess Eloise and Princess Johanna stepped through it, looking like they were going for a walk. Something wasn't right. They were arm-in-arm and laughing, which Hector had not seen them do for years. That made him suspicious, especially given that Jerome and Lorch were not with them.

A few moments later, the two jesters, the scheming Turpentine Snotearrow McCcoonnch and his younger brother, the massive but two-bulbs-short-of-a-tulip-bed Gouache, burst through the door after the girls. They followed, but did not try to catch them. Hector signaled to the Nameless One, and after a sufficient pause, the horses, too, began shadowing the group.

Eloise and Johanna looked tense, and their manner of conversation appeared strained beneath a veneer of joviality. Not too far from the castle, they stopped, consulted, and ran up the nearby Fogging Hill. Why would they go to the place where executions took place? And why try to make it look like a game? Turpy and Gouache watched them ascending and then split up, reaching the top of the hill from opposite sides. Hector and the Nameless One did the same but, given their unwillingness to be seen and how open the exposed hillsides were, they had to let the jesters get a long way ahead of them.

It was a fatal mistake.

Hector lost sight of the sisters as they crested the hill, and then also lost sight of the jesters. Cautiously, he moved upwards.

Then Johanna screamed.

Her screams echoed down the hill. Hector abandoned all caution and galloped as hard as he could. But by the time he got to the top, the two princesses were gone, and so was Gouache. Only Turpy remained, screeching like he'd been stabbed, pounding his head with one fist and clutching the other to his guts in obvious pain as he stumbled his way back down the hill. Hector ran over to where the Nameless One was coming up the other side and asked if he'd seen the princesses.

No.

They charged back to Turpy. "Where are they?" Hector yelled. "Tell me! Where are they?" But Turpy was useless, lost to the mental fragments that rattled in his head. The look in his eyes was deeply disturbing; Hector did not like to guess what might be happening in there.

The two horses scoured the area looking for any sign of the missing princesses, looking for some place they might have hidden—any explanation that did not involve that damned Purple Haze.

And then from 100 lengths away, Hector saw her. Eloise was rolling Gouache out of the fog. From where Hector stood, the big jester looked dead, but—impossibly—Eloise was very much alive. "Princess! Princess Eloise!" he called.

She should have been close enough to hear him, but she gave no sign.

And then she did something monstrous. Eloise turned and rushed back into the Purple Haze.

"No!" Hector yelled. He galloped after her, but slid to a stop at the fog's edge, scared to follow. He took a breath and steadied himself. If she could survive the fog, so could he. Swallowing his fear, he stepped into the shroud of mist.

As soon as his front legs crossed into it, a buzzing sound filled his ears and his legs twitched, then flailed. He went mind-numb and fell hard on his side as he collapsed into an apoplectic attack. The seizures took hold, and did not let go.

ACROSS THE SLOPE OF THE HILL, THE NAMELESS ONE SAW HECTOR'S back legs poking out from the fog, thrashing wildly. He dashed over, unsure what he should do. Why had Hector poked himself into the fog? Had he fallen in? Been lured? Seen something?

And why was Gouache lying face-up, slack-jawed, and mind-numb a dozen lengths away?

Each thrash slid Hector a little further downhill and into the Purple Haze. There was only one thing to do. Silently apologizing to Hector for the pain this would cause, the Nameless One clamped his teeth onto Hector's tailhead, braced himself, and tried to drag him out.

At first he only managed to stop Hector's downward progress. As the thrashing continued, the Nameless One strained against the other horse's weight and, using the movement of the palsy, waggled Hector up the incline. It was slow and difficult. Given how long the seizures were lasting, the Nameless One wondered how much permanent damage there would be, and how much injury he was causing Hector's tail. One might as well be dragged by the nose—it would've been about as comfortable.

Eventually, the Nameless One got Hector completely clear of the fog, and almost immediately the frantic movements stopped. The horse's breathing remained rapid, however, and sweat covered his body. The Nameless One had seen people fall in battle before, and he had a cousin who was prone to apoplectic fits. But this was unlike anything he'd ever encountered. He was unsure whether to run off and find a healer, or stay and hope Hector got better. He chose the latter, figuring that a healer was unlikely to have any useful tools that would help in this situation.

The Nameless One waited, feeling the minutes drag by. Unlike the mind-numb jester, after a quarter of an hour, Hector blinked and came back to consciousness. *Thank Çalaht*, thought the Nameless One.

"What..." slurred Hector.

"Shush," whispered the Nameless One in a gentle tone. It was the first time Hector had ever heard him speak. He didn't know the horse had a voice.

"Was... Was I dying?"

The Nameless One gave a noncommittal shrug, his silence resumed.

After another ten minutes, the Nameless One encouraged Hector to stand. Hector was woozy, but managed to walk back to the castle with the Nameless One to raise the alarm about Gouache. They accompanied half a dozen castle guards and a cart back to Fogging Hill, where the inert, but still breathing, jester's body lay. It took four men and two women to heave the man onto the cart's floor.

The Nameless One and Hector watched the guards leave. As soon as they were out of earshot, Hector said, "I saw the Princess. She... She pushed the jester out of the fog." He whispered, despite them being alone on Fogging Hill.

The Nameless One looked at him, slowly shaking his head in disbelief.

"I know. It's impossible. But I saw what I saw."

The Nameless One glanced left and right—a quick "Where is she?" look.

Hector blinked back tears. "She ran back into the Çalaht-cursed fog. Back into it! I called for her, but she did not hear me."

The Nameless One tilted his head, waiting for an explanation.

"I don't know. It made no sense. But the mist swallowed her right over there. That's why I tried to..." Hector shivered at the memory of collapsing into the mist.

So that was why the Nameless One had found Hector with legs thrashing. He nodded, indicating that he understood, then moved so they stood shoulder. He leaned gently into Hector.

Hector's tears finally broke through. "We lost her," he cried. "Our princess is gone and it is our fault. Somehow, it just is."

The Nameless One took two steps back, stamped the ground, and stared at Hector, hard.

"What?" Hector sniffed.

The Nameless One just stood there holding Hector's eye, unblinking.

Hector was the one who broke eye contact. "OK, OK, I get it. You're right." He drew a deep breath, and let it whoosh out. Hector squared his shoulders. "Right. So, what do we do next?"

The Nameless One pointed to Hector with his chin and mimed eyes closing in sleep.

"You're right. I need to sleep." Hector's head hung, his eyes drooped, and his limbs shook like he'd run a dozen strong lengths. The Nameless One wondered if he was about to cock a back leg and doze off right there. "But given everything that has happened," said Hector, "I don't think we should go back to the Rusted and Runcible. I think we need to be less conspicuous."

The Nameless One nodded in agreement, then indicated that Hector should follow him.

"Where are we going?" asked Hector. "Actually, it doesn't matter. I just hope wherever it is, it has a bed of straw."

3

WHOEVER DID THIS

There was no question the Purple Haze was strange. There was the buzz, for one thing. For another, the mist was not damp, the way one would expect fog to be. When Eloise touched her skin or the bones they sat on, they were dry. Dry to the point of dust. How could there be a dry fog?

The fog also seemed to have a non-specific light source. There was no obvious single point where the sun might be. The fog seemed to create its own light while shrouding the natural light outside it.

And there was something else. Eloise had trouble putting words to it. Her first thought was that something was "calling" to her. But that wasn't quite right. It was more a tugging at her insides. "Beckoning" might have been the way to describe it. But this was soft, like the entreaty of a shadow cast far away. She had to focus to feel it, but it was definitely there.

Eventually, Johanna stood up, brushing dust off her dress. "Come on, El. Let's get out of here."

Eloise didn't move. She was still thinking things through.

"El? Really? This place is horrible."

"Yes, it is." Still, she didn't stand up.

"What's the matter?"

"I'm thinking something I don't want to think, but I have to."

Johanna sat back down. "I know that expression. Whatever it is you're thinking, stop it right now. I mean it. I've seen that look too many times, and no good ever comes of it."

Eloise stared her sister straight in the eyes. "Do you have an answer?"

"An answer to what?"

She pointed at the pile of bones she was sitting on. "Why we don't look like that."

"No, I don't. And frankly, I don't think I want to know."

"There has to be a reason."

"I guess," said Johanna. "Here's what I do know. I hate it here, and the sooner we get out of here, the better. It might take a while to find our way out, so we should get started." Johanna stood and offered Eloise a hand to help her up. Eloise ignored it.

"Whoever created this fog, it was a crime."

"You don't know that."

"Yes, I do."

"You can't possibly know. It's been over two centuries. It could have been anything. It could have been an accident."

"Look around, Jo. Does this look like an accident to you?"

"It could have been."

"Maybe something went wrong. Maybe what happened wasn't what was supposed to happen. But this…" Eloise pointed at the fog, then at the bones everywhere. "This was deliberate. And there's only one explanation that makes any sense." Eloise blinked back tears. She didn't think of herself as a crier. In fact, she was usually the exact opposite. But she had cried more times on this trip than she had in years—probably since she was a toddler.

"Go ahead, El. What makes sense?"

"It's our fault."

There. She'd said it.

"What? That's not right. How could it be our fault?"

"Not you and me. But it was one of us. It was our family."

"Oh. Oh, no." Johanna started sifting the pieces of the puzzle to form the same shape that had formed in Eloise's mind. She sat down again. "You can't use magic against blood."

"Yes."

"So one of our direct blood ancestors..."

"Exactly," said Eloise. "On our mother's side."

"How do you reckon that?"

"Because if it was on our father's side, more people would have been unaffected by the Purple Haze. The de Chëëëkflïïïnt bloodline is all over the Half Kingdom, both with legitimate issue and presumably illicit offspring as well. You can tell from the amount of bones here that there have been a lot of foggings. Surely some of them would be directly related up the line to Father's family. If it had been his side that cast this magic, someone would have walked out of here a long time ago, and everyone would have known more about what the fog was all about. There would have been people sent in to explore it."

"Maybe it kills them—kills us—but more slowly. Maybe they still don't make it out of here."

"Possible," said Eloise. "What I'm thinking isn't without holes."

Johanna picked up the previous thread of logic. "Mother was the first Gumball to marry someone from the Half Kingdom since before it was the Half Kingdom. Since before the fog. So we're almost certainly the first direct blood descendants of whoever created this to have come in here."

They sat there pondering, trying to remember history lessons they'd endured a decade ago. Then at the exact same moment, they said the exact same three words: "Gwendolyn the Irritable."

"She was queen—" started Eloise.

"—when the Purple Haze first appeared," Johanna finished. "And she hated what's-his-face..."

"I don't remember his name either, but you're right, she hated the Northern Lands king. Brüüünööö somebody? Brüüücëëë? It was Brüüü-something."

"Brüüütus Ulcer Tabific Twizzle de Chëëëkflïïïnt," said Johanna, pronouncing the name with an affected rural northern accent.

"How can you possibly remember that?" Eloise grinned.

"Because the initials of his first names formed a word that a bored six-year-old in Histories and Hearsay found amusing." Johanna giggled at the memory.

"I never saw that. Why didn't you tell me?" Eloise nudged her sister with her elbow. "Back then you told me everything."

"Back then I didn't need to tell you everything. You already knew it."

The moment of lightness passed. "You're right. I did," said Eloise. "And so did you."

"Now look at us," said Johanna. "Sitting on a mountain of bones, practically strangers. What happened to us?"

"Life, Court, the Thorning Ceremony, Mother—take your pick. Life happened, I guess."

"I guess."

Another silence fell between them. Eloise took comfort in Johanna's nearness. She even put an arm around Johanna's shoulder and pulled her into a hug. They sat that way for a long time.

"I can't believe I was less than a day away from marrying Uncle Doncaster." Johanna shuddered. "Thank you for coming after me. It must have been hard for you."

"You have no idea," said Eloise.

Finally, it was Eloise who stood. Johanna looked at her. "You've got that look on your face again. Stop it. I really mean it."

"I have to get going."

"Right. Any idea which way is out?"

"I'm not going out."

"I knew you'd say that." Johanna stood as well.

"I have to—"

"I know, I know. You have to go find whatever this is and stop it."

Eloise shrugged. "It was one of us who did it. If anyone can put an end to it, it will be another one of us. I've seen a fogging. For that matter, I've seen *you* fogged. I promised myself I would figure out a way to end it. I'm going to try to keep that promise." Eloise squeezed her sister's arm affectionately. "I'm not asking you to come with me."

"No, you're not." Johanna sighed. "That's not how you work. The last thing I want to do is traipse all over this Çalaht-forsaken hellscape looking for who-knows-what, which, by the way, is clearly lethal. But then, I can imagine that's also the last thing you feel like doing. Plus, you just saved me from a disastrous marriage, so I owe you one."

"No, you don't. You don't owe me anything."

Johanna shrugged that off. "Got any clues which way we should go?"

"Actually, I do. I'm guessing you do, too." Eloise pointed. "That way."

❧ 4 ❧

EIGHT-HOUR CANDLES

Jerome and Lorch had been left waiting in the cold, stuffy room without the benefit of furniture, food, a window to look out of, or any idea what was going on. The two eight-hour candles lighting the stone-walled chamber provided the only indication of how much time was passing, and watching them burn was their only entertainment.

As the candle burned lower, Jerome took to fidgeting, then pacing, then fidgeting while pacing, then pacing and fidgeting faster, and finally pacing backwards as well as forwards while fidgeting with both his claws and his tail.

Halfway through the eight-hour candles, Lorch tried the door, but of course it was locked from the outside.

Lorch had spent the first couple of hours standing at parade rest, still and calm, which only made Jerome more aware of his own twitchy nervousness. As the hours stretched, Lorch finally allowed himself to lean against one of the walls, and eventually he sat. Now and then, he sprang up, thinking he had heard someone coming. And maybe he had, but it had nothing to do with him or Jerome.

As the candle burned below the one hour mark, Jerome started feeling claustrophobic. His breathing quickened and sweat gathered on his fur. He went to the door and called, "Hello! Is anyone out there?" Jerome thought he might have heard a sneeze in response, but it might just have been his imagination. He looked at Lorch. "How long are we supposed to stay in here?"

"I guess until Princess Eloise is done, one way or the other."

Sometime later, the two candles spluttered out at almost exactly the same moment. The darkness didn't help Jerome's state of mind. "Do you think there are jail chiggers in here? I don't think I could take jail chiggers again."

Jerome, Lorch and Eloise had all encountered jail chiggers while sitting in the Southie jail, where they'd been held for a painful period after being arrested in the Sclerotic Wold. The chiggers were used by the authorities for "enhanced discomfort"—mocking, ridiculing, and haranguing inmates, as well as causing awful, mercilessly itchy welts. It had been maddening.

"We are not in jail," said Lorch.

"No, not yet," said Jerome.

"And there are no jail chiggers in here."

"Are you sure? I swear I can hear whispering."

"No one here but us chickens," joked Lorch.

"You know chickens hate that phrase, right?"

"I know. I was just trying to amuse you."

"Do I need to be amused? Yes, I suppose I do." Jerome wiped the sweat dripping off his forehead onto the sleeve of his champion's tunic.

The door handle rattled. "Oh, thank Çalaht," said Jerome. He stood and straightened his clothing, ready leave the room. He heard Lorch rustling to do the same.

The hall was as dark as night, and lit by candles in sconces that were evenly spaced along the hall. Through the open door, 15 guards entered the room, swords drawn. There were 20 pikemen behind them, their spears pointing directly at Lorch and Jerome's chests.

A uniformed badger stepped through the arc of weaponry. "You two," he snarled. "I'm placing you under arrest."

"You can't arrest us," said Jerome. "We're with Princess Eloise."

"It would appear I can."

"On what charges? We've done nothing wrong. We've just sat here. For far too long, I might add. And without tea."

The badger tilted his head and stroked his chin. "How about, 'Entering a royal building with untoward intent'? That sounds plausible enough."

"That's ridiculous."

The badger walked around Jerome, then pointed to the two closest guards. "Search them."

"Certainly not!" said Jerome.

"Champion Abernatheen de Chipmunk, I suggest you submit," said Lorch. "We don't have a lot of options."

"See, one of you has some sense."

One guard searched Lorch, while the other tried to pat down Jerome, who giggled and flinched. "Sorry. Ticklish." The guard tried again, and finally had to hold Jerome down with one hand while frisking him with the other. Among the personal items Jerome was carrying, he found a small, embroidered, felt-lined pouch. The guard handed this to the badger. "Hey, that's mine," said Jerome. "It was a gift."

The badger ignored him and examined the pouch. He sniffed it, opened it, sniffed it again, and held it closer to a light. Suddenly he laughed, a genuine, deep, belly laugh. "Oh, my goodness. What were you thinking?"

"What? Thinking what?"

"There's got to be, what, an eighth of a weight, maybe a tenth of a weight, of prattleweed here."

"So what? It was a gift from the Southie envoy at my Champion's Naming."

"I don't care if our good King Doncaster himself gave it to you. Possession of this much proscribed herbage is all I need." He turned to Lorch. "And you, good sir, are an accessory."

Lorch did not reply.

"Now, come. I have different accommodation for you two. Follow." The badger turned and headed out the doorway.

They followed.

Jerome, desperate to ignore the rising panic he was feeling, chattered questions and demanded to see Eloise, but neither the badger nor the soldiers paid him any mind. Fifteen minutes and three flights of downward stairs later, Jerome and Lorch were ushered into separate cells in the dungeons. Behind them, impenetrable, iron-reinforced doors clanged shut, leaving them in darkness again.

❦ 5 ❦

SPEAKER FOR THE INDIGENT

Hector and the Nameless One stood at the castle gates, laden with bundles of burlap sacks. The guards blocked the entrance as a line formed behind them. "Oats. I told you, they're oats," said Hector. "We're supposed to deliver half of these to the kitchen, and half to the stables. Please, just let us do our job."

"There are a couple of problems with that statement," said the head guard. He was wheat-stalk thin, barely old enough to sport the wisp of chin hair he had managed to grow. He wore an impeccably tailored uniform and a face marred by a combination of acne pock-marks and knife scars that suggested difficult teenage years. "First, you have no scrollwork with you. No notices of sale, consignment notes, nor bills of lading. You have no receipts, invoices, or promissory documents. You don't even have a hand-scrawled note telling you where the goods should go, nor proof that these are approved sacks of oats. Do you care to comment on that?"

"All I can tell you is that if I don't get this to the scullery, Çalaht only knows what will happen." Hector tried to make it look like he was shuffling nervously, but his years of training as a Horse Guard made a mockery of this. Hector could no more look oppressed and harassed than he could look unkempt. The inherent perfection of his body, coat, and mane were a force of nature, and did not lend themselves to fakery.

The head guard ignored Hector's comment. "Then there's the small matter of this." He walked over to his desk and picked up a parchment. Unscrolling it, he held it up for Hector and the Nameless One to see. At the top, the parchment read, "Nope Don't Let In No Matter What's Going On." Beneath it were rather unskilled drawings of Hector and the Nameless One. The artist hadn't come anywhere near capturing Hector's magnificence, nor the sure look in the Nameless One's eye, but it was definitely a passable resemblance. "You're on my Nope Don't Let In No Matter What's Going On list," said the guard. "That's a clear indicator that nope, I'm not going to let you in no matter what's going on."

Hector looked at the Nameless One, who shook his head slowly. It didn't seem like it was worth pursuing this. They stepped away from the castle gate so that others could get checked through.

Another disappointment in a lengthening list.

Two days.

It had been just over two days since Hector had seen Eloise go back into the Purple Haze. Two days of recovering from whatever happened to him when he went in after her. Two days of debating and arguing with the Nameless One about what do next, and whether there was any point in staying in the Half Kingdom waiting for the princesses to reappear. Two days of worry, fear, and running through worst-case scenarios in his head. Two days of looking out for Princess Eloise and not seeing her, while also seeing her everywhere, in every vaguely princess-shaped person. Two days of wondering if they should send news home to the king and queen in Brague, and of discussing whether the princess would want him to do so sooner, or if he should give her more time.

Two very long, very bad days, which were only getting worse.

The midday sun made a half-hearted attempt to push warmth through the gray, uninspired sky, but to little effect. Hector and the Nameless One watched the gate from two dozen paces away as, for the most part, the guards allowed a flow of merchants, minor royals, workers, and merchants into the castle grounds—none of them, apparently, appearing on the Nope Don't Let In No Matter What's Going On scroll. A smaller, yet still steady trickle of people moved in the opposite direction, exiting the castle grounds—horses and donkeys with unladen carts, messengers, and even the odd necromancer. It irked Hector that so many could move in and out, while he and the Nameless One could not even peek around the corner of the wall.

The Nameless One snorted to get Hector's attention, then pointed with his chin. At first, Hector couldn't tell what had caught his eye. Then he saw it—a one-armed capuchin with a satchel slung over his shoulder, carrying a fishbowl with a jellyfish in it. That wasn't so unusual, but the fishbowl was decorated with the guild robes. The capuchin strode away from the castle like he was late for an appointment.

"Excuse me! Excuse me!" called Hector. He and the Nameless One trotted over to the capuchin. "Excuse me," repeated Hector. "Are you the Speaker for the Indigent?"

The capuchin set down the fishbowl on the cobblestone road and assumed a waiting posture. "Ah, you saw the robes." The voice came from the jellyfish, bubbling up out of a slurry of brine in the glass bowl. The capuchin made perfectly synchronized gestures to accompany the jelly fish's words. "I normally take them off before I leave the castle, but today I was rushing. I'm Kёёёvin. Kёёёvin Ïïïgnatius Bümbёr-shööt, Speaker for the Indigent." He wafted a couple of tentacles toward the capuchin. "This is my associate, Fïïïnn. What do you need, young equine?"

Hector hadn't been called "young" for years. He wondered how old the jellyfish was. "My name is Hector de Pferd, and I believe my two friends are being held captive in the castle. Is it possible you might have spoken with them? A human and a chipmunk?"

The capuchin tilted his head and mimed deep thought, stroking his chin with his one hand. The jellyfish rotated in his bowl, tentacles wafting, body tilted at the same angle as the capuchin's head. "Have they been there more than, say, three months?"

"No. Just a couple of days."

"Then it's not likely I've encountered them. I'm currently on Wing..." The jellyfish sloshed around and seemed to look at Fïïïnn, who paused, flipped open his satchel, peeked at a scroll, then made a gesture. The jellyfish turned back around. "Wing R of the dungeons. If they've only been there a couple of days, they are unlikely to have been banished to Wing R—they would not have been taunted enough yet. But a thorough search of my records will have to wait. I'm sorry I can't remember off the top of my gelatinous bell, but the dungeons are full as always, and it's not like I can get to everyone. Things slip my mind. Memory like a goldfish."

This was a phrase that goldfish found offensive (although their memories were so bad they never remembered long enough to maintain their offense). So, while this was a stereotype, it was one base on truth, as jellyfish also had short memories. They were usually employed in positions that were repetitive, very, very simple, or did not require much grasp of detail. This memory problem, along with their mobility problems, meant that professional occupations were completely ill-suited to them. That this one had risen to the role of Speaker for the Indigent was either a testament to a particularly unjellyfishlike tenacity or was deliberate judicial sabotage. Hector suspected both.

"Come to my chambers in the Low Street in three hours, and I'll gather details. But for now, I must away." With that, the capuchin bowed gracefully, picked up the fishbowl, nodded, and was gone.

6

IN THE FOG

They walked in the direction that Eloise had pointed, the direction of the hushed, shadowy tug on her soul. Johanna admitted she could feel something too, but it was more like a light push on the back of her head than a pull from the front.

It took what seemed like forever for them to pick their way off the mountain of bones. The piled bodies looked mainly human, though there were plenty of other species as well, including, if Eloise was reading the skeletons right, an emu, a trio of walruses, and something she couldn't recognize, but which was either a gibbon or a baboon. All recipients of the Half Kingdom's particular flavor of justice, Eloise assumed, given that the pile sloped sharply away from where she and Johanna had landed, suggesting that its source was Fogging Hill.

Eventually, Eloise and Johanna made it to solid ground, although it was unlike anything either of them had ever touched. The soil was devoid of life. Whatever force sucked the flesh from the bones had done the same to the land itself. As they traversed it, their feet sank a few weak lengths into the dead, dry surface, each step swirling up a small cloud of fine dust particles. They were soon covered from head to foot in a light dusting of it and began breathing through cloths to keep it out of their mouths and lungs.

They walked for what felt like an eternity, but might have been just a few hours. The limited visibility within the fog gave few clues about the passage of time. Eloise spent the time looking down to make sure she didn't step in anything dangerous, and to focus on that inner tug.

At one point, Johanna, who was a few paces ahead, stopped. "Look."

"It's... It's a sign of some sort." Eloise moved closer, then wiped it with the hem of her travel cloak. Caked dust fell in a single sheet and sent plumes flying when it hit the dusty ground. Eloise squinted at the lettering that was revealed. "Welcome to Süüünnÿÿÿ Glëëën."

"A village," said Johanna.

They walked along the road into a place where people had lived two centuries before. The buildings were simple, made of wood or mud brick. The unimaginative dwellings and shops had belonged to people long since removed from the timeline of history. The thatched roofs were caked in dust like a macabre gray snowfall. Some doors stood open, yawning, blind to the passage of years. Others were shut tight, keeping the worst of the dust at bay.

Eloise accidentally kicked something. "By Çalaht's stretched thumbs," she swore when she looked down.

It was a skull. She'd dislodged a skull from a spine. She looked more closely at the skeleton. It was two skeletons—a mother and daughter, she guessed from the relative sizes and the fact that the now headless one lay near a market basket.

As they looked around, they realized that skeletons of long-dead people lay everywhere. It had been one thing to see skeletons in a pile near the edge of the fog. And they'd seen plenty of them along the way. But to see a whole village that had succumbed in a single moment was a whole other thing.

"This place gives me the creeps," said Eloise.

"Me, too. It's like the whole hamlet turned into an alfresco cemetery."

Eloise and Johanna silently, respectfully, went from house to house and shop to shop, examining them through the mist. The dust lay every-where, thick on door frames, carpeted across steps and porches, and heaped on lintels. If a door was open, the building's inside lay as caked as the outside. Here and there, they found the remains of burned-out buildings, consumed by a long-ago fire.

The unremembered dead told little stories of their demise, apparently having passed away suddenly in the middle of whatever they were doing—tending shop, making a meal, talking to a friend, dragging a cart. The largest group was in a building that had once been a public inn. There, two score people lay buried partly visible, like skeletons after a sandstorm.

"Look at them all," said Johanna. "It's like a fairy-tale with a wicked sorcerer who's cast an evil sleeping spell. They lay down right where they were and never got up again."

That was when Eloise noticed something. "Look, Jo. Look at their arms."

Johanna stepped around the skeletons, leaning in close to see what Eloise was talking about.

"They all look like they're trying to grab something," said Eloise.

"Not just something, but the same thing," said Johanna. "They are all reaching in the same direction."

"Stay here a minute." Eloise hurried into the street and quickly moved from building to building, glancing into half a dozen doorways. Then she went back to the inn. "Everyone is reaching like that. Adults, chil-dren, babies. Everyone."

Johanna shuddered. "They're reaching in the direction we're headed. It's like they are reaching for the thing we are looking for."

"It reminds me of Gouache," said Eloise. "He did the same thing during his seizure. It was like he was trying to grasp something."

"Gouache? Seizure?"

Eloise filled Johanna in on what had happened with the jester, including, uncomfortably, the part where she had saved his life before coming after her sister. To Eloise's surprise, Johanna smiled at the story. "I'm glad you got him out," said Johanna. "He's dim, but he's sweet. And I could listen to his version of 'Three Bags of Groats for My Sweetheart' all day."

Just the mention of the title immediately lodged the song in both their heads, and as they tracked through the barrens of fog, it quickly became their unofficial travel anthem.

Time had no meaning in the fog. There was the same dull, purplish light and the same dry, windless mist wherever they looked and however long they walked up and down the hills and valleys of this forgotten village. There was no sense of day or night, nothing for the body's rhythms to latch onto. The two princesses walked, rested, walked, rested. It could have been hours or days, or even months.

At one point, Johanna asked, "Are you hungry?"

"Yes. But I don't feel like I need to eat. What about you?"

"Same. Thirsty?"

Eloise nodded. "Parched. My mouth is dry and dusty, but my body doesn't crave water."

"Same." Johanna shook her head, disbelieving. "It's like the fog is keeping us alive. It killed everyone else, but us, it seems to like."

"I wouldn't personalize it that way," said Eloise. "It's just a force. It might sustain us, but it's draining as well."

"Hmm. Maybe."

On they walked, seemingly forever. Sometimes they spoke. Sometimes they held hands. Sometimes they spread apart a little so they could be with their thoughts.

Now and then, Johanna would hear Eloise mumbling "Hum thrum," or "clawing" or "merged."

"Stop it, Eloise. You sound like a crazy person muttering their way through the streets of Brague."

"Sorry."

"What is that you're saying, anyway?"

"You remember Jerome's Naming Ceremony?"

Johanna smiled. "It seems like it was years ago, but yes, I remember. It was spectacular."

Eloise felt a flush of embarrassment at the memory, but let it slide. "Seer Maybelle had a vision right beforehand. It was triggered when she touched me."

"I didn't know that."

"I've been thinking about what she said. 'Day and night merged. The hum thrums through the bones. That which was once in hand but was lost, can be found again, still in hand, unreached by the clawing of the doomed.'"

"Well, that's a pretty good description of where we're at," said Johanna. "There's no day or night. And that buzzing is getting louder all the time. Did you know you hum 'Three Bags of Groats for My Sweetheart' at the same pitch as the hum when you're lost in thought? It's like it has soaked into you."

"I had no idea. Anyway, I've been thinking about the last part of what she said. The 'clawing of the doomed' bit seems obvious now. All those dead people reaching. But the 'That which was once in hand but was lost, can be found again' bit..."

"... Means there's *something* somewhere that can be found," said Johanna.

"Yes, I think so."

"I guess we'll know it when we see it."

"Let's hope so."

7

THE TAUNTER

Jerome knew he was a complete mess. There was a small part of his mind that was calm and rational enough to consider at the way he was manically running around the dungeon cell and think, "This isn't a good look." And yet, here he was, barely functioning, wild with panic, chattering constantly, and scampering himself to exhaustion. The calmish part of his mind wondered how long he could keep this up, but the rest was too occupied with half-crazed raving to to pay much attention.

He guessed from the number of meals that had been slid into the room and ignored that it had been eight days since they had first stepped into Castle Blotch. So, seven and a half days since he'd been thrown into this cesspit of ague and infection. The displaced part of his mind wondered if maybe his running was an attempt to outrun the inevitable sickness. Obviously, that was stupid. He knew it was stupid. But this was a place where such stupidity went unchecked. Apart from the dull eyes of the indeterminate shapes who stood guard outside the dungeon door, there was no one to watch or comment as one's sanity slipped out of one's head and rotted on the floor along with the unidentifiable organic matter that mulched there.

The grinding boredom of Jerome's agitated movement was only broken up by the visits of his taunter, Gääärvan. Gääärvan was a massive lemur, whose taunter's robes of silver and navy were perfectly accessorized by his silver spectacles and manicured nails. He was careful to keep the magnificent striped rings of his tail out of the dreck of the cell. There seemed to be no pattern to when he'd show up, but his taunting sessions were announced by the single candle that screamed its light into the cell's darkness. Gääärvan took his taunting duties very, very seriously. Mainly, this consisted of haranguing and deriding, but sometimes it also included mocking, ridiculing, uncalled-for rudeness, sarcastic commentary, and general garden-variety unkindness.

It drove Jerome crazy, and made him yearn for the excruciating discomfort of the jail chiggers he'd endured in the Southie jail.

Of course, that was the point.

"Hello, scut," said Gääärvan when he stepped into Jerome's cell for the sixth time in who knew how many days. "Still smelling like a rafflesia in its full corpse odor blossom, I see. Suits your worthlessness, I guess, although it makes those around you dislike you even more." Jerome retreated to the far corner of the dungeon, where he crouched down and tried to plug up his ears. But the lemur would have none of it.

"Remove your hands from your ears, or I'll have the guards tie them to the iron ring again. You remember how much you enjoyed that last time, don't you?"

Jerome forced his hands to his sides, stood, and faced the lemur. He'd learned that this was the best of his unappealing choices.

A guard brought in a chair and table, placing them in the exact center of the cell. Gääärvan unrolled the scroll of parchment he used to make notes during their "discussions," spreading it out on the table. He took three small lead cubes from his pocket and weighed down the scroll's corners with them, using the candle holder to hold down the fourth. The guard, a muscled civet with few teeth and fewer words, stood to the side, ready to intervene if Jerome tried to get physical. But over the first five sessions, Jerome had learned that was not a good idea.

"Shall we pick up where we left off? I think so," Gääärvan said. "Tell me your name."

Jerome swallowed, saying nothing.

"I said, tell me your name."

"Jerome Abernatheen de Chipmunk."

Gääärvan ticked. "Clearly you are too stupid to remember what I said last time. Try again, scut."

Jerome spoke through clamped teeth. "I am Nothingness Personified. Nothing Incarnate. I am Naught."

"That wasn't so hard now, was it? Now say it again so you commit it to that thick, brainless rat skull of yours."

"I am a chipmunk. We are rodents, not rats."

"Say. It. Again."

"I am Nothingness Personified. Nothing Incarnate. I am Naught."

The lemur noted something on the scroll. "I've learned a little more about you since we last chatted. I had no idea you were such a disappointment to your mother. What a flawed, miserable person. No talent for the family business. No help for your mother after your loser of a father passed over, and we know he's not standing with Çalaht if there's any justice in the world. I heard about your Naming Ceremony. The shame you caused your princess must have been excruciating. It is amazing she didn't punt you from Court then and there. And where is your princess? Why has she not sent for you, or come after you? Because you are a drag, a burden, a stone around the neck of a royal who hasn't exactly set Court alight with her brilliance, that's why. Frankly, it's a wonder that you have lived long enough to blunder your way to this cesspool of a dungeon."

On and on he went, every word a poison dart aimed at Jerome's core, each inflicting particular damage.

The cell door clanged opened, and Jerome watched the scullery mare nose in a squeaking tea cart. This was different. Jerome's whiskers twitched as he smelled the aroma—haggleberry tea. A good one.

The taunter moved his scroll to make way, and set two cups and saucers on his table, along with a plate of poppyseed biscuits. The lemur carefully poured tea into both cups and placed two biscuits on each saucer. Jerome couldn't help himself; his mind and nose clicked into aficionado mode. Delicately sniffing the air, he was surprised at what it told him. This was a sublime variety of haggleberry tea, grown in a cooler region of the Central Ranges. Berries of Ultimate Bliss blend. Four—no, five years old, harvested at the end of an unusually dry, cool growing season. The haggle-berries from that year were renowned for a smokey, woody bass note that somehow tricked the tongue into thinking of wild sour cherries, but those flavors only slipped through when the tea was cold brewed, then heated slowly, over four hours, to the proper serving temperature. Tea buffs speculated that somewhere in the chain of production, someone, possibly the person responsible for removing the toxins from the berries, had exerted a weak magic on the product, giving it a unique taste.

Emotionally battered as he was, Jerome wondered how it could be that someone whose job it was to reduce him to a pliant puddle of nerves could also possess a palate attuned to the particularly complex, exquisite blend of flavors steaming from that cup.

And there were two cups set out. Was someone else expected?

Was one for him?

Jerome didn't dare believe that. But, oh, Çalaht soliciting sacraments, he was desperate for a cuppa. Despite himself, hope blossomed. Maybe he could wrangle his way to a sip of that divine brew. After days in panic, a cup of that tea would hit him like a waterfall of relief.

Gääärvan stopped his verbal bombardment, blew across the rim of his cup, then sipped. When he saw the look of satisfaction cross the lemur face, Jerome's desire deepened. "That's something. That's really some-thing," sighed Gääärvan.

Jerome stood silently. His tail quivered, his mouth watered, and his mind raced. He had to get some of that tea.

"The blend is Berries of Ultimate Bliss," said Gääärvan. "From the cool, dry spell five years ago."

"I thought it might be," said Jerome. "It's meant to be good."

"Good? That description is willful ignorance. The tea is legendary. Le-gen-dar-y."

"Well, yes," agreed Jerome. "Legendary."

Another sip.

Jerome's mouth flooded with desire. "How did you come by it?"

The lemur waved a paw to indicate the surrounding castle. "There are connections." He sipped again with exaggerated pleasure. "So you've never had it before?"

"No. I have smelled it from across a room and have read about it. But it was considered an extravagance in my home, despite connections I might or might not have had. Can you..." Jerome hesitated, not sure if he wanted to know the answer or not.

"Can I what?"

"Can you taste the wild cherries?"

The lemur looked offended. "Are you questioning my brewing skills? Of course I can taste the wild *sour* cherries. That is the point! That is the trill note that graces the top end of the flavor range." The lemur eyed Jerome. "Would you like to try some?"

Jerome wanted to say "no." If the past behavior of the taunter was anything to go by, this would not end well. But jail had taken its toll, and he could not help himself. "Yes. Yes, please."

Gääärvan looked like he was considering his options, although it was equally likely that he was just pretending. Finally, he set down his cup, walked over to Jerome and leaned down. He whispered conspiratorially. "Say your name willingly and with conviction—so I believe you—and I will give you a cup of Berries of Ultimate Bliss tea."

That seemed a reasonable price. He was being forced to say it anyway, so he may as well get something out of it. And what a something!

"Agreed."

Gääärvan went back to his seat and took another sip. He nodded at Jerome. "Go ahead."

Jerome swallowed. "I am Nothingness Personified. Nothing Incarnate. I am Naught."

The lemur shook his head slowly. "No. I'm not feeling that. You're going to have to try again."

"I am Nothingness Personified. Nothing Incarnate. I am Naught." Louder this time.

"Nope."

The tea was calling him. Jerome launched himself into it. "I am Nothingness Personified. Nothing Incarnate. I am Naught." Earnest. Then yelling. Then quietly. Over and over.

"I am Nothingness Personified. Nothing Incarnate. I am Naught. I am Nothingness Personified. Nothing Incarnate. I am Naught."

The more he said it, the more he came to believe it. It took on its own momentum in his head, until it came out like a curse mixed with self-loathing.

"That one," said Gääärvan. "That one I believed. Stop now."

Jerome panted from the exertion.

Gääärvan picked up the tea pot and filled the second cup. He picked it up and stepped back to where Jerome stood, trembling. A puzzled look crossed his face. "But there's something I don't understand."

Jerome looked him in the eyes. "W-what?"

He waved the cup. "Why would I give such a fine thing as this to someone who is a nothing, a naught, like you yourself just convinced me you were?"

Then he poured the Berries of Ultimate Bliss on the ground at Jerome's feet.

Jerome crumpled in on himself, sobbing, oblivious to anything around him.

Gääärvan smiled. He called for the guard to open the door.

"Mission accomplished, for now anyway," he said to the guard. "See you in a bit."

❦   8   ❦

THE TAUNTER'S APPRENTICE

Lorch's taunter was a ferret named Glorious Ordnung Planter IV, but he'd been nervous when he'd first entered the dungeon cell, and had introduced himself with the nickname that had followed him since childhood—Bungle.

Bungle had dun-colored fur, a lazy eye, and a plethora of tics, including a cheek twitch that acted like a comma, an ear twitch of a period, and an eyelid flutter that served as an exclamation mark. His silver taunter's robes looked second-hand, and had been altered to fit his particular shape by someone who seemed to wield a needle and thread as instruments of war, not of fashion. He, too, had had a table, scroll, and tea brought into the cell. He and Lorch sat across from each other, both enjoying an unremarkable, yet passable, haggleberry tea.

"You don't mind if I give you a few pointers, do you?" asked Lorch.

"No, no, no. Please do!" twitched the ferret. "If I'm going to get this taunting business right, then I have to take constructive feedback."

"I think you'll get the hang of it, eventually. You just need practice. I mean, you've only just become an apprentice taunter. Everyone has to start at the beginning." Lorch sipped. "The key is, you have to take control of the situation. I mean, you've been lovely, and I think you're a fine person, but that's not really what you're going for, is it?"

"No, it's not. 'Intimidation. Domination. Interrogation. Humiliation.' Those are the watchwords of our trade. My mother even embroidered them into a pillow cover for me."

"She sounds lovely, your mother."

"Oh, she is, she is! The best, really. She was the one who got me this job. Through her connections to the Taunter's Guild."

"It's nice that she's so encouraging. Not everyone has that. My mother was the same. 'Lorch Lacksneck, my boy, if you put your mind to it, you can be a guard.'"

"My mother said something similar," said Bungle. "Although it was more like, 'Stop being daft. Stand up. And hunker down. You've got this in you.' Similarish, anyway."

"Well, I think your mother was right. You've got the stuff to be a good taunter. This is your first solo taunting. I don't think you should expect too much on your first go. You'll get the hang of it."

The ferret nibbled a poppyseed biscuit. "Please, have another."

"No, no. But thank you," said Lorch. "I think you should try another taunt or two."

The ferret stopped, his teeth just short of another chomp. Chagrined, he put the biscuit down. "Of course, of course. I suppose you're right."

"I'll let you know what I think." Lorch took a last sip of tea, straightened himself, clasped his hands in his lap, and waited for Bungle to let fly.

Bungle stood on his chair, smoothed down his robe, and cleared his throat. "Would you mind standing?"

"Try again."

"Right, right, right. Stand up?"

"More of a command. Less of a question."

"Stand up."

"This time like you mean it."

Bungle pointed at Lorch. "Stand up."

"Better. I like that you're using a gesture. That adds to it. I might suggest you don't crook your finger, though. It looks like you're pointing at the wall."

"Oh, sorry."

"No, no. You're the taunter. Don't apologize."

"Right, sorry."

Lorch looked at him.

"I just apologized again, didn't I?"

"Yep."

"Sor—"

Lorch put up a hand to stop him. "Also, this time, try putting a little snarl in your voice. Like you're trying to scare a child."

"Oh! I would never do that. That would be mean."

"Well, being mean is sort of at the core of being a taunter, isn't it?"

"Not to children."

"True. Anyway, snarl?"

"Stand up."

"More snarl. Come on, give it to me."

"Stand up, you jackaboot."

"Jackaboot?"

"Yes, jackaboot."

Lorch furrowed his brow. "Is that a word?"

"I, I think so?"

"I don't think it quite worked. Try again."

Bungle cleared his throat. "Stand up, you lout!"

Lorch delicately pushed back his chair from the table and stood.

"Really? Did you really feel it? I think I felt it."

"I thought it was a very good effort. I felt it warranted me standing up."

"Well, that's a relief. You really are being most kind about this."

"I know what it's like. When I first became a guard, I could barely hold a sword. And now look at me! I'm in a dungeon and everything—all in the line of duty. I've adventured, traveled the land, and even protected a princess. Who would have thought?"

He put a hand on the ferret's shoulder. "Someday you will be a great taunter. You will taunt merchants and mendicants, royals and ragamuffins, the lowly and the mighty. You just have to learn your craft, is all."

Tears welled in the ferret's eyes. He sniffed and dabbed his eyes with the corner of his napkin. "I wish my Guild Master had that much confidence in me. He let me pass my apprenticeship, which is the only reason I'm here. But he's not nearly as helpful as you. 'Be vicious! Rip out their metaphoric guts! Make them weep!' That's the kind of thing he says. A bit short on the practicalities. I've seen my master at work. He can reduce lifelong criminals to blubbering with just half a dozen words and a raised eyebrow. He really is that good."

Bungle stood and walked around Lorch, trying to act fierce. He did what he could to keep the hem of his silver robe out of the dreck on the ground, but it was difficult and his shoes squelched unpleasantly. "I do wish conditions were nicer in here. It would make everything so much more pleasant."

"Can't disagree with you there," said Lorch.

"I mean, it's not the worst dungeon I've ever seen. But I wouldn't want to spend too much time here, if you know what I mean."

"Well, dungeons are dungeons. You don't expect service like an inn when you're in one. Salubrious it is not."

"No, I would certainly not call it salubrious."

"Care for another go?" asked Lorch.

Bungle drew himself up to full height, and even stood on his back legs. "You are worthlessness itself."

"Not a bad start. Keep going."

Bungle slumped. "I'm just not feeling it. I mean, what's my motivation? What am I trying to achieve here?"

"It's a taunting session. You can make me feel bad. Now focus."

"OK, here goes. You are a lout."

"Keep going."

"You are a wastrel, a layabout, and have bad personal hygiene."

"That's sort of getting there. You need to find things that are personal to the individual you are taunting. Otherwise, it's just name-calling."

"What do you mean?"

"Let's say I was taunting you. I might say, 'Your fur is the color of an ill-kept dungheap.' Or, 'You speak like someone stole half of your vowels.' That sort of thing."

Bungle sat back in his chair. "You're a natural."

"Well, don't worry too much. I'm happy to help you practice, and it looks like I'm stuck here a while. You've got plenty of time."

"But that's the thing—I don't think I do. I heard His Jesterness advocating to His Majesty that you should both be done away with. If I'm going to get this taunting done, I have to do it ASAP."

"Done away with?"

"I know. Just when I've found someone who can help me."

"As in, done away with permanently?"

"Yes. I fear I may only have a few days to achieve tauntedness."

But Lorch had stopped paying attention. He hadn't realized his situation was so dire. How could he possibly escape?

❀ 9 ❀

INTERVENTION

The dust defined their existence. It caked their clothes, it coated their skin, and it seemed to lighten their hair. Soon they looked like white ghosts moving through a bardo plane of forgotten dreams.

On they walked across empty hills and plains, breathing dust, following the pointing fingers of any skeletons they saw. Hours would pass without them speaking. And then one would fill the space with talk. Eloise told Johanna about her journey and all the people she'd met. Johanna spoke of plants and gardening, and sometimes, for a laugh, would quiz Eloise on the intricacies of Protocol.

After one of the longer stretches of silence, Johanna cleared her throat, and said, "You know, I should have been firstborn."

"Oh, come on, Johanna. Don't be silly." They were crossing a field that had once been a farmer's paddock. The wooden post-and-rail fencing was now just a faint reminder of all that had been lost to the fog. There was no way to tell what had once grown here. Eloise cheered herself with the thought that it might rye or caraway, which she tolerated, but did not relish, and not oats or corn, both of which she liked and would hated to have had ruined.

"It is the truth."

"Look. We're twins. One of us had to come out first. It happened to be me."

"There is no 'happened' about it."

Eloise stopped. "How can you possibly know that?"

"We were three. I remember it well because we were wearing those little green dresses with the dark red bows. That was when they used to dress us as twins."

"I remember those dresses. There were matching green slippers, and we'd slide across the floor in the Receiving Room while Mother and Father did whatever."

"I'd forgotten the sliding, but you're right, I remember the slippers," said Johanna. "Well, it was nap time. I remember, because you snored, even back then."

"I don't snore!"

"Ask Jerome. You snore. And you snored then, too. Come on, let's keep walking." Johanna looped her arm through Eloise's and drew her on. "Mother came in with Seer Maybelle. I didn't want them to know I wasn't asleep, so I hid under the blanket. Seer Maybelle said something about us being a perfect Firstborn and a perfect Second Born. And she said she was glad Mother had agreed to her intervention. I had no idea what 'intervention' meant. But the sentence stuck with me because it seemed, I don't know, somehow important. Or meaningful."

"Why is this the first I've heard of this?"

"Because at first I didn't know what it meant. And then, when I was a few years older, I worked it out. And I was angry. So angry. Livid. Then a few years later, I realized I was powerless to do anything about it. So I wallowed in that powerlessness and tried to make those around me pay."

"Why mention it now?"

"You like numbers. What are the odds that we emerge from this fog alive?"

Eloise shrugged. "I genuinely don't know. There's nothing living here at all, and it looks like that's been the case forever. Why would we have a different outcome, unless there's some connection to the magic? I can feel the fog affecting me. I'm sure you feel it too. I don't think it's exactly doing us any good. And if we find whatever it is, we have no idea what we're dealing with or how to do anything about it. So the odds of surviving? I put them somewhere between unlikely and catastrophically unlikely."

"Then perhaps things should be said that otherwise wouldn't. Plus, I've realized something."

They stopped talking to focus on scaling a low boulder. Eloise gave Johanna a boost up with laced fingers, then found minute cracks that gave her enough purchase to haul herself up and over. The stopped conversation stayed stopped.

Was Johanna telling her the truth? Had there been an intervention? Should she be worried about something Johanna heard when she was three? But if what her sister said was true, then the core circumstance that defined Eloise's life—being heir to the Western Lands and All That Really Matters—was the result of an old chipmunk's meddling. She had nothing but respect for Seer Maybelle, and what she foresaw was, in one way or another, inexorable. But how different her life would have been if she was second born.

And maybe she should have been. Maybe Seer Maybelle had interpreted the Unseen incorrectly. Eloise had learned long ago in Oracles and Insights that there was always another interpretation, another way to look at things, another equally valid choice of action based on a vision. The more she dwelled on it, the more she believed Johanna—Eloise was firstborn due to a deliberate act, and not nature's perfidy or Çalaht's grace. If that was true, then it undermined her entire sense of self. A gloom settled over her.

She tried to fight off the depression. Maybe the seer's interference *was* an expression of Çalaht's grace. One could know nothing like that for certain. But she *had* been born first, and she *was* the heir. Maybe there was some sort of divine will, and Seer Maybelle was just the instrument of it.

Maybe. But that was all too oogie-boogie for her liking.

This new knowledge ate at her. Maybe Johanna knew it would, and that was why she'd said it. That was not the most charitable thought Eloise might have, but there it was. Spite and jealousy can make you do things. She knew that. Eloise's emotions sloshed inside her from anger to doubt, embarrassment to confusion, from feeling gutted to feeling numb, and then back again. And in that emotional state, the pang of her habits began yelling at her. The filth on her suddenly became intolerable, and counting offered no solace.

Eventually, Johanna said, "I can hear you thinking all the way over here. Trust me, whatever is running through your head, I've already traveled that way a hundred thousand times. But you haven't asked me the obvious question."

Eloise looked at her sister. "What? What obvious question? Do you mean, why would you poison my mind like this? Or, how could I ever sit on Mother's throne without thinking that really it ought to be you? Or perhaps, why don't I just curl up here and join all the other bones?" Eloise sat down on a stump. There didn't seem much point in continuing.

"Don't be so dramatic. That's my department." Johanna brushed the dust from a flat bit of rock, merely rearranging it rather than making the rock cleaner, and sat next to Eloise. From habit, she primly tucked her skirts beneath her legs, as they had been taught in Deportment and Comportment. "El, what was the last thing I said?"

"That perhaps things need to be said."

"After that."

Eloise thought again. "That you have realized something. What, Jo? What, pray tell, have you realized?" She didn't mean to sound so snippy.

"I've realized that Seer Maybelle and Mother made the right choice. You really are the best heir. And I'm better suited to Second Born." Again, she tried unsuccessfully to brush some of the dust away from the stone. "You're more patient with people than me. You're tenacious. You might have your quirks, yes, but you care about people much more than I do. And, I'm not sure how to put this, but you think like someone who should be queen. Mother is the same. She thinks like a queen. Like, I would have just tried to get out of the fog. But you wanted to do something about it. That's the kind of thing I'm talking about."

Eloise just listened, letting Johanna have her say. "That's why I decided to tell you about the intervention thing. I wanted you to hear it from me, and not Mother or Seer Maybelle or anyone else. And I wanted you to know I'm OK with it."

"Really?"

"Truly."

"Because that's a change."

"Yes. Definitely a change. Feel free to be Heir to the Western Lands and All That Really Matters to your heart's content."

Eloise reached out and took Johanna's hand. She closed her eyes, and they sat that way for a while, quietly, in the middle of the wasteland. Eloise thought about the orderly, clean, somewhat predictable life that awaited her somewhere to the southwest, and about the differences that being Firstborn had made, and would continue to make, should they get out of this place alive. She still felt the gnawing doubt in her stomach that Johanna's revelation had caused.

Then she decided to let it go, at least for now.

Eloise kissed the back of Johanna's grime-encrusted hand and gave it a small squeeze. "Thank you."

Johanna squeezed back. "Don't thank me. All I did was rain on your reign."

"You told me the truth."

"The truth can be overvalued."

"The truth matters. And knowing is always better than not knowing."

"I suppose. Although, sometimes I wish I didn't."

They rested in silence. Then Eloise stood. "Let's go find this whatever-it-is."

THE WAIT IS NOT THE HARDEST PART

The Nameless One had found them an absolute dive of a stable called the Splintered Dray. Hector did not give it much mind, but was grateful that it did not take long for the Nameless One to secure a private and clean stall for them—surprisingly clean, given how filthy the public bar area was. The Nameless One's initial encounter with the innkeeper had seemed awfully familiar, but Hector, still addled, from the Purple Haze, had been too drained to care, and had fallen asleep moments after he'd collapsed onto the fresh bed of straw.

Hector and the Nameless One had spent a lot of time waiting. Days of waiting, watching, hoping. They waited in shifts and in different places, so that one of them could see if there was any sign of the princesses coming out of the cursed fog, while the other tried to figure out what had happened to Lorch and Jerome. For days, there was no hint of the guard nor the champion from within the castle. Daily they touched base with the Speaker for the Indigent, but the jellyfish could only respond with a shrug from his capuchin. The castle had swallowed Lorch and Jerome as completely as the fog had swallowed the twins.

Hector had to consciously keep the fear that was clutching his insides at bay as the possibility that Eloise was dead slowly hardened toward certainty. But he refused to give up, and was bolstered by the fact that the Nameless One remained resolutely hopeful that something would turn up. Hector's mind raced constantly, trying to find some constructive action he could take. Sleep came hard, and infrequently.

The waiting itself was not hard. What Hector found impossible to tolerate was how useless he felt.

Their next breakthrough came a week after the disappearances. It was night, and Hector was sitting alone in their room at the Splintered Dray with a small trough of rice wine and a sour mood. From down the hall there came a giggle, and the giggle grew louder as it approached their stall. There was a knock at the door, and at Hector's "Come in," the Nameless One entered the stall with an exceedingly cute filly who had a coppery sheen to her mane and coat, and was dressed in a home-spun tunic, an apron and cap—the outfit of a scullery mare.

"Hiya, sweets," she said. "My name's Kiiit. Pleased to be making your acquaintance." She nuzzled the Nameless One's neck, and brushed her wither against his, then sauntered over to Hector, who scrambled to his hooves.

"Pleased to meet you, Mistress Kiiit."

"Sweetie Pie here told me you were good-looking, but my, oh, my I had no idea how right he'd be. I'm partial to shades of midnight." She sidled over to him and giggled again. "You smell lovely!" Then she craned her neck to look back at the Nameless One and said, "And so do you. I'm not playing favorites."

Hector felt blood rush to his cheeks. "Mistress Kiiit, how may I be of service?"

She let that one hang in the air a little too long for polite company, then giggled once more. "I would love to take you up on that, Good Sir. And who knows, maybe I still will." She pranced the few steps back to the Nameless One. "Sweetie Pie here made it clear that you're trying to find out about your friends in the dungeon."

"Dungeon?"

"A human and a rat?"

"Rat? Do you mean a chipmunk?"

"Chipmunk. Rat. Whatever. Rodents confuse me. Plus, it's hard to see down there." She leaned in to the Nameless One again. Her behavior was much more familiar than Hector was comfortable with, but the Nameless One didn't seem to mind. This was a side of him that Hector had not seen before.

"How did they end up in the dungeon?" asked Hector.

"That I can't tell you. I just make the food and drag it down to them."

"So they're alive."

"They were at evening slop time."

"Slop time?"

"Yeah. The scuts get slop twice a day."

"Scuts?"

"Scuts. You know—scuts, because they're worthless, and if they live long enough, they do the scut work."

"Charming," said Hector. Clearly, Kiïit meant no harm. This manner of speaking was just her way. But the casualness with which she referred to Lorch and Jerome's incarceration grated on Hector's nerves. "So, how are they?"

"The human..."

"Lorch."

"The Lorch is doing okay, methinks," said Kiïit. "He's quiet. Maybe even serene, from what I can tell. Guards tell me he spends a lot of his time sitting cross-legged, making the same sounds over and over again. Sort of like a moan, but not like he's in pain or anything, just repetitious. Now and then, he stands up and moves real slow and deliberate, like he was gonna beat you up in very creative ways, but only if you were a tortoise or something and couldn't get away. Your Lorch eats what he's given and has been polite every time."

"And Jerome?"

"Jerome's the rat? Sorry, chipmunk? If I've ever seen anyone who is completely unsuited to life in a dungeon, it'd be your Jerome," she said. "He chatters incessantly, and nonsensically. He runs from one end of the dungeon to the other, which doesn't take very long. He is bouncing off the walls, and that's an actual thing. As for eating? Barely anything. Perhaps the slop is not to his taste. Can chipmunks even eat turnip, rutabaga, and snotweed slop?"

"This is not good," Hector said to the Nameless One, who nodded in grim agreement. "Mistress Kïïït, what can you say of the goings-on in the castle?"

Kïïït's chirpy manner drooped. "Aye, it's been miserable, that's for sure. His Jesterness, Master Turpentine Snotearrow McCcoonnch, is right sore all the time."

"Oh?"

"Unbearable, he is. His brother, Mr Gouache, lies in his bed, mind-numb to the world, and His Jesterness, Master Turpentine Snotearrow McCcoonnch, snarls his way from one end of the castle to the other when he's not attending His Highness or sitting with his brother. A more vicious mood I've not seen from him before, and that is saying something." She turned, fluttered her eyelashes a few times at the Nameless One, then continued. "His Jesterness, Master Turpentine Snotearrow McCcoonnch, was right horrible to the apothecary, the healers, the priests, even the prelate, because none of them could do anything for Gouache. Mr Gouache lies on his pallet, motionless, sightless, silent, taking neither food nor water, yet he does not diminish. It is like his body has become detached from time. He's not dead, but it's hard to tell the difference, save for the lack of smell. But I tell you, I do what I can to stay out of the way of His Jesterness, Master Turpentine Snotearrow McCcoonnch. His tongue lashings are horrible."

The mare drifted a step or two over, to where she could reach Hector's trough of rice wine and, without asking permission, slurped down a couple of gulps. It was much too familiar an act from someone Hector had only just met.

"Please, have the rest," said Hector.

"You mean that?" Without waiting for a reply, the mare guzzled it down.

"What else can you tell us?" prompted Hector. "Perhaps something of the king?"

"His Highness, King Doncaster, has been a right grouch too. He says nothing is ever right, and that it was the servants who scared off the Princess Mistress Johanna, because we're all worthless and not worth our weight in dust and dirt, and then he slams the door and smokes the stuff that we're not supposed to know anything about—the stuff that makes him want to chat and lets His Jesterness, Master Turpentine Snotearrow McCcoonnch, put ideas in his head, which, and I'm talking out of school here, he does all the time, but at least it makes the king less of a bear—sorry, no offense to bears. But anyway, a king's supposed to decide things, and it don't look like the king's doing much deciding at the moment. Whereas deciding is all that His Jesterness, Master Turpentine Snotearrow McCcoonnch, seems to be doing at the moment, and the decisions are not very nice."

The room went quiet.

"How are we going to get Lorch and Jerome out?" Hector asked the mare. "There must be a way."

"That's funny," said Kiïit. "Them dungeons is like a river. They flow in one direction, Sugar Socks. The scuts flow in, but they only flow out once they no longer be breathing. That's the way of dungeons. Is that not that way in the place where you come from?"

The Nameless One gave a noncommittal bob of his head.

"But never you two mind," said Kĩĩit. "Them two be there, and we three be here. Now, which of you two sweetie pies is going to buy me a trough of mash? Oh heck, you both can. That'd be OK with me."

Hector's back stiffened, put off by the scullery mare's manner. "Thank you for your kind offer of company, and for letting us know what is going on with our friends. I shall leave you in the capable companionship of my friend, as I have thoughts to gather. My friend will delight in buying you a trough of mash as a small thank you for your time. Allow me to bid you a good night, Mistress Kĩĩit. You've been most helpful."

The scullery mare, less stable from having slugged down the rice wine, gave a fair shot at a curtsy. "Good sir," she slurred, then turned for the door.

The Nameless One opened the stable door for Kĩĩit and let her lead out. As he stepped out the door, he turned and looked back at Hector, giving a sad shake of his head. Hector could tell that it would not be long before the Nameless One allowed the scullery mare to be distracted by some other sweetie pie propping up the bar of the Splintered Dray. There was thinking to be done, and fast.

＊ II ＊

BURNED ONIONS

They crested a rise, and Eloise almost died.

She was two steps in front of Johanna, lost in thoughts of groats and getting irritated with the buzzing in her head, which continued to grow louder.

"Stop!" yelled Johanna.

Eloise froze, puzzled.

Then she saw it. Three steps ahead, shrouded in the mist, the ground disappeared. Not a taper, but a drop. "Oh."

They took a careful step forward.

"It's... It's a cliff," said Johanna.

Eloise tossed a stone over the edge. It clattered, echoing a long way down. "Çalaht's chin warts, that was close."

Johanna shook her head slowly. "That would not have been good."

"No. No, it wouldn't have been." She gave her sister's arm a squeeze. "Thanks, Jo."

They stood still, considering.

"Do you feel it?" asked Eloise.

"The tug? Yes. More than ever."

"Me, too. Like it wants me to go over the cliff."

"I don't get the sense it's trying to get me to plummet. Just to go down."

"How? Are we supposed to fly?"

They circled the rim, looking for a path or some kind of trail marking. If it had once been there, it was long gone. What they found was an old rope. It was tied around a boulder and dangled over the cliff face. "This can't seriously be it," said Johanna.

"It looks like it's been put here deliberately."

Eloise pulled up the rope from the depths of the fog to see what was there, and if it would be safe to climb down. The rope was long. Scary long. Which meant the cliff was probably scary high. The rope showed minor fraying, and the hemp felt slightly brittle. They tested it by pulling on it as hard as they could.

"It seems sound enough," said Eloise. "I'll go first."

"I might let you," said Johanna. "You were always better at this sort of thing."

"It's nothing you haven't done on the Skills Course at home."

"That was, what, 20 lengths? Twenty-five, tops? From the sound of the rock you dropped over, and the length of the rope, this is ten times that, easy. Yeah, you can go first."

They fed the rope carefully over the side so it did not tangle going down. Then Eloise stood with her back to the drop and her face to the boulder. She picked up the rope, stepped over it, and threaded it through her legs. Wrapping it behind her and around the top of her right thigh, she brought it in front, crossed the rope over her chest and took it over her left shoulder. She then crossed it behind her so she could grab it with her right hand near her right thigh. Eloise loosely held the forward feed of the rope with her left hand for balance, and prepared to use her right hand to control how fast she went down.

Eloise leaned a little to put a strain on the rope and decided it would either hold or it wouldn't. This was her best choice, so it would have to do. With a long, slow breath, she eased back over the fog-bound nothingness below. Keeping her feet carefully positioned against the sheer wall, she used her weight and her right hand to feed through the rope, which slid around her as she walked her way down. It rubbed hard against her left shoulder, and Eloise worried what it might do to her travel cloak, but it was working.

As she descended, Eloise considered what it would take to get back up. Going up, if they had to, would be a whole different matter, but that was always the case. She looked for handholds she might use for an ascent. There weren't a lot there.

Hand cramping and shoulder rubbed like a bad sunburn, Eloise finally touched down onto the rock-strewn sand at the bottom. Only then did she realize how hard she'd been breathing. But she'd made it, thank Çalaht.

"All yours," she called.

Up above, Eloise could not see Johanna wrapping herself in the rope, so she watched the rope jiggling, imagining what was probably happening: around the thigh, across the front, over the shoulder, across the back, and ready. Then nothing. Johanna was stalling. This was definitely not her idea of fun.

"Trust the rope," Eloise called up to her. "It's solid. And whatever you do, don't let go with your right hand."

"I know that, thank you," Johanna yelled back. "I'm too tense to come up with a suitable snappy retort. You'll have to fill in one of your own."

"I'll let you know what I come up with."

"If I die, tell Mother I'm sorry."

"Sorry for what?"

"Does it matter? Just say I'm sorry. That should cover all contingencies."

It was an odd conversation to be shouting across such a distance. "Right. Will do. But you'll be fine."

Eloise studied the rope movements as Johanna worked her way down. She slipped once, and then a second time a few minutes later—Eloise could tell from the sudden jerk of the rope and the mist-muffled cursing. But Johanna stayed steady, righted herself, and continued.

At the bottom, Johanna shrugged off the rope and massaged her shoulder. The material of her dress had rubbed away, and there was a patch of raw skin peeking through the damaged cloth. "I hope there's a different way up."

"Me, too. But I doubt it."

Eloise closed her eyes and focused. The pull on her was very specific now. If it had felt like a call from a shadow when she was at the foot of Fogging Hill, here it was like a herald, yelling in her face.

The land at the bottom of the cliff was covered in rocks and pebbles below the thick dust. Close to the cliff wall, there were a few tree carcasses, but twenty lengths away from it, the remains of any vegetation disappeared. They did not come across any dwellings, or any other built structure.

Eloise gasped and pointed. "Look!"

It was a woman, her hair white, her clothing antiquated, her flesh withered, but still most definitely attached to her body, unlike everything else they'd seen in this fog. The corpse sat in a nook formed by stones, leaning back like she had tried to get comfortable before passing away. The woman's death mask was tortured agony.

Carefully, they walked toward her. The buzzing in their heads got louder and louder, almost unbearably so, until they came within three lengths of the body, when suddenly it stopped. "Whoa!" said Eloise.

She put a finger in her ear and shook, like she was clearing it of water after a swim.

Johanna pressed her palms against her temples, then closed her eyes, sighing. "Çalaht hanging noodles from her ears, what a blessed relief."

They both took a moment to enjoy the unexpected reprieve, then edged closer to the woman's remains, coming within a length of her.

"Goodness, she's a mess," said Johanna. "Maybe not as much of a mess as some of the skeletons we've seen, but, ouch, look at that." The body's left arm had bone poking out of the skin in three places. Her left leg was similarly mangled, twisted into an unnatural angle, like a child's rag doll set upon by a mean older brother.

"That would have hurt," said Eloise.

The shattered arm rested on an open wooden box with a padded lining. Clutched in her right hand, which even now gripped like a vice, was a glowing emerald-green stone the size of a grapefruit—a grapefruit that had won Biggest in Show at the Celebration des Pamplemousses, perhaps, but still a grapefruit. "That's it, Jo," whispered Eloise. "That's the thing I can feel."

"Yes. What is it?"

Eloise shook her head. "No idea."

"Guh."

"Gah!" screamed Eloise. The corpse had made a noise. Both girls reflexively jumped away from the body, landing back in the buzzing zone. The sound hit Eloise like a stone, and she jerked forward again to make it stop. With testing, she found the spot where the noise stopped. Johanna did the same.

The corpse's lips quivered, then opened a weak length or two. "Guh. Gwh."

"Holy Çalaht banging bongos," said Eloise. "She's alive."

Carefully, they approached her. "Goodwoman. Goodwoman," said Eloise gently. "Can you hear me?"

"Gweh," the old woman moaned. "Gweh."

"Are you in pain?" asked Johanna.

"Gwehn." The sound slipped out of her like a rustle of parchment.

Eloise reached out to put a hand on the woman's right knee, but jerked her arm back almost immediately as a shock practically knocked Eloise over. "What the…"

She leaned in, careful not to get too close, and spoke loudly toward the woman's ear. "Goodwoman? Goodwoman, can we help you?"

The woman opened ancient eyes. She blinked glacially, once, twice. "Gwennie?" she slurred. "Gwennie? You?"

"Goodwoman, my name is Eloise. This is my sister, Johanna."

The woman sighed the slowest, saddest sigh Eloise had ever heard. "Not Gweh." She sank back in on herself, closing her eyes again.

Eloise stepped away and motioned for Johanna to come closer. "What is going on here?"

"I'm not sure. But look at her. Look at the way she's dressed. She's been here a while. What happened when you tried to touch her?"

"I couldn't get near her. Coming close was like shaking hands with a delegation of shockfish."

They went back to her, getting as near as was safe. Eloise knelt so she could hover near one ear, and Johanna did the same with the other. "Goodwoman! What is your name!" yelled Eloise.

"No." The woman wheezed, and sluggishly opened her eyes again.

"Pardon?" yelled Johanna.

"No. Need. Yell. Not. Deaf."

Eloise guessed that was more words than the woman had spoken in decades. She spoke in the same cadence of disused speech as the Nameless One had. "My apologies," said Eloise at a normal volume. "Goodwoman, may I ask your name?"

The woman carefully turned her head slightly, being careful not to move any of the rest of her body. She looked at Eloise. "You have her eyes. Strange."

"Whose eyes?"

"Gwen's."

"Gwen?"

"My sister. Gwen."

"You can't be," said Johanna, mostly to herself. "That's not possible."

"What, Jo?" asked Eloise.

"Goodwoman, is your name 'Melveeta?'"

Eloise looked at Johanna, shocked. "It can't be."

The woman started to swivel her head toward Johanna, but winced at the movement. Johanna moved around and knelt next to Eloise. She accidentally got too close to the woman, and recoiled at the shock.

"Careful there," said the old woman. "How do you know my name?"

"We have read of you," said Johanna. "In Histories and Hearsay. Melveeta the Elusive, who mysteriously disappeared while serving as champion to Gwendolyn the Irritable."

There was a pause, and then the woman's mouth stretched and quivered. Eloise feared she would fall into a palsied fit like Gouache. How could she help her if she couldn't touch her?

But this was no fit. This was something different.

Laughter.

She was laughing, making as little movement as possible.

"Gwendolyn the Irritable? That's how my Gwennie is remembered?" More low chuckling. "Oh, she would hate that. She would truly hate that." She chuckled a little more. "That I'm 'the Elusive' and she's 'the Irritable'—that would burn her onions, for sure."

"How can we help you, Goodwoman Melv—" Eloise corrected herself. "Apologies. How can we help you, Champion Melveeta Gumball? I'm sorry, I don't know your full name."

The woman ignored the incomplete formality, and a sad look came over her. "How did she die?"

Eloise and Johanna looked at each other. Eloise gave her an "I don't know" look.

"Surely my Gwennie is as dead as I am not. You said you read of her in your histories. How did she die?"

"I believe she died of old age," said Johanna. "But it has been more than ten score years, and there have been many queens since then. I fear I cannot tell you for certain."

"Old age?" repeated Melveeta. "Well, more burned onions, then. Gwennie always wanted to go out in a blaze of glory. Gwendolyn the Great or Gwendolyn the Conqueror, fallen to the sword in the great fight." The unfamiliar effort of talking clearly tired her, and she slowed. "I have had a while to think on our foolishness. I did not know it had been more than ten score years. It could have been a thousand or a few dozen. But foolishness it was. And I am the greatest fool of all."

And with that, Eloise and Johanna watched the oldest living human, the greatest mass murderer in the history of the realms and their distant auntie, doze off into a senescent, drool-specked nap.

NO SUPPOSED ABOUT IT

While Melveeta slept, Eloise and Johanna discussed what they might do for her, but there weren't many options. Touching her seemed out of the question. Moving her, or helping her move herself, also seemed beyond possibility, given how broken her body was and how much pain the slightest movement seemed to cause her. Besides, where would they take her? Up the cliff?

Then there was the small matter of whatever it was she was holding—clearly a magical object, and probably the one they sought. They couldn't do anything until they had a sense of how it was involved with the Purple Haze.

All they could do was wait in the small space between the woman and the wall of buzzing, and let her rest. They, too, slipped into sleep.

Melveeta woke with a startled jolt that racked her body with pain, causing her to howl. Eloise and Johanna woke with a shock, but all they could do was let Melveeta's wave of pain subside. When it finally passed, the old woman said, "I used to do that all the time. Over the years, I taught myself to be as still, dull, and quiet as possible. Having you here has agitated me."

"Champion Melveeta," said Eloise gently, "can you tell us what happened?"

"Do you know what that is?" Her eyes darted to the glowing stone she clenched.

"No," said Johanna. "Clearly it is magical."

"No guesses?"

"If I were to hazard one, it would be the Star of Whatever," said Eloise.

"So the knowledge remains."

"To be honest, not really," said Johanna. "We are told that it probably existed. It was alleged to have disappeared under the reign of Gwendolyn the Irritable—sorry—under Queen Gwendolyn. It was supposed to have been powerful, but no one knows in what way."

"'Supposed to have been powerful'? There is no 'supposed' about it. Look at me! Look how broken I am. Yet I have lived two centuries and more. I cannot release it. It will not let me die, though I have certainly tried hard enough. There is enough power in the Star of Whatever to draw the magic from ten villages around!"

"No," said Eloise. "If what you said is true and this is the Star of Whatever, then it is much, much more powerful than that."

Eloise and Johanna told her of the Purple Haze, the damage it had done to the Half Kingdom, the mass of deaths when it was first unleashed, the devastation to the land, and the thousands upon thousands of deaths it had caused since, from ships tossed into it during storms to monarchs deliberately using it for foggings.

Tears ran down the woman's face. Quiet sobs shook her chest. "I'm so sorry," she whispered, not to Eloise or Johanna, but to the ghosts in her memories. "I'm so, so sorry."

❧ 13 ❧

A STAR IS BORN

Melveeta told her story like she had been rehearsing it forever. But it was a tale being told for the first time, so was still rough in the delivery.

"I was not my sister's first champion," she finally began.

⁂

PRESUMABLY, I WAS NOT HER LAST, IF SHE PASSED OF OLD AGE. BUT she honored me as champion, and I served her and her interests as best I could for twenty-three years, until I ended up here.

Gwendolyn became queen very young, and there were many who opposed her. She dealt with that by becoming the toughest biscuit in the basket, with a complete intolerance of nonsense. Still, she proved to be an excellent queen, with a skill for balancing the petty needs of Court with the genuine needs of people. If she's not remembered for that, then history is remiss.

But she was flawed, as people are. There's no getting around that. Name it and she suffered it. Pride. Avarice. Jealousy. Gluttony. Wrath. Overcoming these was part of what made her great, when she was great. Succumbing to them is what brought her low. And it was the Star of Whatever that brought her lowest.

Gwendolyn always had a fascination with magic, although she had no natural talent for it herself. This was frustrating for her, with so much magic all around her. She became obsessed with magical artifacts, which she collected and studied, hoping they might extend her mundane abilities. Gwendolyn's desperation for her own magic made her vulnerable to hucksters and charlatans, who promised much and delivered nothing. Most of what she gathered proved ordinary—trinkets without a hint of enchantment.

But then there were those things that most definitely had magical qualities, even if they were strange. There was her Brass Snoreless Weasel of Lassitude, which could put people into an unnaturally deep and completely quiet sleep. There was the Marble Olive of Pulchritudinous Bounty, captured during a raid on the far ends of the Eastern Lands, which could double the size and volume of an olive tree's harvest when planted below it. Unfortunately, it was of limited value since it was the only one, and it only affected one tree at a time. You would have heard of the Bident of Trapezius, a two-pronged pitchfork you could stab into a person? If they were particularly pure of heart, it would pass through them as if they were smoke. Then there were the Shoes of Elevatorius, which looked like two small upturned soup cauldrons about ten weak lengths deep, with antlers. When worn on the feet they disappeared and charmed everyone into believing the wearer was ten weak lengths taller than they actually were. She even came to possess the Chimichanga of Veracity, which, when nibbled, acted as a truth serum.

As champion, I traveled with her, and was always on the lookout for possibly magical pieces my queen might find interesting. Near a quaint, cheerful village called Unmitigated Catastrophic Disappointment, which was not that far from Blisteringly Overwhelming Defeat, I met a tinker who promised me that the case he was trying to sell would be a treasure trove of magical wonder that would help "our beloved Her Highness Gwendolyn live forever." Despite the fact that this was utter tosh, on a whim, I paid him his pittance and took the cheap wooden box.

I forgot about it until we were back at Castle de Brague, and my groom brought it to me after unpacking. I picked through the contents, immediately discarding a nose ring, a polished disc that looked like a blank for striking a coin, and a crust of bagel purporting to be from the first bagel ever boiled and not just baked.

I was regretting even the measly sum I had paid when I felt something smooth and solid in the box. When I touched it, it lit with a small glow, a light no brighter than that shone by a geriatric lightning bug. I took it out of the box. The stone, the size of a decent goiter, was wrapped in a hessian rag and looked like it had been tossed into the bottom of the case to add weight.

When it came in contact with my bare skin, it brightened even more. I rushed to Gwendolyn to show her what I'd found. She was pleased, until the moment I handed it to her and the light faded. In my hands, it looked like it was powered by a handful of glowworms. In hers, nothing.

"Well, it's at least a bit magical, I guess we can say that," said Gwendolyn. "Let's see what it is capable of, and start working on a name."

The name thing was important to us, if perhaps silly. All the great magical artifacts had catchy names, and we kept hoping we might get to name something one day. Our favorites were not things Gwendolyn owned—the Chuckling Spear, the Helmet of Formidable Wonder, the Foundation Garments of Doom, the Unpronounceable Cauldron of nïägäÿrtdnädräöbgnïwärdëhtötkcäbtïëkätëkässsëndöögröfrët- tëbgnïhtëmöshtïwpüëmöctndlüöcüöÿgnïddïkëböttögëvüöŸ, and of course, Bob. With our magical stone, we wanted a name that could stand with those greats.

But we did not understand what the thing could do—it's not like it came with an instruction scroll—and good names have to tie in with the thing itself. The "star" part was easy, since it glowed. So we called it the Star of Whatever, knowing we'd eventually get something better.

However, once we started using that name in front of the research mages, it stuck, and any effort to change it failed to take hold.

The research mages could sense it was powerful, which pleased the queen, but were baffled as to how one unlocked its possibilities. When they approached the stone with their usual tools of detection and testing—wands, divining rods, calipers, and savants (both idiot and non-idiot)—all the magic boffins could do was scratch their heads. The stone defied them.

The stone defied everyone.

Except me. I was the one who worked it out, and even that was an accident. I got in the habit of carrying the Star of Whatever around with me. I liked the look of the glow, and the fact that it responded to me. It was too large to fit conveniently in a pocket, so I fashioned a close-fitting, shoulder-slung pouch that I wore under my clothing.

It was the court jester who provided the breakthrough clue. Nostrum Kruscheltante used magic in his entertaining. He could juggle nine balls in his sleep, and once juggled 15 for five minutes—a staggering performance. He was performing for Gwendolyn, who saw me passing in the hall and called me in to watch with her. As soon as I entered the room, Nostrum fumbled his clubs. He looked confused, but picked them up again to resume. But for the first time in his jestering career, he was unable keep more than two going, and even that was a struggle.

I lost interest and begged my leave. Gwendolyn waved me off, and as soon as I was out of the room, Nostrum regained his rhythm and had a half-dozen clubs flying. My sister called me back, and again, Nostrum dropped them all. When it happened a third time, we became curious. We tested how close I had to be for Nostrum to have a problem. We considered if the way I walked into the room made a difference, or the words I spoke. Eventually, I began removing objects from my person, leaving them at what seemed a safe distance. With the Star of Whatever in the hallway, the change was immediate. Nostrum flicked eight rings in the air in a perfect cascade. We found that having the Star within ten lengths when I could see him, or five lengths on the other side of a stone wall, was enough to render him a bumbling klutz.

The Star of Whatever affected his magic.

It affected everyone's magic. That's why the research mages couldn't crack it. They were using magic to figure out magic, but the Star muffled it.

I worked with it when I could, and got a sense of its proclivities. I could control it enough to dampen all the magic in a room, but it remained more of a curiosity than anything else.

And then Gwendolyn had her heart broken, and everything changed.

❦ 14 ❦

GAZUMPED

King Brüüütus was a fop, a dandy, a coxcomb, and he and my Gwen fell hopelessly in love. They met on a battlefield, their two armies ready to face each other over some squabble I no longer recall. Following Protocol, the two leaders met to parlay. Usually this was a formality before bloodshed, a pro forma attempt to resolve their differences and avoid the fight. To everyone's surprise, they did more than that. They emerged from the two-day tête-à-tête engaged, and, we soon found out, expecting. It would be a match for the ages— the ruling monarchs of two great realms joining into a single grand land and a joint throne.

It should have been wonderful.

The two went their separate ways, as both had realms to run, and unions like that are complex things to structure. Love notes criss-crossed the two realms, and I'd never seen Gwendolyn happier.

Things went wrong around the time the blessed impending event was becoming visible. Plans to unify the kingdom and the queendom became bogged down in stubbornness among the negotiators. Promised trade delegations failed to arrive and expected shipments were diverted to other lands. Worst of all, communication that had once been sweet and playful became terse and sparse, then stopped altogether.

Something was amiss.

Emissaries were sent, as well as spies, and what they both found gutted Gwendolyn. Brüüütus had not only taken up with another, but had quietly married her. He no longer had thoughts of a grand unified realm, nor of Gwendolyn at all. The woman in question was a little-known minor noble, which led to inevitable speculation that the king had been ensorcelled.

Something broke in my sister. She stopped calling the future queen or king inside her "Blossom," instead referring to the baby as "The Parasite."

⁂

"HOLD IT, HOLD IT, HOLD IT," INTERRUPTED JOHANNA. "ARE YOU saying Queen Aubrey the Parasitic got that nickname from her mother? That's horrible."

"So she's remembered that way, is she?" said Melveeta.

"I thought it was for extravagant living on the public purse, or a comment on her relationship with her suitors or advisors. But for her to be named such even before birth? And to have to carry that her entire life? Dreadful."

"But you referred to her as 'Queen' Aubrey. So she must have ruled."

"Late in life, and badly," said Johanna. "She was ill-suited to the task, and was probably more relieved than anyone to have passed away after a few scant months on the throne."

"You have to remember I've only ever known her as a swaddled baby blob being held by someone who wasn't the queen. My last memory of her was her spitting up on a rather expensive dress. That she disappointed later in life comes as little surprise, given my sister's antipathy."

Johanna shook her head, and she and Eloise let Melveeta continue.

THE IRRITABILITY OF WHICH YOU SPOKE FLARED UP THEN. Gwendolyn's hatred of the Northo king festered, growing in parallel with the child. It was hard for me to tell which irked her more, having been gazumped in love or losing the chance to double her sphere of rule.

One day, half a year after her encounter with Brüüütus, Queen Gwendolyn called me to her private chamber. "Melveeta, it vexes me greatly that this has happened. I've decided to do something about it."

"Yes, my Queen." I didn't like the exaggeratedly calm tone she used. I'd heard it enough to know it bode ill.

"I shall assume control of the Northern Lands. They were promised to me, as was he. The Parasite is proof enough of that. I intend to make sure that promise is kept."

"How do you plan to do that? His armies defend him. His castle is fortified, with both guards and enchantments—just like yours. We are as likely to breach his defenses as he would be ours. In other words, not very." It was not totally unlike Gwendolyn to squander lives or resources on vanity projects, but there was always a logic to them. She must have come up with something.

"We have something they do not."

"What is that?"

"The Star of Whatever. It, and you."

"What?"

"It is time the Star stopped being a toy and was honed for practical use."

"Nonsense. The thing is little more than a party trick."

"I believe you have not been trying hard enough, Champion Melveeta Gumball. I think it can be channeled to greater use. I need what it can do—but more, bigger. You will apply yourself, Mel. You will learn to extend the range of the Star of Whatever, to focus its knack for magical dampening as a weapon. And you will do that now. I will have the Northern Lands. This..." She pointed at her growing belly. "This thing will grow up in the world that was promised to me. And you and this 'party trick' will help me do it."

"Yes, my queen."

I devoted myself to the task. Gwendolyn was right, as she so often was —there was more hidden in the Star of Whatever than in any magical object I'd ever handled. With time, I learned to control it, to deploy its strengths, to hide its weaknesses, to use intention, will, spells, and incantations to amplify its talents and direct its effects. I worked out how to augment its power using a kind of magical gray fogginess, and went from being able to disrupt a magical juggler to deploying the fog in the middle of the Mages' Guild headquarters and disabling everyone in the building.

What was the difference to my previous attempts to harness the Star? I had a purpose. My queen had asked me to use the Star of Whatever for her benefit. I would not fail her.

There are those who say all things contain consciousness. Çalahtists and philosophers can debate that all they want, but here is my truth: the Star of Whatever had a spark of something that was akin to the spark of something in people. I connected with it very personally. As I grew to know it, I felt a sense of "self" residing it it. It responded to the attention, and like any muscle exercised, it became stronger and more capable.

Gwendolyn's child was born, and immediately handed off to a wet nurse.

I continued to train and learn. I tested it on small villages and hamlets, spreading the fog and drawing down all magic, then withdrawing the fog and letting magic return.

After weeks of intense work, I knew the Star of Whatever was ready—that the two of us were ready.

Gwendolyn and I shaped a plan. She would travel unannounced to Stained Rock to present Brüüütus with his daughter at Castle Blotch. We would take a force with us that was large enough to be effective, but small enough not to look like a real threat. Once inside the castle, I'd deploy the Star of Whatever, knocking out their magical protections, and our guards would assume control. And if Brüüütus was, indeed, under the influence of an enchantment, then it would fall away too, and perhaps he'd see Gwendolyn as he had before. But by then, that was a matter of lesser importance.

The northerners must have realized something was up. We had to practically shove our way through the gate at the Adequate Wall. Northo troops shadowed our every movement, and we couldn't get close to the Castle Blotch gates, much less find a way in. Gwendolyn, already aggrieved, did not exactly take it well. Through her messengers, she tried cajoling, invective, reasoning, even caroling. But the responses she received gave no satisfaction.

When Gwendolyn tried sending me in on my own as her emissary, I met particularly rude and immutable resistance.

We were stymied. We had a force that was too small to mount a direct assault, but too large (not to mention the child) to mount a sneak attack.

It was time for Plan B.

Müüüdy Wäääters was the busiest port in the Northern Lands. Its water was not so much muddy as prone to unpredictable outbreaks that would choke the harbor with a blanket of blueish algal sludge. Air bubbling up through the blue gunk would produce sounds like moans and wails. Northo sailors called these mournful algae noises "singing the blues," and Müüüdy Wäääters was famous for it.

While Gwendolyn retreated from the Stained Rock town walls and waited for me to access the castle and cover it in the magical foggy grayness, I charged off to a smaller, more distant port, hired a boat and sailed for Müüüdy Wäääters. My plan was to assume a trader's costume, blend in with arrivals, and make my way to Stained Rock under pretense of commerce.

Unfortunately, the harbor was singing the loudest blues in living memory. It was like a noisy, bluesy tapioca pudding. With that much algae choking the port, there was no way the captain was willing to risk getting stuck in it. He point-blank refused to take me in. The trip was a waste of precious time and valuable coin.

So. Plan C.

❧ 15 ❧

PLUMMET

For Plan C, I'd take a small boat and row it into Transporters of Not Necessarily Registered, Approved, or Properly Taxed Goods Cove, then climb up the wall behind the cascading waters of Certain Falls. Smugglers leave a rope tied there so they can make the treacherous ascent and haul up their goods, so I'd climb that. I'd then cross overland, approaching Stained Rock from a deceptive angle, somehow sneak past the town gates, and get close enough to the castle to cast my spell. When Gwendolyn saw the gray mist from where she waited, she'd approach and take control of the castle. The rest of the plan would follow the same route as Plan A.

It should have worked, too, but for my own failings. I caught a favorable tide, beached the boat, and picked my way through the dense brush toward the falls. The cove was choked with rash nettle, no doubt deliberately planted to discourage casual visitors. More than one plant brushed my skin, setting off its infernal itch.

Certain Falls was a thing of beauty. It wasn't the highest or widest waterfall in the realm, but it splashed into a clear, blue pool, and had a permanent rainbow gracing the mist the falls threw off. I knew a rope would be coiled on a ledge above head height, hidden from anyone who didn't know where or what they were looking for. I found the narrow slip of relatively dry rock between the falling water and the cliff face, and shimmied up to where the rope waited.

I made sure the Star of Whatever was secure, and climbed, trusting my fate to Çalaht and the rope. I tried not to think about how treacherous the rock wall was, nor how treacherous smugglers were, or whether those two things would overlap.

You've come down that cliff face, so you have a sense of the skill and caution needed to ascend it. It was trebly difficult for me. Rushing water would pummel me if I leaned the wrong way. Anything that might be gripped was slick with slime. The rope itself was greasy with ancient wet. The nagging red skin irritation of rash nettle blossomed into full white-headed pustules that, if broken, would bleed and spread the itch.

So, I was careful. Obsessively, hysterically cautious. I moved very deliberately, always making sure I had three solid points of contact with the wall. The climb took hours, as expected. I pushed through the fatigue of exertion and the pain in my fingers by thinking of how my queen was waiting for me, and how her destiny waited on me as well.

My extreme care fell short by a single foothold.

Just one.

From what you've told me, I've spent two centuries thinking about those moments of failure. One more careful foothold, and everything would have been different.

I've played back the moment in my head like a bard rehearsing. My right hand gripped the rope a length away from the top, clutching as best I could to the dank hemp. The fingers of my left hand curled into a crack that was two weak lengths deep at most. I slowly shifted my weight from my left foot to my right, then lifted the left one toward the spot where I could ease up and over the ledge. That's when the tiny divot that my right foot was lodged into broke away, showering fragments down to the rocks below. I dangled, trying to wrap a leg around the rope.

If it had happened an hour before, I would have had the strength to find purchase again. But I was beyond exhausted, soaked by the waterfall, and rash nettle pustules shot pain and itch through my fingers. I'm not making excuses. I should have succeeded.

Instead, I lost my grip and slipped off the rope.

I hit an overhang with my arm, fracturing it, glanced against the cliff wall, then careened off a narrow shelf where I had previously rested. That sent me slowly spinning like a drunken carter's wheel. My instinct was to curl into a protective ball, but I resisted, instead trying to fly toward the water and not the rocks that ringed it. Fly? Ha! A delicious moment of wishful thinking. I plummeted. What I did was akin to what a sack of rotting yam off-cuts might do if tossed from a Çalahtist devotional house steeple onto a cobblestone road.

I landed hard on my side, hitting a cluster of small boulders, then slid off into a patch of rash nettle. My left arm had broken two more times, and, well, you've seen what happened to my hip and leg. That I survived was a fluke, but I had little time for that, as I was in more pain than I could ever have imagined.

Despair fought with agony for my attention. I was alive, if you could call it that, but I had let down my queen. There was no way I could get up that cliff face again. She was waiting for a gray fog that would never come.

I cupped a mouthful of water from the pool, then half-crawled, half-dragged my shattered body away from it. I'm sure I fainted, because I clearly recall waking to a face full of rash nettle. Somehow I reached this place where you found me, which had the advantage of shade and a lighter covering of the cursed plant. If I had known I would be here the next 200 years, I might not have chosen a spot that faced the cliff, where my principal entertainment would be retracing the path of my fall.

Amazingly, the Star of Whatever was still strapped to me. It slowly dawned on me that I might still do something.

I rested, practicing what I have practiced ever since—moving as little as possible to avoid the torment of broken bones and smashed organs. I shrank my world to a single goal: live long enough to cast the strength of the Star of Whatever toward the castle at Stained Rock, and help my queen one last time.

Hatred grew as I fumbled the Star of Whatever out of its box. A hatred for King Brüüütus. This was all his fault. If he had stayed true to my sister, ensorcelled or not, I would not be a wrecked, miserable wretch at the bottom of a cliff. Mine was no small antipathy. Hate filled every fiber of my being, fueled by the rash nettle pustules that inspired delirium, sharpened by arm bones piercing skin, and leg bones grinding together at demented angles, my guts reduced to unrecognizable soup—all this was brought into sharp focus by the feeling that my life force was ebbing away too quickly to achieve my task. That feeling circled around on itself, igniting even more anguished hatred.

What I was about to attempt, one way or another, would be the last significant act of my life, a final chance to serve Queen Gwendolyn. I grasped the Star of Whatever with the hand of my good arm and focused all my remaining energy on a single thing—casting a spell that sent magic toward the castle at Stained Rock.

Ah, the spell.

The spell was a grotesque perfection. The extremity of my situation amplified its birth. The genuine madness created by pain, itch and hate seeped into the Star as I cast the spell. Certain that this mangled body would expire soon, I put my all into this last act of power. I gave it everything and then I gave it more. The spell was infused with hatred. Hatred and disappointment, frustration and rage, a mania of gnawing itch and an all-consuming yearning for a pot of Northern Lands wart cream and its lilac caress. All of this flooded into the Star of Whatever as I chanted the incantation.

Then the Star of Whatever did something I had not thought a magical object could do—it took over. It gobbled up everything I gave it, then extracted more. The spell gripped the tissue and sinew of my body, taking all for itself. Anything I was or had was lost to the Star of

Whatever's control, and when it loosed the spell like an arrow toward Castle Blotch, I could do nothing but watch the purple, foggy manifestation slice away from me.

I knew this spell was unlike anything anyone had ever cast before, a perfect confluence of ingredients. Who would cast a spell while in such a state, using such a rare tool? No one.

Together, the Star and the spell enveloped me, imprisoned me, froze me in time. Death refused to come. I had no idea what, if anything, had been achieved. Had the spell crossed the many strong lengths to Stained Rock? And if it had, did it dim the magical fortifications of Castle Blotch? I allowed myself the comfort of imagining it had, and that Gwendolyn had seen the lavender mist in the distance and used its cover to charge the castle and wrest control.

From what you've said, I understand there's no way she could have. So even that is now taken from me.

I expected it might be a while before the spell's effects faded enough for me to free myself from its grip. I tried to position myself in the least painful way, ready to wait it out. The spell's hold and my own pain limited my options to the briefest exertions. With time, I learned to put myself into a kind of fugue state, breathing as little as possible, moving even less. The rash nettle sores itched, but I locked away the part of my mind that might care. As the center point of the Star's spell, I neither healed—which would have required more energy than the Star would give me—nor deteriorate, presumably because I was crucial to the spell's existence.

Time passed, measured by inhales, exhales, and slow changes to the world around me. I bore witness to the withering of the land nearby, the curling up of the plants, the death of trees. I was intensely aware of the complete silence. There were no voices of any kind. Not the chatter of bugs, nor the high-pitched gossip of flies. Nothing. Then my one source of variation, the movement of water down the cliff face, slowed to a trickle, then a drip, then dried completely. Certain Falls met a certain finish.

Next came the dust. The world around me became filmed with dust, which settled over everything except me. The Star or the spell or both kept me clear.

❦

"SUCH IS HOW I REMAINED," said MELVEETA. "SOMETIMES MY MIND was quiescent, which might have looked something like peace from the outside. But most often, it was active, filled with thoughts chasing each other in circles of recrimination, horrific imagining, boredom, fulsome self-aggrandizement, and even more plentiful self-loathing. Then you showed up and told me of destruction far worse than any possibility I'd ever tortured myself with."

She went quiet. There was nothing more to say. Eventually, she muttered, "So here we are."

"Yes, Champion Melveeta," said Eloise. "Here we are."

❧ 16 ❧

JUDGMENT

Jerome had no idea how long he'd been in the dungeon cell when he was finally hauled out, wrists bound, snout muzzled, and feet hobbled by chains. The emotional battering he'd received had left him drained, woozy, and depressed. It seemed like a long time since he'd stopped bouncing around the cell in panic, but his sore muscles told him there was still a lot of recovering to do. He should have had more of an emotional reaction to finally getting out of the Çalaht-cursed dungeon, but he was numb to the change. Plus, there was the insult of the guard carrying him by the scruff of the neck instead of allowing him to walk. His limp acquiescence came naturally and easily.

Lorch, too, had emerged from his cell bound, gagged, and hobbled. At least he was allowed the dignity of walking. Lorch had given Jerome a concerned look, but had been shoved toward the stairs before he could say anything. The clink, clink, clink of chains on stone accompanied their ascent.

They were taken to an outside yard where they joined a dozen other prisoners, eight humans, a python with an eye patch, a bilby with a truncated tail who looked more like someone's granny than someone who ought to be in prison, and the roughest-looking gecko Jerome had ever seen. Guards bucketed them all with cold, brackish water to remove the worst of their grime, then kept them shivering in a wan sun patch while they dried from sopping to an unpleasant dampness. Jerome's guard picked him up, shook him to get more of the water off him, then said to the other guards, "That'll do. The king'll be waiting."

The king. They were going before the king? Jerome's muzzy thoughts gathered a bit. This was either very, very good or very, very bad. Had Eloise intervened? He hoped so. That would mean he was out of the cell once and for all. Or was this just an extension of the tauntings? He couldn't take more of those. And to be taunted in front of the king? Or by the king? It was a sign of how fragile he'd become that even at this little emotional hiccup, Jerome's panic rose.

He looked ahead at Lorch and saw calm. Lorch was wet, goose-fleshed, and thinner than before, but calm. Jerome tried to draw some of that calm into himself as he was carried by the back of his neck.

The line of prisoners clinked and sloshed their way through a maze of cold, dimly lit hallways until they reached a solid wooden door. "Stand and wait in silence," commanded the lead guard, and the line of prisoners shuffled to a stop. Jerome's guard let him go, dropping him behind Lorch at the end of the line, where he landed hard and twisted a bound ankle.

One by one, the prisoners were led through the door. In the moments it was open, Jerome could see hints of formal proceedings, but the room was brilliantly lit, so most of what he saw was a painful glare of light. Sometimes he thought he could hear a wail or a moan from within, but mostly he heard the breathing, shuffling and chattering teeth of chilled impatience from both guards and inmates. Only the python seemed not to care about the cold, although he was decidedly sluggish when it was his turn to go into the room.

Whatever was going on in there, it seemed to take forever. Now and then, the door would open and the next prisoner would go inside as someone said their name. Them the door would close, leaving the rest of them in the dank hallway. Jerome would have tried to talk to Lorch, but there wasn't much he could say through his damp gag.

After what seemed like forever, the door cracked open for Lorch, who held himself straight, and strode forward as best he could in leg irons. Unlike the previous prisoners, it was only a few moments before the door opened again, and Jerome found himself nudged forward by a guard's boot. He blinked himself into the brightness of the room, and followed the trail of wetness to where Lorch still stood. He heard someone say, "This is his accomplice, Jerome Abernatheen de Chipmunk, also from the court at Castle de Brague."

"I know who they are," snarled Doncaster.

So the king was, indeed, there. As Jerome's eyes adjusted to the light, he looked to where the voice had come from. Doncaster sat on a low dais, surrounded by three scribes scratching quills on parchment, recording everything that took place. To Jerome's horror, Doncaster's jester, Turpy, was there too, his hand heavily bandaged and his arm in a sling. Jerome's breathing quickened, and he tried to control his jester phobia. As he did so, he could see that something was changed about Turpy. He'd seemed evil enough when Jerome had encountered him before, but now a darkness pervaded his eyes, and a manic nervousness kept him perpetually moving, leaning in and whispering to the king over and over. The word "unhinged" came to mind, but then, given his current state, who was Jerome to judge?

Doncaster looked somewhere between bored and steely. On a low table next to him sat a bowl of roasted peanuts still in their shells. Doncaster idly picked one up, cracked it in his teeth, pulled out the nut, and flicked the shell to the ground in front of him. From the pile of shells on the floor, it was clear this had been going on a while.

"Excuse me, Your Highness. Might I have a word, please?" The watery voice came from Jerome's left.

"The Speaker for the Indigent may approach the throne," said Doncaster, flipping a shell fragment onto the pile.

Jerome watched as a one-armed capuchin picked up a fishbowl from a table and carried it to within a length of the throne. He set it down and assumed a waiting position. Doncaster flicked another peanut shell fragment, which landed just to the side of the fishbowl. Jerome suddenly worked out that the gray-bluish mass in the bowl was a jellyfish.

"Your Highness, unlike the people who have come before you so far today, I have not yet had a chance to confer with these prisoners. I would request that the case be recessed until I have had a chance to properly prepare it."

"Denied." The suddenness of Doncaster's pronouncement shocked the room.

The jellyfish continued, undeterred. "King Doncaster, the crown's own justice demands I represent them properly. How can I do that if I'm not able to speak with them and hear their side of the matters under charge?"

"I said, denied. There will be no recess."

Jerome had been transfixed by the scene before him, especially the way the capuchin could gesture so expressively with this one arm in exact harmony with the jellyfish. It was like his own brain was sitting there in that glass bowl.

"Then at least let me speak to them now for a few minutes. I've only seen the charges against them this morning."

Turpy leaned in and whispered, but Doncaster waved him away irritably. "The charges are clear enough, are they not?" The king turned to one of the scribes. "Read them out."

The scribe to his left set down her quill, picked up a scroll and cleared her throat. In a voice like a squeaking carriage wheel, she read, "Disturbing the peace. Showing disrespect to a royally designated representative of the crown. Entering a royal building with malicious intent. Treasonous plotting against the crown. Conspiring and plotting against the Royal Personage in miscellaneous and nefarious ways. Encouraging sedition. Aiding and abetting the removal of the king's property." The scribe set down her scroll and picked up her quill, ready to resume writing.

"Your Highness, these are serious charges. Surely you can spare me a few minutes to confer with the accused?"

The king dug at a molar with the nail of his pinky. "Fine, then. You may have ten minutes while I go and find a toothpick."

"Thank you, Your Highness," said the jellyfish. "Your consideration of the prisoners is most appreciated." But Doncaster was already up and out the door, followed closely by Turpy.

The capuchin picked up the fishbowl and brought it to where Lorch and Jerome stood. He set it down on the ground and was gesturing almost immediately. "First, I'm Këëëvin Ïïïgnatius Göööbermouch, Speaker for the Indigent. This is my associate, Fïïïnn. I bring greetings from your friends, Hector and the one who does not speak. They told me to look out for you, but I had no idea where in the dungeons you were. I'm sorry you won't be able to speak to me, as there's no time for me to file a motion to have your gags removed—just nod or shake your head as is appropriate. First, is any of this true?"

Lorch shook his head, a firm "no." Jerome shrugged his shoulders. The bit about conspiring and plotting against the Royal Personage in miscellaneous and nefarious ways probably wasn't too far from the truth, if he was honest. Certainly, he'd easily have admitted as much to his taunter. Maybe he had. It was all a blur.

"Whether it is or isn't, your case is grim. I don't know what you did to anger His Highness so much. Perhaps it was that jester who was angered. It's hard to tell sometimes where one starts and the other stops. But it seems like every charge that could be laid is being pressed. My goal is to slow down the proceedings. If I can introduce a delay, then maybe the heat of this annoyance will dissipate, giving His Highness a chance to reconsider. Do you agree with this strategy?"

Lorch nodded, but Jerome just offered another shrug.

"So, please let me ask you a few questions," said the jellyfish. "What exactly does it mean that you..."

The door opened and Doncaster strode back in poking at the same molar. "All right, I found a toothpick. Let's get on with this." Turpy hovered as always, as Doncaster sat back down.

The capuchin picked up the fishbowl and set it back on the table. "If it pleases Your Highness, I would like to start by saying—"

"Guilty."

"I beg your pardon, Your Highness?"

"Did I not speak clearly enough? All those things. Guilty. Above all, the abetting of the removal of my property."

"Your property, Your Highness?"

"My fiancée." Doncaster stood and pointed at the prisoners. "I announced I was taking a queen, and you two were part of ruining that. Where is she?" The gagged accused said nothing. "It is as I said. Guilty on all counts. I condemn them to fogging." Then Doncaster picked up a handful of peanuts, put them in his pocket, and walked out of the room. Turpy cracked a malicious smile and followed.

The last thing Jerome heard before he fainted was the jellyfish saying, "Well, that's less than ideal."

17

THE HOPE OF DWINDLING

Johanna broke the silence that lingered after Melveeta's tale. "So, what do we do?"

Melveeta's eyes darted in her direction. "Is that not obvious? The spell must end."

"Yes, that much I'd worked out. But how?"

"It requires more than me alone. We must link together in physical and spiritual connection. The spell was cast in hatred and pain. If it will be undone, it will be through the opposite. The most likely key to triggering its end is love. We must overwhelm it with love. That, plus something else. Perhaps not the opposite of pain and itch, but rather, an intense desire for relief."

"Again, how?"

"Both of us have tried to come near you," added Eloise. "It's nigh on impossible."

"You must go past 'nigh'." Anger and desperation flashed across Melveeta's face. "I will not spend another two centuries stranded at the center of a magical monster. I cannot do it on my own. I've proven that to myself for five lifespans. But this must end, and it must end now."

"What do you propose?" asked Eloise.

"You two must push through the protective layer of the spell around me. Each of you will take one of my hands and join hands yourselves. One of you will hold the Star of Whatever with me, and between the three of us, we will create a vortex of power. That should provide me with enough support to deal with the spark of life within the Star, and with the spell."

"How do we know this will work?" asked Johanna.

"We don't. This could go very badly in many ways. We might not be strong enough to end it, in which case the two of you could end up stuck here as well. Or we could end the spell, but in doing so, release a power that obliterates us. Or we could end up not stopping the spell, but influence it enough so it changes, but not necessarily in a way that is desirable. Shall I continue?"

"No, thank you," said Johanna. "I get the idea." She moved to Melveeta's left, positioning herself so she would not be the one to grasp the Star of Whatever, which was in the Melveeta's right hand.

"Be careful with that side," Melveeta said to Johanna. "Try not to jostle me. It hurts enough as it is."

"Of course. May I ask what will happen if we can actually end the spell?"

"It will not vanish like a weakling flame going out. It will dissipate slowly, fading with time. It has had centuries to establish itself. Who knows how long it will take to disappear completely? Some elements of the spell will dwindle quickly, while others will linger, possibly forever. I can't say which elements will do what, or how. I just hope I'm not here to see it."

"Pardon?" asked Eloise. But she knew exactly what Melveeta meant.

"If Çalaht has any mercy in her, then I, too, shall dwindle," Melveeta allowed herself a sigh. "I've long given up the idea I might be privileged to stand at her side. I have no expectation I will see her gap-toothed smile. I have caused too much ill. But I hope she will at least let me have the dignity of simply passing away, though I have my doubts. I fear her sense of humor will be such that she'll force me to keep living. I do not relish that possibility."

Eloise felt an incredible mix of emotions. The old woman's spell was the most destructive thing that had ever been inflicted upon the world. Yet Eloise could not help seeing Melveeta as a person. She tried to imagine spending so long in such pain, unmoving, itchy, and staring endlessly at the cliff that had been the source of that pain. And it must be dreadful to know her spell had probably had an effect on the world, but not knowing the extent, or if anything had come of it.

But then, wasn't that the case for everyone? How could anyone know what one's presence did in the world? It wasn't always clear what was good and what was bad, and good intentions could certainly have disastrous results. Her mother once talked to Eloise about making decisions, the way a queen must. She'd said, "You'll make many rulings. Some will be good, some will be bad, some will be profound, and some will pass like wisps of dust in a föhn. The problem is, despite what you think you might be doing, you will never truly know which is which until much, much later, if ever."

Someday, Eloise thought, she would be the one doing the ruling. Her choices would affect real people's lives. Sure, she could second guess everything. But down that path lay paralysis and inaction. Like her mother—and, she realized, like Melveeta—she would just have to try to do what was best for the queendom, and hope she didn't end up at the bottom of a cliff with a crippled body and a voracious spell sucking the life out of the world around her.

Eloise tried to consider Melveeta dispassionately. She had been loyal to her queen, sacrificing everything for her sovereign. It was clear that her actions, such as they were, had come from her heart. She'd endured centuries of the worst pain that any person might ever experience. Had she suffered enough already? On the scales of history, did that counterbalance the diablerie she'd set upon the world?

But ultimately, this was not about Melveeta. This was about the spell. The old woman's spiritual redemption did not come into it. Plus, it didn't help to personalize everything. Just as Eloise had said to Johanna earlier, the spell was just a force. A force that needed to be stopped.

"Could we possibly start?" whispered Melveeta. "I've been waiting a long, long time. Too long."

Johanna looked at Eloise, and raised a single, questioning eyebrow. There was so much to read in that look—a mix of "Do you really want to do this?" and "This is beyond stupid," along with "What are the odds we end up stuck in this thing?" plus a sarcastic "I can't wait to endure the worst pain I've ever felt in my life."

Eloise settled next to Johanna where she could take Melveeta's right hand and the Star of Whatever. She reached for Johanna and gave her a small "I'm ready" squeeze.

Johanna returned the squeeze, then said, "OK, let's do it." Then they reached for Melveeta, coming into contact with the shell of the spell.

❧ 18 ❧

THE HIGH TONGUE

Hector and the Nameless One were staking out the town market near the main entry gate to Castle Blotch. They'd tried each of the castle entrances in the past few days, both directly and in disguise, with no success.

Each horse contemplated what remained of his plate of scones and haggleberry jam, purchased from a stall in the market. "I think I might prefer fig marmalade to haggleberry jam, although this jam is nice, and doesn't have the toxic tang you sometimes get with haggleberry condiments," said Hector.

The Nameless One nodded, and took another delicate nip from his plate.

The scones were a rare indulgence. Coin was tight, but their days had been long, full of uncertainty and anxiety, and frustrating, as they tried to gather information from people who were either ignorant of anything useful or disinclined share what they knew. Beyond what they had learned from the scullery mare, news was sparse. Hector thought they needed something to brighten them up while they waited for the news broadcast.

Not long after, the morning herald (as opposed to the mourning herald) emerged from the castle gate clanging his bell and shouting "Öööy vëëëy, öööy vëëëy, öööy vëëëy, ïïit's öööne öööf thöööse nëëëws däääys." Tall even for a northern man, he wore the tunic and buttons of an official court herald, and his baritone was rich and loud enough to be heard a quarter strong length away.

The problem was his accent. They'd heard him previous mornings and found that even the locals had trouble understanding him. "I wonder how he got the job as herald," said Hector across a final mouthful of scone. "I can barely work out a word he says. Do you think that's a deliberate strategy to obscure official information?"

The Nameless One shrugged, but motioned that they should move closer in, along with the rest of the market crowd.

The herald clanged his bell a few more times, then tucked it under his arm, stepped up onto a low platform, and unscrolled his decree sheet. "Thëëërëëë ääärëëë sëëëvëëëral röööyäääl pröööclääämäääätïïïöööns ääänd ääännöööuncëëëments tööödäääy."

"Oh for the love of Çalaht, Jäääkëëë, speak the High Tongue." The comment came from a brussels sprouts monger. "Ïï cäään't üüünderstääänd äää wöööörd yööööüüü'rëëë säääyïïïing," he mocked.

The herald's face flushed. "Ïï äääm spëëëäääkïïïing thëëë Hïïïïïgh Töööngüüüëëë, Bäääärt."

That brought more laughter.

"My old granny wouldn't understand what you were saying," said the brussels sprouts guy. "And her accent was so strong, her kids could barely understand her. Speak the High Tongue proper, good man."

"Fïne, Bärt," the herald said with deliberate enunciation. "Ï'll spëak thë Hïgh Töngue möre hïghly sö yöu änd yöur grän cän underständ thë ïmportant nëws fröm thë cästle, yöööüüü gïïït."

There followed a dull litany of petty pronouncements similar to those Hector and the Nameless One had heard on each of the previous ten days. The Middle Street re-cobblestoning project was behind schedule, as cobblers had mistakenly been hired to do the work, not stoners, so the road would remain unusable for another fortnight. The Spice Mongers Guild had agreed to join the Condiments Exchange, with futures trading set to begin the following week. The general prohibition against snoring in public had been upheld on appeal. A box containing 13 dried mushrooms, a lock of hair, and a blood-specked nail file had been turned in to the "Löst and Föünd." The owner was welcome to come and claim after answering a few questions.

On and on Jäääkëëë heralded, covering all kinds of mundane matters that would only ever interest the locals. Hector noticed that the market-goers and stall holders drifted back to buying and selling, although they kept a respectful silence so they did not disturb those who were still listening.

"Fïnally," he finally said, "by röyal pröclamations, ön the mörrow, the Cröwn's justice shall be fulfilled. Three miscreants, five felons, a pair of ne'er-do-wells, and twö cönspirators against the king have been adjudged guilty and shall be fogged. Gather ye upon Fogging Hill at midday to bear witness to the lawful and just ënfogment of said persons, whose deeds range from rampant thievery to treasonous plotting against the Crown and conspiring against the Royal Personage in miscellaneous and nefarious ways."

No one seemed to overly care that the herald had just announced public foggings, but it bothered Hector. A lot. And "treasonous plotting against the Crown and conspiring against the Royal Personage in miscellaneous and nefarious ways"? What was that supposed to mean? Did someone spill soup on him or something?

The Nameless One snorted quietly to get Hector's attention, then fixed him with a look that clearly said, "Go ask him."

"Ask who what?"

The Nameless One nodded his head toward the herald.

"Him? What am I supposed to ask him?"

But the Nameless One was already trotting over to where the herald sat on a bench next to his platform, pocketing a few coins for the private messages he was being asked to deliver. It took Hector a few seconds reach his side.

Jäääkëëë the herald looked up at the horses. "Yëëës?"

"Hi. I'm Hector."

"Hi Hëëëctööör. Ïïi'm Jäääkëëë. Whääät cäään I dööö fööör yöööüüü?"

"I'm hoping you can tell me something about the people being fogged tomorrow."

"Yëëës?"

"Do you have their names?"

"Nööö. Nööö, nööö, nööö. Nööö."

"Their species?"

"Nöööpëëë. Sööörry. Thääät's prïïvïïlëëëgëëëd ïïnfööörmääätïïööön thääät Ïïi dööön't rëëëmëëëmbëëër ööör hääävëëë äääccëëëss tööö."

The Nameless One exhaled an exasperated sigh. He reached around to his side, mouthed open a saddlebag, and fished out three coins. He held them in his teeth, offering them to the herald.

Hector shook his head. "Don't insult our new companion. As a dedicated public servant, he'll not be open to such measures."

The herald shifted back to his more understandable way of speaking to facilitate the transaction. "Nö öffence täken. Yöur frïend's gësture öf ëncouragement ïs përsuasive." He held out his palm and let the Nameless One drop in the coins. "Ät yöur sërvice, göod sïrs."

Hector peppered the herald with questions, and determined that, while the man did not know the names of those being fogged and had not been there when judgment was passed, he had glanced out his window and seen them as they walked or were dragged back to the dungeons. If their order had been kept the same, and usually it was, then the three miscreants were all human—a man and two women—

the five felons comprised four humans and a rabitty-looking bandicoot-like thing who looked as if she was more likely to bake you scones than commit a felony, the two ne'er-do-wells were some sort of snake and some sort of lizard, and the conspirators were a human and a rat.

"Are you sure it was a rat?" asked Hector. "Not a chipmunk?"

"I dön't knöw. Rödënts cönfüsë më. Ärë thösë thë önës wïth thë skïnnÿ täïls?"

"Bushy. Chipmunks have bushy tails."

"Hmmmm... Mäybë." The herald rubbed the coins together as he thought. Hector wasn't sure if he was hinting that he wanted more coin, or if it was idle movement. "Hë wäs dänglïng bÿ thë bäck öf hïs nëck, sëë. Sö thë täïl wäs tückëd üp ündërnëäth. Ä bït härd tö sëë ïts büshïnëss ör läck thërëöf. Büt thë blökë wäs prëtty strïkïng. Täll. Wälkëd lïkë hë wäs süpërïör tö whät wäs göïng ön. Ör ät lëäst rëfüsïng tö lët ït gët thë bëttër öf hïm."

"Wearing Westie guard clothes?"

"Ï'm nöt müch öf önë för fäshïön. Cöuldn't säÿ." The herald stood from his bench. "Ïf thërë's nöthïng ëlsë yöü gööd sïrs nëëd, Ï müst bë mäkïng mÿ wäÿ bäck ïnsïdë för lünch.

Hector and the Nameless One watched the herald go, his bell still under his arm, clanking mutedly with his steps. "For someone in charge of communications, he really doesn't communicate all that much," said Hector. "I'm not sure you got your three coins' worth."

The Nameless One shrugged, then fixed Hector with a look.

"I don't know," said Hector. "But I agree. We have to rescue them. Somehow."

❧ 19 ❧

THE SPARK OF SOMETHING

It was like reaching into the sun itself. Approaching Melveeta's hand felt to Eloise like forcing her arm through a red-hot custard cooked of iron and rage. It would have been easier to snatch a coal from the heart of a blacksmith's furnace, grab a razordisc in mid-flight without losing fingers, or negotiate visitation rights between estranged hornets. Searing agony shot through her.

The proximity to such power filled Eloise with both dread and curiosity. This was strong magic—magic from Back When. It had been so long since anyone had experienced such old magic that no one remembered what it was like. Actually, that wasn't quite true, Eloise thought. There was Melveeta. And there were those who were sentenced to fogging, but she doubted they appreciated the experience.

Eloise could tell the exact moment when Johanna made contact because Melveeta jerked at her touch. Eloise knew she only had a dozen weak lengths to go before she reached the stone, but it felt like a thousand strong lengths of torment. She blocked out everything. There was just her hand and the stone. She pushed hard, and her fingertips finally met the smooth, faceted surface of the Star of Whatever.

It was unlike anything she'd ever felt before. Immediately, an intense energy burst through her. She laughed and cried at the same time. Reaching a little further, she felt the dry, bone-thin hand that clutched the stone. Eloise wrapped her fingers around both the hand and the Star, and the world shivered as she, Melveeta and Johanna formed a closed circle. The twins were subsumed into the roil of the spell, and the protective layer that surrounded Melveeta expanded outward with a soft pop, enclosing them.

They were part of it now.

"Well, well, look at that," mused Melveeta. Inside the spell, her voice was unexpectedly louder, her manner stronger. "That tells me so much."

"I beg your pardon?" asked Eloise.

"Well, for one, you are not dead."

Suddenly, Johanna lapsed into mind-numbness, slumping onto Melveeta's crumpled leg and arm. Melveeta yelled reflexively, then gritted her teeth to stop herself. Eloise pulled Johanna, trying to drag her back upright, but Melveeta stopped her. "She must keep the contact. If she slips off completely, you'll have to reconnect her. Once was plenty. Leave her as she is."

"As you wish."

"Has this one not built up her tolerance for proximity to magic?"

"There is not much magic in the world. So, no, she hasn't. No one has."

"Oh." Melveeta carefully shrugged, repositioning herself to ease the pressure of Johanna's weight.

"Excuse me," said Eloise, "but what did you mean by, 'For one, you are not dead.'?"

"There was some likelihood that when you touched the Star, it would turn you to dust."

"What!"

"I couldn't know for sure. I've only seen it happen once before. Maybe twice."

"You're—you're serious!"

"Deadly serious. But here you are, both alive. So not to worry."

"'Not to worry'? You trifle with my life—our lives!" Melveeta's coldness nettled her. "Why?"

"Because."

"That is no answer."

"Because there is only one way that I can see to affect this spell, and that is for me to add something beyond myself. Of course I would stake your lives against that possibility. What would you do if you were me?" Melveeta shook her head, annoyed. "Don't be a child. I told you it could go wrong. Have you not been at risk since you stepped into the spell's magical mist? You told me yourself of all the bones you found."

It was all Eloise could do to maintain contact with the papery, bird's claw of a hand. "You are a mad woman."

Melveeta chuckled a mirthless bark. "I will hardly argue with you on that account. But consider—you two somehow managed to get this close to me. You are my first opportunity to change the spell since I cast it. I would not let that pass."

Eloise looked at her. "You still haven't figured it out. Don't you know how we managed to come this far?"

"A Çalaht-inspired miracle, I guess. Whatever you did, I am in no position to question such unexpected fortune."

"'You cannot use magic against blood,'" Eloise quoted.

"You recite me a line from a nursery rhyme?"

"That's from a nursery rhyme?"

Melveeta's eyes lost focus as she retrieved a memory. "'Knackknick, chili stick, periwinkle, spud. No kiss for my sweetheart, no magic against blood.' Goodness, I haven't thought of that in a long, long time."

"I've not heard that one before."

"I learned it before I could walk." Melveeta looked slowly from Eloise to Johanna and back. "So, you are Gumballs?"

"That I sit before you is proof."

"Cousins?"

"Distant nieces, I think."

"Curious." Melveeta looked at Eloise anew. "I *thought* you had her eyes."

Eloise still felt peeved. She nodded toward Johanna. "Why have I not collapsed the same way she has?"

"Everyone reacts to magic differently. Lapsing into mind-numbness is not uncommon for those unused to it. But probably, it is because of the Star. You're touching it. Can you feel it?"

"Feel the Star? Yes, my hand is on it."

"That is not what I meant. Close your eyes."

Eloise was reluctant to do so. But it wasn't like Melveeta could jump on her. So she shut her eyes and concentrated, sorting through the sensations rushing around and through her. She flitted from feelings to thoughts and back. Eloise grasped at every nuance, every tendril, every wrinkle of the Star and the subtleties of the spell. At the same time, she kept up her guard just in case—although she had no idea in case of what.

It was immediately clear there was a distinct difference between the Star of Whatever and the spell that gushed from it. It was like the distinction between volcano and lava flow—related, but decidedly different. Eloise continued to probe at the churn of it all with her mind and feelings, but it was like trying to understand the nature of a spring breeze in the middle of a slashing gale.

And then, there it was! The spark of something allowed itself to be glimpsed. It was different to any person—human or non-human— Eloise had ever encountered, but there was definitely an existence there. How very strange. The sense of it made her feel like she should introduce herself, or maybe invite it to tea. And maybe she was projecting, but it seemed to Eloise that the Star of Whatever was sending out something toward her, too. Perhaps a query? If she had to convey it, the communication would have been expressed as a single punctuation mark—a "?". The tiny whatever-it-was felt like it was checking her out. Trying to get to know her, maybe? Assessing her?

What was clear to Eloise was that it did not feel evil. That surprised her, given how much evil it had been a party to. Then again, maybe "evil" was a label, a point of view tied to an agenda. It was, as she'd said to Johanna, just a force.

Maybe. Now she wasn't so sure.

Eloise opened her eyes. "Yes. I sense it," she said. "It seems to be—I'm not sure of the right word—curious, perhaps?"

"Yes, child. It wonders who you are, and why I am no longer the only one touching it. Maybe it is bored with me after so long."

"Has it been that long for it? What is the timescale of a magical stone?"

"Bah! That approaches philosophy," snorted Melveeta. "Philosophy is for dreamers and wastrels. I have no time for useless mental meandering."

Eloise was not enjoying this, and after the possibly-turning-into-dust thing, she'd lost empathy with Melveeta. As fascinating as the strong magic was, Eloise disliked the feeling that it was testing her, looking for vulnerability. She suspected that Melveeta was somehow protecting her, keeping the forces at bay. But from what she'd experienced of Melveeta, she did not trust that protection to last. Eloise wanted to be done.

20

ATTACK OF THE PURPLE HAZE

Just as a gibbous moon heaved itself into the night sky, the Purple Haze attacked. As though infused with a renewed vigor, the mist crept forth, first swallowing Fogging Hill, then slowly consuming the streets and alleys, homes, businesses and people that lay before it. It advanced like a silent nightmare, the stars above seeming to wink out as it went, a curtain of lavender-colored horror slinking its way to the outer walls of Castle Blotch. It plied its menace silently, engulfing all before voices could turn the evening into an agony of shrieks. Instead, they fell convulsing, straining, then lying still for eternity, their souls freed to stand with Çalaht—or not.

By the time the fog reached the east side of the castle walls, a fifth of Stained Rock was effectively gone.

At that moment, Turpy sat next to the inert body of his brother. Gouache's breathing was unchanged—slow, shallow, steady, and with a bizarre three-beat snore. He seemed neither closer to life, nor further from it. His face still had the same unnatural slackness it had had borne ever since he'd been discovered at the foot of Fogging

Hill. The look was unnerving, and something Turpy had never seen before.

When Gouache had first been brought back to the castle, they'd tried everything to revive him. But no amount of cheek slapping, nose pinching, medicament dosing, water splashing, prayers to Çalaht, or any of several dozen other treatments and remedies did anything. Gouache just lay there, eyes closed, face weirdly loose, his snore, snore, snore, (pause) snore, snore, snore droning on forever.

Turpy could not help replaying the scene in his mind, how that disgusting, pathetic excuse of a child had somehow broken his thumb to free herself, then slammed into his brother, knocking him down the hill and into the Purple Haze. He didn't remember what happened after that. He was back at the castle having his thumb looked at when, somehow, Gouache had miraculously been found at the fog's edge, looking exactly the way he looked now. "This was her fault" throbbed in Turpy's mind the way his thumb throbbed in its bandages. The apothecary and healer both suggested that he let them cut the shattered digit off, but Turpy refused. Maybe it would heal. He could always remove it later if he had to.

Gouache lay in the room he'd occupied since the two of them had become court jesters. It was a windowless closet of a space lit by a single candle, and decorated with trinkets Gouache had saved from his childhood: a small plush pony, a dried seedpod from an unknown plant he'd found on a family trip to the rainforests of Inner Splutter, and a drawing of the two brothers, done by their mother when they were five and three. It was the only bit of artwork either of them had from her —everything else was held by collectors and was much too expensive for them to afford. Gouache's room held no books, no tools of art, nor anything to suggest that Gouache had much of an interest in the world.

There was, however, something Turpy hadn't seen before. On the bedside table, there was a swatch of purple velvet from one of the dresses Johanna had worn on their trip to Stained Rock. She'd snagged in on a gripper cactus at the Whacking Great Hole. Turpy remembered how upset Johanna was at the tear in one of her favorite travel gowns.

Gouache must have pocketed the cloth as a keepsake. Or maybe he thought he could repair it later. He'd put it on his bedside table next to their portrait. As a reminder of her? It was unusual for Gouache to get attached to anything, let alone any*one*.

Turpy watched his brother's breathing, thumb cradled gingerly in his lap, and wondered how he could turn this disaster around.

THEY DIDN'T KNOW IT, BUT LORCH AND JEROME WERE, IN THAT moment, two of the safest people in all the Half Kingdom. Tucked away in dungeon cells devoid of light or any hint of the outside world, they were also sealed away from the skulking death wrought by the Purple Haze. While hundreds perished, Lorch sat on his pallet, outwardly calm as his mind raced to find some way—any way—to dig himself out of this literal hole.

In the next cell over, Jerome was near catatonic with fear, crying small, gulped prayers to Çalaht, to his mother, to anyone "out there" who might be listening and could do something about this situation. He did not want to die, and he knew in his bones that's what awaited him on the other side of the mist at Fogging Hill.

ACROSS THE CITY, HECTOR AND THE NAMELESS ONE WERE ALSO ignorant to the unfolding tragedy. They, too, were holed up, although their stable at the Splintered Dray was much nicer than Lorch and Jerome's surroundings. Hector had not felt like eating, but the Nameless One had insisted they keep up their strength, so they'd ordered in a couple of hay nets worth of lucerne, half of which still hung there, uneaten. The horses were trying to recall what they could of the fogging they'd seen, and thinking of ways to charge in or somehow disrupt it to save their friends. Hector didn't think they could snatch them away, but maybe they could keep the fogging from taking place. He didn't like their odds.

Still, something had to be done. But what?

KING DONCASTER STOOD IN THE MIDDLE OF THE DESULTORY VEGGIE patch that grew—if you could call it that—just outside the castle's kitchen door. He had genuinely hoped that Johanna might do some good here even if the real reason he had agreed to Turpy's "acquisition" of her was more political than anything else.

But now, that plan lay in ruin.

Turpy had laid it out, a simple two-step process: marry the second born, then wait to inherit (and maybe help that along somehow). It had seemed doable enough, but now, without Johanna, there was no way. After her disappearance, he had raged. He had inveighed. He had snapped and snarled and in quieter moments, smoked and simmered and brooded. At least today he'd been able to deal with two of the accomplices of that failure. Somebody had to pay, and they were a good start.

The past week and a bit had been so trying that Doncaster had allowed himself the benefit of just a little extra prattleweed. It was inconsistent for him to flout his own laws that way, but there were perks to being king, and inconsistency was sometimes one of them.

Doncaster bent down and pulled a carrot from the ground. He brushed off the dirt from the root and looked at it, thinking of that afternoon in her garden at Castle de Brague. This one couldn't hold a candle to hers. There were multiple rooty bits where there should have been one. It was like the carrot had little arms and legs, which made him think twice about wanting to eat it. "You would've done a better job," he mumbled.

Doncaster was still unused to speaking of her in the past tense. But she had gone into the fog, although he didn't know why that lug Gouache had thrown her there. Turpy had witnessed it, though. He'd come back to the castle babbling about what had happened, with his thumb a horrible mess. Then somehow Gouache was there again, and even now, still breathed. None of it made sense. Why would that idiot be the first person to ever come out of the fog? But apparently, he was. It was a mystery.

Doncaster didn't like mysteries.

He tucked the malformed carrot into a pocket, leaving the leafy green top poking out. "Oh well," he thought. "Something else will have to happen for me to take over the Western Lands. Maybe Turpy will come up with another idea."

All the while, Doncaster was oblivious to the Purple Haze laying waste to another slice of his realm. The moment he'd tucked the ill-formed carrot into his pocket, the fog had rolled over the castle walls. As he puzzled through Gouache and the loss of Johanna, and pondered a path to the future that was clearly not going to be, the mist crept up behind him.

Moments later, King Doncaster lay convulsing in the carrot bed.

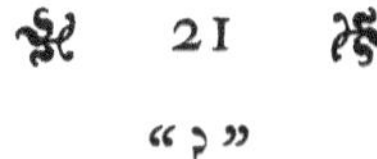

21

" ? "

Melveeta closed her eyes and chanted. The language was odd, and her inflections odder. Eloise was reminded of divination incantations she'd heard years before in her Oracles and Insights classes. That was the closest thing she'd had to magical training, but it was as closely related as molding clay was to gourmet cooking. Melveeta's words were a tongue from another time, and their power was palpable. Eloise stared at Melveeta, losing herself in the tone and rhythm.

The old woman abruptly flashed open her eyes and glared. "Did you not hear what I said before? Do not sit there like a dullard. Close your eyes. Focus on that which will alter the spell. Now I must start again."

Eloise swallowed her irritation at being spoken to that way, and closed her eyes, giving full focus to the spell.

She could sense that the biggest presence in it was the hate that Melveeta had based it on. Her hate was like a cauldron of thick, black rock oil churning at full boil, and amplified by the Star of Whatever, turning what might have been a magical mumble into the world's loudest bellow.

When she was younger, Eloise sometimes wandered around the scrollarium in the Bibliotheca de Records and Regrets, pulling out scrolls at random to see what they might reveal. Most had all the excitement of a ship's manifest. But there was one she remembered that tried to describe what it was like to have magic Back When. In particular, the scroll talked about the uniqueness of an individual's magical expression. "Everyone's magic is different, like the swirls on your fingertips, the flecks in the color of your eyes, or the scribble of your words on parchment." It had made sense, but only theoretically. Now Eloise understood it in her body. The festering hatred in the spell was Melveeta's fingertip swirls. Eloise wondered what her own magical scribble might have looked like if she had lived Back When.

She shifted her attention to feeling love. Love and relief, as Melveeta had directed. Love and relief. Love and relief. She channeled it through her body and down to the hand that held the Star. Love and relief. Deep, abiding love and calm, relaxing relief.

As the old woman continued the unfamiliar syllables, Eloise increased her grip and lifted the stone a few weak lengths. Melveeta's hand tightened reflexively. Slowly, gently, Eloise waggled it slightly, but Melveeta, either unconsciously or deliberately, grasped it even more tightly. Letting the stone drift back to a resting position, Eloise returned her focus to sending love and relief. Love and relief. Love and relief. Love and relief.

Eloise could sense Melveeta addressing the spell, engaging in a sort of dialog. Was she coaxing it? Luring it? Lulling it? Eloise wondered if strong magic was like prophesy, in that it required the application of insight. Or was it more like cooking, where specific actions created predictable results?

More love. More relief. Love, love, love. Relief, relief, relief.

The longer it went on, the less certain Eloise was that Melveeta was actually doing anything. Insight nibbled at Eloise at the periphery of her attention. Clarity tickled at her from afar. Something beckoning for her understanding loomed just out of reach.

Love and relief. Love and relief.

Relief. The relief of a mountain stream against the scorching of summer. The embrace of clean bedding after an exhausting day. The comfort of a massage, of a hug, of a tub of perfectly hot water to thaw from the cold, of having Odmilla comb the unruly obstinance from her hair. The relief of salve on an itch, of water slaking thirst, of sleep for the weary.

And love. Soul-filled, heartfelt, uplifting love. Eloise conjured as many kinds of love as she could think of. The handfasted love of the newly betrothed. The love of fellow travelers, of protectors and protected, of warriors who fought side by side. Love that was eternal. Love that was fleeting. Love that sparkled. Love that burned like a thousand bonfires.

No, that was all in her head. Love had to come from the heart.

What she felt for Jerome, Hector, and the Nameless One certainly felt like a kind of love. Jerome especially, since they'd been friends for so long.

Still not deep enough.

Eloise dug further

Her mother squeezing her shoulder and saying, "Well done." That had happened a few times, and was about as expressive as her mother got. That was love, especially if she peered at it from the right angle.

Walking through an elm forest hand-in-hand with her father, when she was three or four. Him swinging her up into a hug, or dangling her behind him and pretending he couldn't find her. That made her smile, and she felt her heart swell.

That was more like it.

The closeness Eloise had felt toward Johanna when they were younger, and the way they were inseparable. Even now, the love had done its best to flow again between them as they trudged through the Purple Haze wasteland, a flow Eloise hadn't felt since the Thorning Ceremony three years earlier.

The Thorning Ceremony! Eloise recalled as best she could how she had felt at the end of it. She'd been emotionally drained, physically exhausted, and under the influence of the mad monk's breakfast thorn and the visions it induced. The two thorns, which she'd placed at her heart, had opened up a vast feeling of love and connection to everyone there. It had been a while since she'd thought about it, but the reverberating echoes of the feeling were still there. She called forth the memory and sensation of the strands of light that had emanated from her heart, connecting her to those around her, and the love bond she'd felt herself forming with everyone in the room, and then the realm.

Love and relief. Love and relief.

Eloise cracked one eye open to check on Johanna.

Something was wrong.

Johanna's hair! Her hair had gone white! Not just the gray of the dust they'd been covered in since they started this journey. No, there was a distinct discoloration. What had once been the color of a dirt-crusted raven was now, inexplicably, the color of dirt-caked snow. It was the same white as Melveeta's hair.

Eloise wanted to jostle Johanna and make sure she was all right, but she didn't want to disturb Melveeta.

She wondered about her own hair, but it was tied back, so she couldn't see it. Eloise looked down at her hand. It definitely didn't look like it had the last time she'd been clean.

Eloise gasped. Truth sliced into her awareness like a cleaving sword.

Melveeta wasn't lulling or luring anything. She was conspiring and draining. The truth that had called to Eloise was simple: Melveeta was attached to the Star and the spell. She would *never* give either up. This spell was her entire being. She might say she was ready to end it and die, and maybe intellectually she was—but that was the head, not the guts. No amount of mouthing words could compete with the base, animalistic compulsion to live. There was too much vitality in her for that, and too much momentum in the spell. This strange, unnatural life was her one certainty. It was all she knew, and she had known it longer than any living person had known anything.

She would never, ever give up the spell. Not willingly. And Eloise suspected that any such will Melveeta might have would be overwhelmed by the spell itself. The old hag was feeding the girls to the spell. Eloise could sense it getting stronger.

Her intuition told her what she must do, and it filled her with dread.

She forced herself to relax. Love and relief. Love and relief. Love and relief.

Then, as suddenly as she could, Eloise shoved all her weight against the unconscious Johanna, forcing her hard onto Melveeta's shattered leg and arm. The unexpected spike of pain took the woman's breath and attention, giving Eloise her chance. She gripped the glowing stone and pulled with everything she had. Caught unawares and hurting like she hadn't hurt in years, Melveeta was slow to react. Eloise jerked the Star of Whatever back and forth, causing Melveeta even more pain.

Clinging to the Star and tightening her grip on the dead weight of Johanna's hand to keep the circle of power closed, Eloise swiveled her legs around and planted both feet against her ancestor's hip. Then she pulled on the Star while pressing with the full strength of both legs against Melveeta. Melveeta screamed, enraged, and fought to pull the stone back.

There was a sickening tearing sound as the Star of Whatever ripped from Melveeta's hand, her skin coming with it. Eloise fell backward at the sudden release, but kept her feet in contact with Melveeta, preserving the vortex of power. Blood flowed from the gaping wound in Melveeta's hand, and she howled, her unbroken arm flailing around, seeking what had been lost. There was a corresponding thrashing in the torrent of power that was the spell.

But contact had been broken. For the first time in 232 years, the Star of Whatever was no longer directly hooked into the life force of Champion Melveeta Gumball. Eloise cradled the Star as Melveeta screamed out her agony, grief, and loss.

Eloise closed her eyes, feeling for the spark of something in the Star, sending out her own "?". The Star of Whatever responded—another "?". Then a "!", and a "?!?," which struck Eloise as particularly complex. Then the something slipped away, hiding in the raucous force of the spell.

"Shhhh," Eloise whispered to it, even though she no longer sensed the spark. "It is time to be quiet now. Shhhhh, little one. Come on now. Let go."

Suddenly, Melveeta lurched at Eloise, screaming, "Give it back!" That a body so broken could move so decisively took Eloise by surprise. Melveeta landed on her, planting an elbow in Eloise's solar plexus, knocking out her breath. The old woman clawed for the Star with her damaged hand, smearing blood everywhere.

Eloise curled herself into a protective ball, the Star of Whatever nestled against her abdomen. Gasping, she did her best to ignore Melveeta's desperate scratching. Again, Eloise reached out to the spark of something. "It's time to sleep now," she said. "Time to be quiet. Time to rest. You must be tired after so much work. Rest now, little one. Hush now. Sleep."

Eloise kept up the sing-song chant, seeking the spark, calling to it, encouraging, soothing. And she tried not to be distracted by the old woman on top of her—the pummeling, the shrill shrieks, the screech-ing, and the blood spattering her skin, her clothes, her scalp.

There it was again. The spark of something reached out, tentative and shy, "?".

"That's right, little one. It's time to rest now. Sleepy-byes. Easy now, easy. You deserve some quiet time, you really do. Shhhh." She continued her lullaby, trying to interact with it.

Love and relief. Rest and sleep. Love and relief. Rest and sleep.

Then the spark of something seemed to relax. There was an easing, a releasing. "That's right," said Eloise. "Let go. Let it go now. You've done enough." She sent it a ".".

The Star sent Eloise an answering "." and was still.

The air shimmered, and instead of a pop like before, there was a sound that was more like a sigh. Eloise felt a shift in the cascade of magic that shot from the Star, like a tear drying on a cheek.

Then the Star of Whatever let go of the spell completely and fell dormant, its green glow dimming to nothing.

The purple fog was still thick around them, the crackle of magic remained, but its source was gone.

The spell was over.

22

CARROT-PATCH FACEPLANT

A sound like the sighs of a hundred thousand giants groaned across the Half Kingdom. The Purple Haze slowed, then stopped its approach. Then as slowly as it had moved forward, it retreated to where it had spent the previous two centuries.

⁂

THE HALF KINGDOM WOKE TO FRESH DEVASTATION. AS DAWN bloomed, shocked city dwellers found the bodies of friends, relatives, and associates. The section of the city where the Purple Haze had spent what, ultimately, was just a few minutes, was eerily quiet. Not a mammal, reptile, insect, or arachnid had survived.

Well, that wasn't strictly accurate.

One person had not completely succumbed, as the fog had struck him, then let go and receded before finishing him off, a fact that would have irritated Gwendolyn the Irritable, and maybe amused Melveeta the Elusive, had they been witness to it.

It was Kïïït the scullery mare who found the king in a state of mind-numbness similar to His Jesterness Master Turpentine's brother, although she did not connect the two right away.

Kïïït had spent the previous evening at the bar in the Splintered Dray, as unaware as everyone else of what was happening across the city. She'd hoped she might find that nice, quiet Westie stallion again, the bay one who'd been so interested in her, and convince him to share a trough of bran mash. Maybe this time he wouldn't slip off before the evening could fully unfold. He'd been nice, if elusive, and she liked the way he'd smiled at her. He'd treated her with respect, something in short supply from the louts who normally cluttered the equine bar.

Unfortunately, she'd not seen him, so had passed the evening chatting with a couple of out-of-towner donkeys just for the fun of it. She'd staggered into the castle that morning with too little sleep and a head throbbing with the lingering effects of their generosity. Kïïït set about her duties, trying to avoid Cook's bellowed commands. She was grateful when Cook had pointed at a basket and instructed her to grab some veggies from the garden.

When she saw what looked like her sovereign face-planted in the kitchen garden's carrot patch, her first thought was, "Oh Çalaht, he's had a night like mine." She giggled to herself, imagining the king face-first in a trough snorking up brandy mash or gin-soaked oats. She tiptoed close, not sure if she should disturb him. Kings were different, and she'd never spoken to him, much less been this close before. Odd that he was here. But if His Highness wanted to sleep off a binge in a patch of root vegetables, then that must be his royal prerogative.

"Excuse me, Your Majesty?" she whispered.

No response.

Now she was close enough, she heard King Doncaster's low snoring. Not dead, then. That was good. Kïïït wasn't great when it came to dead things. The snoring amused her. It had never occurred to her that a king might snore. Royals should somehow be above such things, all grace and finery.

She took another tentative step toward him, stretched her neck forward, and—she never thought she'd do this—nudged his shoulder. Then she scrambled back two steps, not wanting him to yell at her when he rolled over and woke up.

But he didn't.

"Dead to the world," she thought. "Must have been a heck of a bender to end up like this."

A voice cracked out from behind her. "You there! What have you done?"

Kiïit whirled around, aghast. "I, I... I haven't done anything, Your Jesterness Master Turpentine. I've just come out here. I found him like this."

☙❧

TURPY STRODE TO DONCASTER'S SIDE, TRAMPLING THREE MEAL'S worth of courgettes and carrots as he went. He knelt, felt for a pulse, put his hand over the king's mouth, pinched a cheek, then straightened, puzzled. The king's face had the same unnerving slack look as his brother. Turpy listened. There! There it was. Soft snoring in beats of three.

But how was this possible? How had he encountered the fog?

No matter. He had. Somehow. Turpy's mind raced with possibilities realigning, plotting as fast as he could.

He stood and brushed dirt from his knee, and a strange, tight smile crossed his face. Quickly mastering his features to a blank, he barked, "Go find guards to help get His Majesty to comfort. Not to his room. That's too far. Use the divan in the Throne Room. We must see he is cared for at once. Hurry! I'll wait here with him."

Turpy watched the scullery mare charge toward the kitchen door, then squatted by his king. "Thank you for this gift, My Sovereign. I shall use it well." He reached into his satchel and drew out a leaf of hemp parchment he'd had Doncaster sign months before. It read, "I, King Doncaster Worsted Halva de Chëëëkflïïïnt, after due consideration, thought, ponderation, hereby name, designate, appoint Turpentine Snotearrow McCcoonnch to be Regent of the Half Kingdom in the event, occurrence, happenstance of incapacity, inability, debilitation or absence, nonappearance, not-there-ness of me, myself, I." Turpy had made sure it was properly signed and sealed, and had slipped the duplicate copy into the Hall of Records.

Amazing what one could get someone to do when they had enough prattleweed in their system.

The document had been a just-in-case whim. Turpy never thought he'd need the thing, since Doncaster was as compliant as Turpy needed. Now he was glad he'd acted when the idea had first occurred to him.

Finally, the Half Kingdom was his—at least as long as King Doncaster stayed the way he was, and kept breathing.

❧ 23 ❧

WHERE ONCE THERE WAS SOMETHING

Eloise opened her eyes. Melveeta's face was weak lengths away from her own, stale breath blasting her nostrils. "How did you do that?" she hissed. "You do not know what works. You are ignorant of magical ways."

"Yes, you're right. I am most definitely ignorant." Then Eloise realized that Melveeta's injured hand was above her forehead, her dripping blood trickling down into Eloise's hair.

Her habits reared up, shrieking. This was too much. Eloise lost it.

"Get off! Get off! Get off!"

"What? I can't."

"Can't?"

"Something else broke inside when I threw myself at you."

Eloise had no choice. Keeping the Star of Whatever safely away from Melveeta, she pushed herself out from under the broken woman. Melveeta's breathing was more rapid than before, but then, at that moment, so was Eloise's.

Eloise sat up, and blood dribbled down her cheek. Eyes wide, she scrabbled for something to wipe it off with. Her sleeve? Then it would still be on her. Johanna's clothes? No. Melveeta's? No.

Her travel cloak? Yes. That would have to do.

Eloise snatched up the bottom hem of the cloak and scraped at the coagulating red on her face. Some of it came off, but Eloise knew there was no way she could get it all. Melveeta's blood remained on her, stuck to her face and—ugh!—in her hair. Eloise felt the top of her head. Wet. Oh, Çalaht, this was a disaster. Frantically, she wiped the cloak hem on the top of her head, then looked at it. Red smears. Some of it had come out, but how much of it would stay there until she could find a bath, a stream, a bucket of water, or even a dirty puddle?

Eloise shuddered, and her habits clawed at her to somehow do more. But what more could she do? Try to rub it out with dirt? Pull it out? Cut it off?

Cut it off.

She had to cut off her hair. Right then. She had done it when she was five. She could do it now. Just get it off!

Eloise ran to the box that had been made for the Star of Whatever, flipped open the lid, and nestled it back in the maroon nest of its custom-made padding. Most of Melveeta's palm had sloughed off, but a few bits still clung to the stone, and she had to shove a little harder than she should have to get it to fit. Eloise mentally sent the Star of Whatever a breezy "See you soon!" that she didn't actually mean and had no intention of honoring. She then snapped the lid shut and set the box on a flat, gray stone near where the buzzing in the outside world would start. The Star of Whatever would be visible to Eloise, but a safe distance away from Melveeta, who once again seemed immobile.

Eloise grabbed the small knife she carried from a pocket in her travel cloak, unsheathed it, turned her back to Melveeta and Johanna, and carefully, but as fast as she could, began cutting at her braid. The blade was dull, so instead of slicing, Eloise found herself sawing and hacking.

That would have to do. A distant part of her mind suggested that perhaps this was an overreaction. Well, that part of her mind could just shove a stocking in it. That part of her mind didn't have ancient murderer blood in its hair.

It took almost four minutes, but finally the braid came away in her hand.

It was white—the same stained, dirty white as Johanna's hair. How? What had happened to her black curls?

No time to think about that. She placed the strangely colored stump of hair carefully on the ground, then went after the next handful of strands—the bit on top and in front, closest to where Melveeta had dripped on her. She cut the hair as short as she could. Now that she was dealing with the blood-in-her-hair problem, her breathing went from manic down to overly excited, and Eloise knew it would not be long before it was somewhere close to brisk exercise.

Five minutes later, she made the last cuts.

Hair removed as best she could, Eloise scooped up the fallen locks using dust to keep the bloody bits off her hands, walked to the far side of the buzz-free zone, dropped the messy pile to the ground, and scooped half a dozen handfuls of dust and sand onto it to cover it up.

There, that was better.

Lying on her side, Melveeta stared at her. Eloise ignored her as she gently rolled the old woman onto her back so she wasn't lying on her more broken parts. She swore Melveeta looked even more wrinkled and wizened than when they had first met, but put it down to the odd light and Melveeta's recent flirtation with mobility. Then she checked Johanna, who lay, mouth open, in an unflattering pose that reminded her of a spilled sack of rutabagas. Eloise straightened her sister, who mumbled something about "more spangly bits," then fell back into deep breaths and silence.

Eloise turned back to Melveeta and considered what she saw before her. As she stared at the old woman, Eloise felt something shift, something bubble up inside her—empathy. Suddenly she could see Melveeta for what she was—an old woman from a near-forgotten era who had survived long past the time she should have stopped breathing. Without the spell and the Star of Whatever, she seemed much smaller, much more fragile.

It was sad, in a way.

Eloise leaned over and lifted Melveeta's hand holding her wrist gingerly with two fingers. Blood dripped from the old woman's palm. "I'll bandage that," she said. It was the last thing she wanted to do.

"There is no need."

"Don't be like that. Of course there is." Eloise looked around to see what might be clean enough to use as a makeshift dressing. Perhaps she had something in one of her cloak pockets. She glanced at Melveeta, and wondered if the light was changing somehow—it was definitely becoming less and less flattering.

Eloise looked down at her tunic. Maybe she could tear off a sleeve. Or the hem on Johanna's dress—that might work.

"Look at me, child," said Melveeta. "Can you not see?"

"See what?"

"What is plain. I'm dying."

Eloise's first impulse was to think, "No, you're not." But Melveeta's eyes were rapidly losing their fire. That was what Eloise had been seeing. The light in the fog was not changing. It was the light in Melveeta that was. Without the Star of Whatever and the spell to hold the forces of nature at bay, the weight of centuries was crashing down on her. The years kept at arm's length, the decades of a fractionally-lived life—those two centuries now rushed in, writing cruel words on her face, her hands, her internal organs.

"You can't die. Not yet," said Eloise quietly. "I have too many questions."

Melveeta shook her head slightly. "I don't think anyone but Çalaht can change what is happening."

Eloise pointed to the Star's box. "What am I supposed to do with that thing?"

Melveeta's rapid breathing became wheezier. "Do not let it eat you the way it ate me. Speak to no one of it, and find a way to make sure it is never, ever, ever used again." Her breathing grew faster. Noisy. It gurgled in her lungs and scratched as it left her throat.

Eloise had never seen anyone die before. She'd only ever seen a handful of dearly departed from a distance. If getting Melveeta's blood on her was enough to make her anxieties go apoplectic, she feared what would happen if she had to support the old woman as she drew her last breaths. Who knew what would come out of her when *that* happened.

It's not like she was clueless about death. Eloise had known people who had died, although her parents had protected her from the details. After her Thorning Ceremony, Protocol dictated that she attend funerals. But that was nothing compared to this. To sit by death's side? To hold vigil—and maybe even the hand—of one who was passing to the realms of Çalaht? Her stomach clenched at the yuck of it, her guts telling her to run. Run!

But those thoughts were her habits talking. Eloise knew this was not a time for fleeing. This was a time for staying, for being present.

She rolled up her travel cloak and slid it under Melveeta's head. How long would this take? Would death come to her like a shadow creeping, or like a falling boulder? Would it be hours? Days?

Eloise knelt down next to Melveeta and ran through what she had been taught about death. Most of what she knew centered on the ceremonial activities that took place after the fact. She'd learned a lot about the ways different species held funerals in her Rituals and Rationalizations classes. Tortoises, for example, who lived such long lives, had massively elaborate solemnities that lasted months and involved decorating the shell of the deceased with precious stones that matched their class in society, as well as dancing tortuously slow, mournful death waltzes, and eating a lot of lettuce.

At first, Eloise thought perhaps the complexity of funeral arrangements might mirror the natural age of the species, but that didn't hold. Mayflies were notorious for their garish, outlandish, bacchanalian funerals, adhering to the mayfly adage, "Live fast, die fast, break the bank as you close the door." Ants were the least sentimental. They treated the dead with all the reverence and respect of building materials, which is exactly what they used the bodies for.

Eloise had a fondness for the funeral practices of dugongs, who hired professional keeners to wail on their behalf, while the bereaved spent a week sunning themselves at the departed's favorite seagrass meadow. Oh, and gang-gangs! When one of them passed, their flock would find a nice secluded spot, lay out the body on a bed of plucked grass, and then cover it a foot deep in the seeds of their favorite food. It was said that if the bird had lived a sufficiently upright life, a new tree would spring forth from the pile, eventually contributing to the flock's nourishment. The tree would be forever known by that bird's name.

A cough brought Eloise back. Melveeta was struggling more now. "What can I do for you, Champion Melveeta?" Eloise asked.

She shook her head slightly. "There is naught to be done. Perhaps..." Melveeta's voice cracked. Looking at her was like watching a hundred years rush past in moments. "Perhaps you could make a promise."

"A promise?"

Her voice grew smaller by the moment. "Promise you will not sully my name."

Melveeta was worried about her reputation? At a time like this? Surely her concerns should be elsewhere.

Then again, maybe how others remembered her was all she had left in this world. Sad, really. But Eloise could understand. The old woman might be happier remaining "Melveeta the Elusive" who disappeared into the unknown, rather than becoming "Melveeta, the Destroyer of Half a Kingdom."

Eloise gently took Melveeta's hand, swallowing back her revulsion. "I promise to convey your story faithfully."

The reply was a barely audible, "That will have to do, child."

Suddenly, her eyes fixed on Eloise's and her grip tightened. With a strength drawn from the life force ebbing away, Melveeta said, "I give the Star of Whatever unto thee." There was weight and ceremony in her words. Eloise felt Melveeta release all affinity and connection to the magical stone, and with a shiver, she felt herself become more enmeshed with it.

Eloise swallowed. For good or ill, it was hers now.

Then Melveeta squeezed Eloise's hand hard, and she spasmed, her eyes oscillating. She looked very much like Gouache when they tumbled into the Purple Haze. Except this time, there was nothing Eloise could do to stop it. There was no magical fog to roll Melveeta out of. There was just the shutting down of a tired, old body.

Melveeta's breathing raced, her eyes dilated, and her pulse became herky-jerky like a prattled Flamenco dancer. Her lips moved soundlessly. She was trying to say something. Eloise studied the repeated motions of her mouth.

The silent words were, "Sorry, Gwennie. Sorry I failed you."

And then Eloise saw the mute words change.

"Forgive me."

Over and over and over.

Pity for Melveeta overwhelmed Eloise. "Let Çalaht be in charge of any repercussions that her soul might have to pay," she thought. In this moment, kindness was called for. Kindness and comfort. Eloise considered cradling Melveeta, but did not want to move her. Instead, she took Melveeta's limp hand into both of hers, gently stroking it.

Perhaps human contact might reach through the shroud of oblivion that blanketed her.

"You are forgiven, Champion Melveeta Gumball," said Eloise gently. "You are forgiven—Auntie."

Melveeta's lips curled. A grimace? A smile? Eloise could not tell.

Then the ancient woman's body stretched unnaturally, her back arching, neck straining, limbs juddering. A death dance for one.

It had taken minutes, not hours or days. At first, Eloise was unsure if Melveeta had actually gone, or if something else was supposed to happen.

But no, it was done.

The difference was so clear. Where once there had been a spark of something, now there was nothing.

"May you stand with Çalaht, Auntie," whispered Eloise to the empty husk. "May you feel Her peace. May you see Her gap-toothed radiance."

Eloise folded Melveeta's arms across her chest, and spread her travel cloak over her, making sure her face was covered. "Goodbye, Auntie."

Exhausted, Eloise lay down next to Johanna, spooning into her back, and fell into a dreamless sleep.

24

REGENT

In the Throne Room, Turpy watched as attendants carefully hoisted the unresponsive King Doncaster onto a bed placed exactly halfway between the doorway and the throne, making Doncaster the literal center of attention. They lay him on his back, removed a scraggly carrot from his pocket, and tucked him in, still fully clothed in his regal finery. The servants all bent a knee or curtsied, then stood back, not sure what to do next.

"I'm sure His Highness appreciates your care," said Turpy with all the sincerity of a used carriage salesman. "Now please, send for the apothecary, the healer, the chirurgeon, the herbalist, one of the geomancers, and, I suppose, the Prelate. I'm sure someone will have a good idea of how best to help the king." Turpy knew they wouldn't, as all of them, save the Prelate, had attended Gouache, but the servants didn't know that, and people needed to know the state their king was in. "Oh, and please fetch the First Advisor."

Then Turpy shooed them off to run their errands as he closed the doors to the Throne Room. The king had resumed snoring, a drone in three beats. Turpy knew firsthand that His Majesty's facility for snoring was epic, ranging from bumblebee buzz to the rending of mountains. Doncaster's current tone was toward the benign end of the scale, which Turpy saw as another sign that things were going his way.

The jester looked around to make sure he was on his own, then strode to Doncaster's throne and sat on it. He was surprised by how uncomfortable the teak and ash chair was, even with the cushions. Still, Turpy had long imagined himself doing this, so couldn't help feeling a fluttery thrill.

A knock at the door interrupted him. "His Majesty is not to be disturbed," snapped Turpy, wanting to savor the moment a while longer.

"His Highness sent for me," replied a gruff voice.

"Enter," called Turpy as he stood from the throne and settled himself on one of the scribe's chairs.

First Advisor Këëëvëëën Läääctööösëëë Frühstück came into the room, gasped, and ran to kneel at King Doncaster's side. "Sire? Sire! What has happened to you, my Lord?" Frühstück was a stout man with a military background, who'd gone fleshy with the perks of office. His gray-speckled curls hung loose around his shoulders, his robes were teal and white, and he wore more rings and neck chains than were strictly needed to signify his rank. Frühstück's advice to the king was often not horrible, and Turpy only occasionally had to neutralize it through his own counter-advice—just often enough that the king never considered Frühstück's guidance gospel.

Turpy walked to the kneeling man. "He was found this way this morning by one of the kitchen maids. I have no idea what's happened, but carers are on the way. In the meantime, the king's Declaration of Regency has been put into place."

"His what? I know of no such thing. His Majesty was never exactly big on succession planning."

Turpy pointed to the page on the scribe's table. "There."

Frühstück picked it up, read it, and looked up. "You?" He scrutinized the wax seal's signet impression and the signature. "It seems genuine. I'm... I'm surprised."

"The librarian in the Hall of Records will have the corroborating copy, I'm sure."

"I'll send for it." Frühstück drew a slow breath as he examined the document one more time. There were no other obvious candidates, such as a queen or offspring. The king had long showed the jester much more favor than the First Advisor thought was due. But Frühstück was loyal, and prone to executing tasks when given then. He bowed the barest bow to the jester and said, "I pledge to help you fulfill your role as regent, and hope the king's speedy recovery will mean the burden of that office will not weigh on your shoulders for long. The king's will shall be followed."

Not exactly an oath of loyalty, but it would do. "I can only say it is my humble honor and duty to serve the court and people of this realm. And I have no intention of steering the realm a minute longer than the king's need for me to do so." It was close enough to the truth. For now.

A page burst into the throne room, breathing like he'd sprinted a dozen strong lengths. "Your Highness!" The boy skittered to a stop, confused by the bed and snoring body. "Your Highness?"

"The king is unwell," said Frühstück. "What do you need?"

"The city! So much death. My parents..." Then he dropped to his knees and sobbed.

Reports of the night's devastation trickled, then flooded, into the Throne Room. Everyone who came in knelt to their supine king, wished him a speedy recovery, then delivered their reports to the First Advisor, who deferred to the regent. Within an hour Turpentine Snotearrow McCcoonnch had stabilized his position as acting head of the Half Kingdom. He ordered a contingent of guards into the affected part of the city, ostensibly to prevent looting and ensure the safety of the populace. In fact, it was a show of force in the guise of helpfulness.

He also declared a day of mourning, putting off all "official business, celebrations, and activities" for 24 hours.

While it wasn't his intention, the decree also acted as a temporary stay of execution for 14 sad occupants of the dungeons.

Turpy stayed in the Throne Room all day, busy enough that the pain of his thumb became background noise. After dinner, he instructed a dozen servants to move Gouache and his bed to an out-of-the-way corner of the Throne Room, and even had a pallet brought in for himself. "I want to make sure that if the king awakens and needs anything, I'm here." While that was true enough, it was also true that the Throne Room was much roomier, and had better heating. There was something to be said for comfort if one was going to control a realm.

25

WORLD'S MOST IMPROBABLE

Some indefinable length of time later, Johanna woke.

She was normally slow to wakefulness and best avoided until she'd had a strong haggleberry tea and some toast, preferably with kiwi fruit jam. But this time, Johanna jerked upright into full alertness, looking around frantically as she tried to figure out what was going on. She saw Eloise's travel cloak covering something, noticed that the padded wooden box had moved, and spotted a pile of whitish string poking out from a pile of dirt and dust. Wait, was that a braid of someone's hair? Where did that come from? Also, Melveeta seemed to have escaped.

"El, what happened?" Johanna swiveled to find her sister lying next to her, asleep. She gasped. "Çalaht stippling a stale stollen, El. What happened to your head? Is... is that blood on your face? And where's your hair?"

Eloise blinked awake, groggily touching the top of her head. "Oh, that. Yeah. You missed a bit." Then she sat up and threw her arms around her twin. "You're OK! Thank Çalaht, you're OK."

Johanna held Eloise at arm's length. "What?"

"You were asleep, or mind-numb. Probably mind-numb."

It took a long while to fill her in. Johanna kept interrupting Eloise with questions, pressing her for details, especially about how she'd ended the spell and how Melveeta had died. "I can't believe I missed all of that," she said. "How is it possible I was mind-numb the whole time?"

Eloise felt ludicrous when she spoke of the matter of her hair, but Johanna understood. "Oh, El. You'll have to let me tidy it up for you. And thanks for not wiping the blood on me."

"No worries."

Johanna curled her own hair around an index finger and looked at it. "What? What the..." She brushed it, trying to remove the dirt. "What's happened to my hair?"

"I'm not sure, exactly. Something to do with Melveeta and the spell. I'm sorry." Eloise leaned closer. "Is my face different? I feel like my hands look different."

"It's hard to tell in this light." Johanna looked down at her own hands, then touched her face. "Maybe?"

"Maybe. And maybe more than maybe."

Johanna threw her hair back over her shoulder and shook her head. "I don't know what to say. Part of me wants to run screaming. Part of me is too exhausted. Part of me is numb."

"Yeah," said Eloise. "That sounds about right."

They sat there a long time, taking it all in.

Johanna eventually stood and pulled back the travel cloak to peek at the body. "What?"

Melveeta's corpse had shriveled to an unnatural nothingness. All that remained were shrunken bones, fingernails and toenails, and knotted white hair that had once reached to her waist. Not even her clothing remained. The rapid decay that marked her passing had continued in death, laying visible the bones that once had caused her so much distress. The multiple fractures in her left arm were now innocuous gaps of air. The mangled leg and hip looked curious, rather than cringe-inducing.

"Look," said Johanna, pointing to where the skeleton's stomach would have been. There was a clutch of gemstones polished to smoothness and reflecting the feeble luminescence of the Purple Haze.

Eloise bent down for a closer look. They were the size of the Stone of the Ancestors—about the size of large grapes. Three were a light shade of blue with veins of white running through them. Two were a deep ochre, one was ebony black, one was a deep yellow with black striping, and one was clear enough to see the ground beneath it. "Traveler stones? Witch stones?"

"Both, maybe?" suggested Johanna. "But look how many there are. She must have rattled when she walked."

"Do you think they're real? And have you ever heard of anyone swallowing more than one?"

"Wasn't there a story in Histories and Hearsay about a greedy merchant who swallowed two—a traveler stone to suppress hunger, and a witch stone to foster magic? I remember thinking it an absurd tale. As for them being real..." Johanna shook her head. "Before we met her, I'd have laughed them off as the fancies of bards. But everything else about her was real enough."

"I wonder if they're safe to touch." Eloise held her palm near them to see if they gave off anything she could detect.

"Why would you want to?"

"We should bury her."

Johanna groaned. "That is so like you."

"It seems the right thing to do. Like it or not, she was one of us. It'd be disrespectful to leave her out in the open, and I certainly don't want her spirit to be ground-bound because of unfinished business. But burying her means I'll need to move what's left of her. So I'm wondering what to do with those whatever-they-ares."

Eloise looked at the ground nearby. Rocks littered the area. She tentatively scraped at the dusty soil with her foot, then reached down and did the same with her hands. Below a weak length or two, it was impenetrable. She tried hammering the ground with a rock. Nothing. Eloise sat back on her heels. "How am I going to dig a deep enough hole?"

"You aren't. We'll have to build a cairn." Johanna picked up a stone and laid it at Melveeta's heel. "There. We've started. Now let's finish."

The two set to gathering rocks, first from nearby, then farther and farther away. They placed them around her to form an outline, then, starting at her feet, began to cover her. It was slow, tiring work—the rocks held fast to the earth like they were reluctant to be pressed into this particular task.

When the corpse was covered to the waist, Eloise again considered the handful of stones that once sat in Melveeta's gut. She went to her travel cloak and pulled out a small food sack that had most recently held dried apple. Squatting by the half-finished cairn, she picked up the eight stones and placed them in the bag.

"El, what are you doing?" Johanna put a rock onto the pile at Melveeta's hips.

"Do you want a rational answer or the irrational one?"

"How about both?"

"I thought there might be something in the Bibliotheca de Records and Regrets that might mention the stones, which would help us corroborate her story."

"And the rational one?"

"That was the rational one."

"I couldn't tell. What's the irrational answer, then?"

"The stones don't want to be buried. And they don't want to stay here."

"Oh, really?"

Eloise felt her cheeks redden. "Yes."

"And you know this how?"

"I'm not sure how to explain it. I set a rock for the cairn near them, and just got the sense it was wrong to cover them up." Eloise cinched the drawstring of the bag and put it back into a pocket of her travel cape. "Perhaps it is just intuition. But you might say they told me."

"That's not so strange," said Johanna. She found a pebble and put it on the cairn. "Whenever I bring a rock into my garden, I ask myself if I think it would be happy where I've placed it. If not, I move it. But I wouldn't be swallowing those things any time soon. Who knows what they'd do to you."

"That wasn't on the cards."

"Good. Now, come on. Not that much more to go."

❧

THEY FINISHED COVERING THE SKELETON WITH A GENEROUS MOUND, then stood looking down at it, not sure what to do next. "I have a travel copy of *The Scrolls of Çalaht*. We could read something from that," said Eloise.

"There's that bit where she seeks counsel from the Bog of Impermanence," suggested Johanna. "Or maybe one of the passages from the Scroll of Futility and Pointlessness?"

"That particular scroll always struck me as needlessly dire," said Eloise. "It was never my favorite."

"I know what you mean. All those lists. The 13 Unctuous Acts. The 23 Blessed Obfuscations. The Seven Primary Proclivities. The 19 Heretical Gestures. The 47 Beatific Snorts. The Three Obvious

Truths. The 17 Means of Peaceful Chewing. The 83 Misbegotten Mimicries. The Two Forbidden Notions."

"All nicely prime numbers."

"You're right. I hadn't noticed that before." Johanna pointed at the grave. "She did not strike me as particularly devout."

"Perhaps we give the recitation a miss?"

"We could just stand here awkwardly for a while."

"No. We have to do something. We could say the Recidivist's Lament."

"That's more a coming-of-age thing than a funeral thing."

"True." Eloise thought through the Devotional Utterances she knew by heart. "The Supplicant's Bargain? The Judderer's Exaltation? The Sutured Complaint? The Pedant's Ode? Or how about The Slurred Pious Vague Reference?"

"What, are you planning the devotional for a wedding?"

"You're right. None of those really suits."

A few more moments passed in silence.

"We can't even say, 'She'll be missed'," said Johanna. "There's no one left to miss her."

"There's us."

"Will you miss her?"

"Not really. But we have to say something." Eloise wiped her hands on her breeks. "We can't just walk away. Someone died. Plus, we're at Ground Null of the worst crime ever committed by anyone ever. It seems wrong to just take that Star of Whatever and leave without commemorating it somehow."

They stood in silence, unsure.

"Wait. I have an idea." Eloise picked up her cape and rummaged through its pockets. "I know it's in here somewhere." She dug past her

Livre de Protocol and *Scrolls of Çalabt,* the latter of which, contrary to Odmilla's suggestion, had not saved her life. Not yet, anyway. She felt past the ornamental bags of groats Queen Onomatopoeia had given her, an unexpected crust of bread she doubted even a starving mouse would want to eat, and countless bits of leaf, grime and dust that had accumulated in the corners.

Then she found it—small, dry, smooth, and still wearing its little hat. "Here. Take this."

"An acorn? Why do you have an acorn?"

"Actually, you've held this acorn before." She held it where Johanna could see it, reminding her of its appearance at the Ceremonies of the Stone, and explaining how Hoarfrost de Blotter had given it to her as a parting gift.

"What am I supposed to do with it?"

"Plant it. Right here, right now, using everything you've got—including your weak magic." Eloise waved off Johanna's demurring look. "Oh, please. I know, it's been a taboo topic between us, but you have it. So I say, let a mighty oak spring forth at the very spot where our ancestor's evil magic laid waste to the land. Let it be a statement of life and hope renewed. Even if no one ever sees it, you and I will know it's here."

"Nice. A little corny, but nice." Johanna extended an open palm. "May I have it?" Eloise handed her the acorn, and Johanna curled her fingers around it, closed her eyes in concentration, then popped it in her mouth. As parched as Johanna was, the acorn triggered her saliva, mixing Johanna's essence with the acorn's.

"I can't guarantee anything will happen," slurred Johanna around the acorn. "So, where do you want this wee acorn to go, so it has a chance to become your mighty oak?"

Eloise pointed to a spot a few lengths from Melveeta's head. "There." The girls walked to where she'd pointed.

"Wait," said Eloise, surprised. She tilted her head to listen. "You hear that?"

"Hear what? I don't hear anything."

"Exactly. Look how far we are from her. We're past where the buzzing was."

"Oh, sweet Çalaht shampooing a Shar Pei, what a relief! That infernal sound drove me spare."

"The spell must have begun dissipating, although you wouldn't think it, looking around at the fog."

"Well, that's something. Shall we?" Johanna stared down at the ground. If this had been her garden, she would have worked such lifeless, sandy soil for months, if not years, before putting a seed anywhere near it. But she didn't have that option. Plus, there was no fresh water to give it. Really, it was silly to even consider planting it. The poor thing would be on its own. Well, it would just have to do what it could, and she could only give it as good a start as the conditions allowed.

Johanna knelt, tucking her dress beneath her knees. She put her hands to the ground and scooped a divot, then froze and flattened her palms against the dirt. "Whoa."

"What?"

"Feel that."

Eloise put down her hands. The dry earth felt exactly like the dusty soil she'd dug into when they were deciding what to do with Melveeta's remains. Certainly nothing to "whoa" about. She looked at Johanna and shook her head.

"Really, nothing?"

"No, what do you feel?"

"It's thrumming." Johanna moved her palms, feeling different spots. "It feels like there are a thousand worker bees just under the surface."

"Nope. Not to me." Eloise put her palm exactly where Johanna's had been. Maybe there was a tiny little tingle, but she might have imagined it.

"Interesting," said Johanna. "To me, the land feels the way the air sounded. All buzzy. How can that be if the spell is over and we can't hear the buzz any more?"

"Maybe because it's more physical than air. Maybe it still vibrates, the way a lute string continues vibrating after it's been plucked, even though you can't hear the sound very well anymore."

"Maybe." Johanna scraped down into the earth, forming a hole. Down a few weak lengths, she met resistance, but Johanna persisted, using a small stone to hollow out more depth. She then chipped away at the sides of the hole so the acorn might extend roots into cracks—if it made it that far.

Johanna opened her right palm and dropped the damp acorn into it. She kissed it, slowly, then deliberately wrapped her fingers around it, and closed her eyes. Concentrating all her will into the seed, she cast her mind forward to a time when it would stand as a mature, healthy, wise oak tree. She could see the luster of its leaves, the smooth ridges of its bark, the roots that spread into the ground as far down as the tree was tall.

Then she raised her fist to her mouth, touching her lips to the small opening where her thumb and index finger curled into each other, and blew that future into the seed, anchoring it with her breath and her intention. Once, twice, thrice. Three breaths of life. Three anchors on the future. Then she held the side of her fist for Eloise to blow into. "Your turn."

"What do I do?"

"Blow into it what you wish for it."

Eloise closed her eyes and pictured what she wanted for the oak. She saw the tree surrounded by other oaks, all of them large and magnificent. They lived surrounded by grasses and a riot of plants. Birds picnicked in the oak's limbs. Lovers cooed at each other as they leaned against its welcoming trunk. The tree was happy, as were the people— human and non-human alike—who shared its shade and the beauty of its grove at the bottom of the cliff. Eloise let that sense of happiness fill her, and then she blew once, twice, thrice into the hollow of Johanna's hand. When she opened her eyes, she was almost surprised to see the wasteland still around her.

Johanna closed her eyes once more, wished the acorn well, and placed it lovingly in the hole. Together, she and Eloise scooped the dirt on top, and Johanna patted it down. "Grow well, my friend. Grow well and strong and fast."

The two young women sat back and looked at the spot. Johanna dug a small, circular trench around it so water would collect, if it ever rained. Then they sat in the stillness, letting a sense of finality come over them.

"I think it's time to go back," said Eloise.

"Yes."

Eloise stood, took a deep breath, picked up the wooden box containing the Star of Whatever, and slung its carry strap over her shoulder. There was a sash, which she tied around her hips, securing the box to her. Eloise thought there might have been a drowsy "?" sent in her direction, but she was reluctant to engage with the magical stone again. She'd had plenty of that already.

Next, she settled her travel cloak on her shoulders and tied it at her neck, pushing away her revulsion at the fact that it had so recently been pressed into service as a funeral shroud. She wondered if the ghost, or at least the blood, would ever wash out. That made her think of Seamstress Linttrap, who'd sewn the cloak at such short notice, and who would certainly deliver a mortifying scolding when (OK, if) Eloise made it back and showed her what had become of her handiwork.

With one last look at Melveeta's grave and at the place where they had planted the acorn, Eloise and Johanna turned toward the cliff face, and took their first steps back along the trail of emptiness and death that had led them to this spot. Eloise considered the Star of Whatever on her hip, just out of the way when she swung her arm. She would bring it home and work out who its rightful guardian was. Perhaps her mother would know. And she would bring her sister home, as she had promised she would.

Behind them, the acorn, finding itself nestled in dirt and awash in magic, made the very unusual decision to sprout immediately, defiantly, and definitively. If the sisters had stayed a few minutes longer, they would have seen the first hints of a tendril poking through ground, the world's most improbable oak springing into life from the dust of devastation.

❧ 26 ❧

POORLY EXECUTED

A chill wind whipped the top of Fogging Hill, making the mood even more somber than it usually was for a fogging. Lorch stood with the other 13 condemned, noting there was barely a crowd to bear witness, or family members shedding tears. He assumed most of the city was still bound in grief from the ravages of the Silent Death, as the tragedy two nights prior was being called. He'd heard through the prison grapevine that the name the "Horrific Doom" also had a lot of support. So did the "Widespread Terror" and the "Unexpected Slaughter." A bunch of the prisoners were simply calling it "Aaaaaaaaagh!" despite the lack of specificity. Still, consensus seemed to have formed around the "Silent Death," so the Silent Death it would probably be.

Lorch stood bound, gagged, and shivering like the others. A fearsome collection of guards surrounded them. Jerome was first in line, with Lorch right behind him. Despite the early winter chill, Lorch saw that Jerome was sweating like he had at his Naming Ceremony. He guessed the chipmunk would have been running around in panic, except for the guard who held him dangling by the tail.

Lorch glanced over to where Hector and the Nameless One stood at a respectful distance, and felt a lump in his throat. They looked poised for action, but what could they do, given the number of heavily armed guards? Swooping in heroically seemed their only option—a foolish, low-probability, and likely fatal option.

A woman in purple robes the exact shade of the Purple Haze approached, carrying an armload of scrolls, and trailed by an awkward teenage boy in a similar purple tunic. "G'mid-morning all," she said to the few onlookers. "On behalf of the Foggers' Guild, I'd like to thank you all for coming. The guild appreciates your support and patronage, and you making the effort to be part of today's solemn ceremonies means a lot—to us and the fog-bound as well."

She handed the scrolls to the nervous teen, who fumbled with them, but managed not to drop them. The woman turned to the line of prisoners. "Well, there certainly are a bunch of you today. I'm super sorry we're late, and thanks for waiting." She nodded at the boy. "Öööscar, my new apprentice, here, spilled haggleberry tea on some of the conviction scrolls, and the Guild Master had to redo them. Good thing she has a good memory, or some of you might have been walking free today instead of trundling down toward the mist. Can you imagine? Anyway, g'mid-morning, again. My name is Abigail Bronzer Splintfinger, and I'll be your fogger today. As there are so many of you, I'd appreciate your cooperation so we're not up here in the wind all day. Let's see if we can get through this quickly and with a minimum of fuss, eh?" She smiled at them with a practiced rictus that, to Lorch, looked like it had been taught in a weekend seminar called "Affability Is Within Your Grasp." He wasn't taken in by it, but noticed that it worked at least a little, as two of the prisoners nodded obligingly back to her.

"Rightio, let's get started." She squatted down so she could look Jerome in the eye. "You're up first. If I get the guard to set you down, do you promise to stand properly while I do the reading bits?"

Jerome shuddered, then nodded. Lorch wished he could reach out and steady him, maybe comfort him somehow.

"Very good. Go ahead, Gerald. Let him stand." The guard put Jerome on the ground while the fogger sorted through the scrolls looking for the right one. "Ta da! Got it." She waggled it a little for emphasis, then unscrolled it, pulled her hood over her head, and cleared her throat. She began her recitations using an official voice that sounded to Lorch like she'd learned it at a weekend seminar called "You Too Can Speak with Commanding Tones."

"Jerome Abernatheen de Chipmunk, you are hereby called to account for the following crimes and misdemeanors. Disturbing the peace. Showing disrespect to a royally designated representative of the Crown. Entering a royal building with malicious intent. Treasonous plotting against the Crown. Conspiring and plotting against the Royal Personage in miscellaneous and nefarious ways. Encouraging sedition. Aiding and abetting the removal of the king's property." She curled down the top of the scroll and looked at Jerome. "That's an impressive list, little fella. But 'Disturbing the peace?' Really? I guess we know the real reason you're here, am I right?"

Jerome managed a shrug in response.

The fogger re-scrolled the parchment and resumed her official tone, reciting the rest from memory. "Because you have been convicted of these various and sundry crimes against the Crown and against his people, you have been brought to this place. And so at the command and authorization of His Majesty King Worsted Halva de Chëëëk-flïïïnt, as confirmed by His Jesterness and Regent, Master Turpentine Snotearrow McCcoonnch, I hereby officially proclaim these things to be true, and commend your body and soul to the uncertainty of the fog. Good luck and Çalaht be with you." She tucked the rolled-up scroll into the gap between Jerome's arms, then, with a sweep of her arm, indicated that he should walk into the fog. "Proceed."

Jerome stayed where he was.

"Go ahead, mate," said the fogger.

Jerome didn't budge.

She bent down and patted Jerome's shoulder a little in encouragement. "Off you go. Down the hill."

Jerome shied away from her and stood his ground.

The fogger straightened. "We've got another stander, Geoffrey."

"Yes, ma'am," said the guard, who walked over and squatted next to Jerome. "Bit nervous, are you, mate?"

Lorch knew this routine. He'd seen it when he and the others had witnessed a fogging soon after they arrived in Stained Rock. He knew exactly what Geoffrey was planning on doing. And from the look of it, Jerome knew, too. He tried to move away, keeping out of Geoffrey's reach.

Lorch felt like he had to do something. "Mmm mmmm mmmm," he said through his gag.

Jerome stopped and looked at him, puzzled.

Geoffrey, however, was used to deciphering the mumbles of gagged prisoners. "That's very kind of you to offer to go first," he said to Lorch. "But this fellow's already had the reading out loud bits done, so we may as well let him finish what's been started. You can be next if you like."

Jerome, distracted by Lorch, hadn't seen Geoffrey sidle over while he spoke. The guard shot out an arm and snatched the chipmunk. Jerome squirmed and kicked, but the guard held him firmly. Lorch lunged at the guard, but Geoffrey must have sensed it was coming. He stepped out of the way and stuck out a leg, sending Lorch crashing to the ground. Then Geoffrey turned so he was facing the fog, arced his arm backwards, overhead and around, then flung Jerome like he was a tiny, fur-covered bowling ball. The chipmunk tumbled head over foot down the slope of the hill, bouncing and rolling faster and faster as momentum took hold.

Lorch screamed through his gag.

A few seconds later, Princess Eloise's champion and best friend since childhood, and one of the people Lorch felt personally responsible for (no, it was more than that—Jerome was now his friend, too) pierced the veil of the Purple Haze and disappeared.

Silence. Cold, dead silence.

The fog had claimed another as its own.

For the first time since he'd left Castle de Brague, Lorch's demeanor cracked. Tears fell for his friend. It had really come to this. Jerome was gone.

"Rightio," said Abigail to the others. "That's not so hard, now is it? Let's see—"

She was interrupted by a high-pitched noise coming from down the hill. Lorch turned and looked.

It was Jerome. He shot out of the fog in blind, frenzied terror, screaming through his gag.

"What the..." said the fogger. She pulled back her hood to get a better look. "Geoffrey?"

"Yes, Abigail?"

"What's going on?"

"I don't know, ma'am. I've never seen one come out."

"Me either."

Lorch watched as Jerome screeched back up the hill. If the chipmunk had any measure of wit about him, he would not have chosen to run straight back to where he'd started. But rational thought was not high on Jerome's list, and within moments he was standing next to where Lorch lay, chest heaving, eyes wild.

Relief flooded through Lorch. How was this possible?

The fogger nodded to the guard, and before Lorch knew what was happening, Geoffrey had picked Jerome up again. This time, he threw him high and long, trying to get the ferociously wriggling chipmunk as far into the fog as he could.

Again, Lorch screamed.

Again, there was cold, dead silence as the mist welcomed a soul.

They all watched and waited, letting the silence gather.

This time, nothing. No sound. No chipmunk.

"Thank you, Geoffrey," said Abigail. "That seems to have done it." She waited a few more moments, and then, satisfied that all was right, pulled up her hood to again cover her face. "Rightio. I'll just—"

As suddenly as before, Jerome came screaming out the mist.

The fogger stared, watching Jerome zigzag crazily across the slope. "Çalaht painting pointillist portraits, what is going on with the Purple Haze today?" She looked at the prisoners, then the guards, as though somehow they might have an answer, then glared at her apprentice, like it might be his fault. She pointed at Jerome, exasperated. "Geoffrey, could you gather him for me?"

Lorch stood, ready to run after Jerome as well, but another guard yanked on the rope that bound him. He'd never get away.

Geoffrey nodded to Abigail, then trotted down the hill. It took a few minutes of playing chase, but the guard eventually zagged against Jerome's zig, and plucked him up.

Abigail had pulled out a small bound volume from her robes called *Fogging: A Handbook for Consigning the Adjudged into the Purple Haze*. Frowning, she quickly flipped to the table of contents. "Quietening screamers. Dealing with standers. Proper scroll handling. Collecting fees," she mumbled. "Well, this is embarrassing. There's nothing here about the fog not working." Abigail tossed the book at her apprentice. "See if you can find something relevant. Geoffrey. Hand the rat to someone else, grab one of the others—her," she said pointing to the nice old bilby. "Find a spare length of rope and follow me."

Lorch watched as Hector and the Nameless One trailed along behind the fogger, as close as they could get, trying to see what she had in mind. Abigail and Geoffrey took the bilby down toward the mist, tied a length of rope around the old one's waist, did a quick version of the official recitation, then had her walk in and out of the fog. They tried tossing her, rolling her, having her walk both backwards and forwards. Each time, the bilby re-emerged, looking like she was ready to bake a few more scones.

They trudged back to the top of Fogging Hill, purple robes flapping in the cold wind. The fogger addressed the row of prisoners. "I'm super sorry, everyone, but the Purple Haze appears to be malfunctioning this morning. I'm sure it's a temporary glitch, but I'm going to have to put the ceremonies on hold. You'll need to return to your dungeons and come back another time, once we sort things out. I'm sorry for any inconvenience, and feel free to direct any complaints to the Director of Communications, care of Foggers' Guild Hall."

With that, she turned and strode off to speak to her Guild Master, her apprentice fumbling along behind her like one of Çalaht's trained fleas.

Lorch's legs went rubbery and he could barely walk back to the castle. He'd live to see another day.

27

ONWARD, THROUGH THE FOG

Hector and the Nameless One watched the guards shuffle the line of prisoners back toward the castle.

"What happened?" asked Hector. "How come the mist didn't do to Jerome or that bilby what it did to me?"

The Nameless One gave an I-have-no-idea shrug as he turned and walked downhill toward the fog to get a closer look. Hector followed, feeling his guts tighten as he drew nearer. The memory of dropping into convulsing mind-numbness was still excruciatingly fresh.

Up close, the Purple Haze looked exactly as it had before—thick, impenetrable, foreboding, and oddly luminescent. But Jerome had emerged, as had that nice old bilby. Something had changed.

Hector did not like the thought of what he had to do, but steeled himself to do it anyway. "Will you grab my tail?"

The Nameless One nodded reluctant agreement. He stepped behind Hector, took a firm mouthful of tail, and braced himself against the slope.

The last time Hector went into the fog, it was on impulse. The mist had not so much hit him as taken him over. He didn't remember it as being particularly painful. There was just a sudden loss of body control, collapsing to the ground, the quake of the first tremors, and then nothing else. The next thing he recalled was coming back to awareness, woozy and with the world's sorest tailhead.

Hector mustered his calm with a long, deep breath, and carefully stretched out his nose so it breached the Purple Haze. Nothing. He moved one step forward, leaning in so his neck was in, then all the way to his wither. The faint buzzing sound that had been there last time was gone. Odd. Another small step, and another, until all that remained outside was his tail. He could breathe in there. The smell was neutral, if dank. Visibility was maybe three lengths at the most, but there was a complete lack of writhing on the ground and uncontrollable kicking.

Hector backed out. "Right then. Something's definitely changed, but who knows how long for." he said. "You stay here and watch out for Lorch and Jerome. I'm going in to—"

The Nameless One snorted. He took two steps toward the fog and positioned himself where Hector had been. When Hector didn't move, he swished his tail, then held it up for Hector to grab.

"You don't have to do this. Only one of us needs to put ourselves at risk. Who knows what's in there? If both of us don't come back, what will become of the others? What if the princesses return while we're both in there? And if all of us are doomed, who will report to the Queen and King?"

The Nameless One swished again, irritable this time.

"Fine. You really are as stubborn as that human you let ride you." Hector set his legs against the slope, clamped down on the Nameless One's tail, and said, "Ready" through clenched teeth.

The Nameless One, too, was able to go into the fog and return unharmed.

"Right, then. Let's go find them," said Hector. "Or what's left of them."

28

PERSIMMON KNEE

The trip up the cliff might have been easier than the one Melveeta had faced, but it was hardly a biscuit walk. The cliff was taller than anything Eloise had ever climbed before, and she knew it would take her hours to make her way up the sheer face. There weren't the slippery handholds or the threat of being pummeled by cascading water, but the dust-encrusted rock face presented plenty of opportunities for disaster. Dried moss that gave way. Handholds that had to be cleared of powder to ensure she did not slip. Eloise decided to free climb it, rather than depend on the dangling rope—she worried that it provided a false sense of security. She made sure it was properly tied around Johanna's waist and thighs so she could help her sister when it came her turn—assuming she didn't crash to her death first—then, with a last hug for good luck, began her ascent.

It did not start well. Just two lengths up, Eloise's left foot slipped from an easy crack, and she banged her knee trying to regain purchase. Her breeks protected her skin from breaking, but it stung.

"Good for you, El," said Johanna just below her.

"What's that supposed to mean?"

"Just that you've gotten the scary slip out of the way. There's always one. So now you can just get on with the rest of it, no problem."

This, of course, made no sense. So Eloise just said, "No problem?"

"Scoot along. You'll be fine."

Eloise accepted the vote of confidence for what it was and turned her attention back to the wall.

The climb took everything—all of her attention, all of her strength, all of her grit. By the time she found a spot halfway up where she could rest, Eloise was soaked in sweat, and her hands ached from the strain. Her left knee pounded out the rhythm of her heartbeat, which made it hard to properly push up with her legs instead of pulling with her arms. The Star of Whatever, which was strapped to her, was not so heavy it affected her balance, but she was constantly aware of it bobbing along with her, which irritated her for no reason other than that she was feeling resentment toward it. Which was dumb. She might as well resent a spatula for flipping a pancake.

Her thoughts spiraled toward, "This is spectacularly impossible." Not helpful. So when Eloise resumed, she tried to take refuge in her counting. First it was her knee throbs, but that just brought attention to the problem instead of distracting her from it. She changed to counting her breaths, but she kept thinking about how much dust she was breathing in. Next, she tried counting shapes in the cliff wall that might be construed to look like letters. That worked better. Once she'd collected a few letters, she started forming words from them. She spelled (and immediately discarded) "splat" and "slip." By three quarters of the way up, she had the right letters for "dummkopf" and "splenetic." She almost lost her grip around "leporine," and had a heart-swallowing recovery at "mellifluous," which kept her pulse racing to "bric-a-brac" and on to "lackadaisical." By "vituperous," she was starting to see the top edge, and with "cattywampus," the end was only a score or so lengths away.

Eloise forced herself to keep it slow and steady. "Liturgical." "Bilateral." "Flustered." Reach, grasp, check, raise, steady, look for the next move, repeat. "Ostensible." That led her to a really good foothold at "obstreperous" and a difficult press up through a narrow gap with "ostentatious." "Eloquence." "Fastidious." "Judicious"—no, "judiciously." Wait, that meant several of the previous handful of words could have been made "ly" adverbs. Oh, well. No need to go back and do that, even in her head.

Her arms burned. Her legs felt like they wanted to file for divorce. She guessed her left knee was taking on the color and shape of a persimmon. Up and up she climbed, until she could think, "Four more words, and I'll be there."

Left foot and up. "Cantankerous."

Right foot and up. "Zoologically."

Left food and up. "Widdershins."

That's when she got stuck. She was one handhold away from being able to haul herself up and over to safety. She was ready with the word: "indemnification." That, or "indefatigable." She had the letters for either, but she didn't feel the latter, so it seemed wrong to use it.

What she didn't have was anywhere to grab or step.

"How's it going up there?" yelled Johanna, invisible in the mists below.

Eloise glanced down. She'd long since climbed out of Johanna's visible range, so her sister was clueless as to her progress. Johanna had been waiting for some sign that Eloise was OK, or for her to make a sudden, downward-directed appearance. "Hanging in there," Eloise yelled back.

"Very droll. But good to hear."

Eloise scanned the area for options. Nothing within reach to the left or up. There was a spot not too far from her right foot where the stone looked different from its surrounding. It was a lighter color, like it had been bleached, or chipped away somehow.

Or maybe it had broken off.

Eloise gasped. She knew precisely where she was and what had happened. She pictured Melveeta clinging to this exact same position, looking at the exact same spot in the stone, seeing something that was no longer there. Without really wanting to, Eloise played out Melveeta's last moments on the cliff. Her stomach dropped just thinking about it.

She looked at the discolored place in the cliff face. The foothold in what Eloise called Melveeta's "whoops-a-daisy spot" was shallow, and certainly shallower than it had been two centuries before. But Eloise had to admit it was probably her best chance.

Fine. Forewarned and forearmed and all that. She'd just have to do what Melveeta hadn't—succeed.

As carefully and mindfully as she could, Eloise reached her right foot toward the divot in the cliff. The angle was awkward, but she jammed a decent percentage of her toes into it. Making sure she was steady on her other foot and locked on with both hands, she shifted her weight to increase the pressure on the foothold.

Without warning, the rock under pressure gave way. Fragments clattered to the depths below. Her foot, suddenly unsupported, slid precipitously along the stone.

But Eloise was ready. "Rock!" she yelled, so Johanna could take cover. Heart racing, she held fast with her hands and shifted her weight back to the left. Then she looked upward at the cliff and said, "Really? The same thing? Do you have something against my family?"

The cliff did not respond.

Eloise figured actions spoke louder than words, for both her and the cliff. Without giving it another moment, she placed her foot in exactly the same spot, noted there was a bit more room there now, said a quiet, "Behave yourself, now" to the cliff, then stepped into the crack, lifted herself up, grasped the top lip and hauled herself over.

"Indemnification," she said to herself. "And indefatigable." She allowed herself both, figuring she'd earned them, and added "persnickety" as a bonus.

She was safe. Thank Çalaht.

Eloise lay on her back looking at the Purple Haze above, imagining blue sky instead. She let her muscles and knee hold a group discussion about the folly of everything she had just done.

"El?" came the shouted question.

"Sorry, Jo," Eloise called back. "I just made it. Tell me when you're ready to start."

"Ready."

"Right. Give me a minute." Eloise pushed away her fatigue and sat up. She could rest later.

She found a relatively comfortable spot near the boulder where they'd first found the rope. She wanted a place where she could plant her feet against the boulder and brace herself with both legs out straight. The climb angle was steep, which meant less rubbing on the rope, but there would be more chance of a pendulum swing if Johanna fell. Eloise had to make sure she would not be spun around or pulled out of position by a fall. Anchoring herself in place would have been a lot better, but she didn't have the gear for that.

Eloise made sure her right leg was the one in the direction of Johanna's rope, so if there was a fall, the sudden strain would not be on the leg with the persimmon knee. That meant threading the rope so she guided it with her right hand, had the rope wrapped around her hip and below the Star of Whatever box, which would help keep it from riding up, and using her left hand as a brake. "I'm ready when you are," she called.

"Ready to climb," said Johanna. Even at this distance, Eloise could hear the reluctance in her voice.

"On belay!"

There was a definite hesitation. Eloise imagined Johanna steeling herself and even knew the exact expression she'd have—doubt giving way to resolve. She'd seen it when they'd played one-on-one hockey sacking games when Johanna was behind and time was running out. She'd seen it before a test in Johanna's least favorite subjects, like Numerals and Quandaries or Rotes and Recitations, the former of which Eloise had loved and the latter of which she'd always thought should have been right up Johanna's cobblestone road, but wasn't.

Eloise waited.

Finally, one word echoed upward. "Climbing."

Eloise smiled, and called back, "Climb on."

There was the very faintest of grunts, and she could tell that Johanna was on her way. Eloise carefully took up the slack, pulling back with her right hand and forward with her left to slide the rope behind her, then reaching forward with her right above her left, pinching the two lines together with her right hand and thumb, and gliding her braking hand back to her left hip, making sure never to let go. Johanna could climb faster, since she had the safety of the rope, but after a while, Eloise could tell it was not going as well as Johanna would have liked. Her calls of "slack" and "up rope" became more irritated as the minutes crawled into hours, and eventually, the climbing became punctuated with oaths and swearing, with a saltiness Eloise had not heard before from her sister.

Twice, Johanna cried, "Falling," which gave Eloise time to brace the braking rope against a coming fall. Once, Johanna fell before she was able to yell a warning, catching Eloise by surprise.

Johanna's voice became clearer as she fought her way up the cliff. Eventually, Eloise saw the top of her head emerging through the fog. "You're doing great, Jo."

Johanna shot her sister a look that could have ignited the bark of an ironwood tree. "Yeah, I'm doing just peachy." Johanna was scratched and scraped. Her hands looked like she'd been scrubbing them with a wire brush, and her dress desperately needed repair. Eloise assumed she herself looked just as bad.

Eventually, Johanna made it to the same place where Eloise and Melveeta both got stuck. "Watch out for that spot with your right foot," said Eloise. "It's not very nice."

Johanna looked up at her. "First, I think it was a bad life choice to have free climbed this thing. Really. I mean, what were we thinking?"

Eloise shrugged. "It had to be done."

"Second, I think you are a hero for having done it. I keep thinking about Melveeta doing this with a waterfall pounding away next to her. It would have been a miracle for her to get this far. Either she was part spider, or prone to even worse life choices than you."

With one final effort, Johanna scrambled over the lip of the cliff. As soon as she was safe, she began crying. "I never want to do anything like that ever again. Give me a patch of ground, a few seeds, and a watering bucket any day."

Eloise disentangled herself from the rope and gave her sister a hug. "Yes, and to think some people do this for fun."

"Thanks for helping me get up."

"No problem."

"Oh, sorry." Johanna leaned away from her sister, then yelled, "Belay off!"

"Oh, right," laughed Eloise. "Off belay!"

Eloise giggled at the deliberate absurdity and her relief at both of them having made it. Johanna must have felt the same, because she caught the giggles as well. That made Eloise laugh more, which spilled back onto her sister. They laughed the laugh of soldiers who'd made it through a disastrous battle and then had to cook dinner.

Eloise was still chucking as she untied the knots from Johanna's hips and slid the rope back down over the cliff.

"Why do that? Why not leave it up here?"

Eloise lifted a shoulder. "I figured we should leave it the way we found it,"

"Whatever," said Johanna. "I never want to see that thing again."

"I agree. How do you feel? We should probably rest before we get going."

"A rest would be nice."

They leaned against the boulder and fell asleep within seconds. Eloise dreamed of flailing for handholds and footholds on an endless rocky landscape. She kept slipping, never quite making it to the top. In her dream, the Star of Whatever chatted away on her hip. It nattered about nothing, a word salad of slightly magical nonsense, peppered with what could only be interpreted as snarky commentary about Eloise's climbing technique.

"El, wake up," said Johanna. "You're snoring."

Eloise snorted awake. "I don't snore."

"You snore like the illegitimate offspring of a rip saw and a bombard who grew up and apprenticed with a professional keener."

"Wow. Been waiting long to use that one?"

"A while."

"Feel better?"

"Enough."

"Shall we head back?"

"Yes, let's."

They stood and began retracing their footsteps backwards through the dust.

29

DISTURBANCE IN THE DUST

The number of bones was astonishing. They were stifle-deep and higher, stretching ever onward as the horses slowly moved through them. Hector's mind reeled. So much death. It was an accumulation of suffering worse than any war he'd ever heard of. Even as he focused on keeping his footing, Hector imagined how each of these bodies was once a person more or less like him, and how they must have twitched and flailed the way he did when they were fogged. The accumulated misery overwhelmed him.

It was soon obvious just how hard it would be to find anything in particular. Within the narrow circle of visibility, all the bones clustered around them looked about the same. The skeleton fragments were devoid of flesh, hair, clothing, or anything that might identify who someone was. Plus, all of it was caked in an obscuring layer of dust, like a haunted castle that had lain dormant for centuries. They'd entered the fog where they'd last seen Eloise, at the spot where she'd left Gouache, and with careful exploration, found the exact two spots where Jerome had rushed out, identifiable by chipmunk-sized disturbances in the dust. But once they were a few lengths in, their surroundings blended into sameness.

It was hard, but Hector forced himself to remember that he needed to look for two different things—the royal remains of the princesses or some evidence they might still live. The latter seemed stunningly unlikely. How could they possibly survive in a place like this? Still, Hector forced himself to leave it at least in the category of "possible," because doing otherwise was just too upsetting.

He began identifying different species—dogs, snakes, kangaroos, and turtles were easy enough, and could be ignored. So could anything with a tail, carapace or exoskeleton. They scoured the fog for hours, first near where they'd come in, then further from the edge. The bones they walked on sometimes gave way beneath them, and Hector feared that whatever clue they needed would disappear accidentally.

When nothing turned up, they picked their way down a dicey ridge, which opened up a whole new area of remains, and hours more looking.

Suddenly, Hector stopped. Something about the bone pile to his left caught his eye. The carpet of dust was different, like something had disturbed its uniformity. "Something, or someone, has been here," he muttered. He looked up. A sheer wall rose above him. It was what he and the Nameless One had carefully walked down not far from the edge of the Purple Haze. Could someone have come over that and survived? Maybe. "Come look at this," he called to the Nameless One.

The two of them studied the spot, trying to figure out what had happened without getting so close that they would disturb it. Hector tried to picture one or both of the princesses at that spot. If they had stood, or sat, or lay there, would it have created this kind of change to the dust? Maybe. He squinted into the fog, stepping carefully. Had they walked away? Crawled? Limped?

There was a sudden rumble, and Hector felt the bones beneath him shift. Without warning, the hill of death beneath them collapsed and the horses plunged in a chaotic avalanche of skulls, ribs, hands, teeth, and claws.

It was hard to tell just how far they slid—three score lengths at least—before they came to a sudden, crunching halt. Debris rained onto them for a full minute after, then silence. Silence, and a choking cloud of dust that clogged their noses and mouths and limited visibility to half a length at most.

Carefully, they got to their hooves. No sudden, sharp pains, so nothing was broken, although Hector suspected he'd bruised a rib, and the Nameless One had a nasty scrape where a broken femur had tried to impale him. He'd lost a decent patch of hair, but his skin was unbroken.

"We had something there," snapped Hector. "And now, it's gone. It could be they are also gone. We could stand on their tibias and be none the wiser." He stamped once in frustration, bringing another rain of bones sliding down on them. "Plus, I have no idea where we are now."

The Nameless One nodded in agreement, then shook to remove the dust from his coat. Even more cautiously than before, he began walking in an ever-widening outward spiral.

"I see. Good idea." Hector fell in line behind him, keeping an exact distance away. They risked complete disorientation, but it was the one way they could think of to find a hint of where they'd previously been, and maybe pick up some hint of a trail, if there was one.

It was impossible to know where they had been before the fall, or if what was there had even been significant. The whole area was an impenetrable jumble. For all Hector knew, they were standing on the princesses' skeletons.

But he refused to stop. If there was a chance of finding anything out, Hector had to take it.

The choking dust cloud raised by the avalanche meant that their progress was marked by coughs, blowing noses, and grit-filled hoicks. On and on they looked. Occasionally, they rested. It was not strenuous, because they moved so slowly, but the constant vigilance about where they put their feet, and the unending, focused searching were fatiguing.

Eventually, their widening circle took them to the edge of the collapse. The first thing they found was the spot where they'd descended. "Good," thought Hector. He knew, more or less, where "out" was—up and over.

Staying on the already disturbed side, they carefully scrutinized every square length. But the cloud raised by the crash was settling, and soon, any hint of previous disturbance would vanish beneath a fresh layer of who-knew-what-those-dust-particles-were-from. Their search seemed to take forever, and now, they were running out of time.

"What a minute," said Hector. "Look. Look, look, look!"

After a day and a half of straining their eyes and breathing air thick enough to chew, Hector and the Nameless One saw marks that could only have been caused by two bipeds moving side-by-side. They were not exactly footsteps—the terrain they walked on was too irregular for that. But most definitely, a path of disturbance led away from where the two horses stood.

Hope flowered in Hector's chest. It looked like the two princesses might somehow, miraculously, have survived entry into the Purple Haze and continued on.

The Nameless One looked around, puzzled. He turned, then turned again, making sure his orientation was correct.

"What?"

The Nameless One pointed in the direction they'd come from, then turned around and pointed toward the path they had discovered. He did it again for emphasis.

"Çalaht hauling hay bales, you're right. What in all the realms would make them decide to stay in here, instead of leaving as fast as they could?"

The two stood still, contemplating. Hector felt a mix of emotions sloshing around inside—confusion, concern, hope, despair.

It was then that Hector saw how the undisturbed bodies were positioned. They were stretching. Stretching or reaching for something—all in the same direction. It looked like the skeletons were reaching for the path. Of course, it was the other way around. The path went in the direction of the reaching.

Hector pointed it out, adding, "That means this probably wasn't a random direction. Some decision drove the choice."

The Nameless One nodded, seeing the logic.

"I say we follow this and see what we find."

Again, agreement.

Hector paused. "You know, there's no guarantee they made this path."

This time the Nameless One shook his head. His meaning was clear: "It's them. Let's go."

Hector let the Nameless One lead the way. They kept a couple of lengths away from what Hector now thought of as "the Princess Path," walking where they could still see it, but wouldn't trample it, and picked their way further into the Purple Haze.

❅ 30 ❆

PECKISH

Eloise didn't relish walking back to Stained Rock, but there seemed to be no other choice. She and Johanna trudged across an uninterrupted wasteland, keeping their focus downward, since visibility remained a few lengths at most in the purple-tinged luminescence.

At one point Johanna broke the silence with a question. "How long?"

"How long what?"

"How long do you think it's been? It feels like I've never done anything else in my life."

"I have no idea," said Eloise. "I've been looking for hints of day or night, but haven't seen anything at all."

"Me either."

They continued. Eloise tried not to step on their previous footprints. She wasn't sure if this was her habits speaking somehow, or if she just liked the visual of two sets of footprint pairs stretching endlessly in opposite directions.

Eventually, Johanna spoke again. "Guess."

"Guess what?"

"Guess how long it has been. An hour? A year? A score of years?"

"I've already said. I can't tell."

"Exactly," said Johanna. "Exactly."

"What's your point?"

Johanna jogged a few steps to catch up with Eloise. "Melveeta had no idea how long she'd been there. She knew it had been a while, but the scope of time she had been away took her by surprise."

"So?"

"So, the same might happen to us. We've been slogging through this magical soup," Johanna waved at the fog around them, "for Çalaht knows how long. What if we get back and it has been a hundred years or more?"

"I don't know."

"It would be like it was for Melveeta when we showed up. Everyone we know—knew—will be dead. Their children will be dead. Their grand-children would be enfeebled and tottering toward their graves. Court would have moved on. Would Mother and Father have had other children to replace the two princesses lost forever to the fog? Would anyone even know what happened to us? There weren't exactly a lot of witnesses—just Gouache and Turpy. You left Gouache behind mind-numb, and I wouldn't trust Turpy to be a reliable source information. Would the line of succession in the Western Lands and All That Really Matters have been thrown into chaos? Could Mother even give birth again? She's only done it the one time with us. It's not like she's prolific."

"Hold on, I'm still back at 'magical soup.'"

"We could have missed decades of wars, or an epoch of prosperity, or a century of peace. A volcano could have wiped out the world beyond this cursed mist, or the Gööödeling Sea could have risen and swamped half the realms. Anything could have happened."

"Very dramatic."

"I'm serious, El. What becomes of us if we get back and the rest of life has just, just—moved on?"

Eloise looked at her, thoughtful. "What if…"

"Yes?"

She reached out and took Johanna's hand. "What if the magical soup works the other way? What if we get back and it has been, say, ten minutes and no one has even noticed we've been gone?"

"Less dramatic."

"Yes. And what if we get back, and everything is just sort of normal?"

"Also less dramatic." Johanna sighed. "But from observation, I think your scenario is less likely."

"Why do you say that?"

"Because Melveeta was not surprised by how little time had passed, but by how much. So she had been there longer than she thought. Not shorter."

"She was in a lot of pain," said Eloise. "That could alter her sense of time as well. Even something as simple as a splinter under your fingernail can make time slow way down."

"I suppose."

Eloise gave her sister's hand a small squeeze. "I know a way we can find out. "

"How?"

"By getting back. How about we just do that?"

"Agreed."

They walked. They slept. Sometimes they talked. Mostly they focused on the trail of their steps. Now when she saw the remains of people straining in vain toward where the Star had been, Eloise felt no curiosity, just sadness, a dull ache for those who lost their lives due to a personal squabble between two half-remembered monarchs.

A colossal waste.

Eloise already had a good example of how not to run a queendom in her grandmother, Eloise Hydra Gumball I. Although One was long dead when the twins were born, Eloise had read plenty of history scrolls, and none of them were kind. Nor were the stories her mother told. From One, Eloise had learned not to let the queendom suffer, no matter how brutalized one's heart felt.

But now she knew that Gwendolyn the Irritable had plunged half a realm into irretrievable death and chaos for exactly the same reason. Gwendolyn hadn't directly told Melveeta to cast the spell that created the Purple Haze. By Melveeta's telling, the original plan had been much more contained. But if the Star of Whatever was the tip of the arrow, and Melveeta its shaft and fletching, then Gwendolyn was most definitely the archer. She sent that weapon of destruction out into the world with a purpose, so its consequences must lie at her feet.

It was a lot to think about. Eloise wasn't sure the unknowns of unintended consequences were the best traveling companions when walking a long way in the private hush of fog.

It was Johanna who first noticed the change. Her initial realization came in six simple words: "I'm feeling a little bit peckish."

"Hmmm." Eloise had been dwelling on Johanna's worries about arriving back—if there was a back for them to get to—a few lifetimes after they should have. None of the implications were pleasant.

"Are you?"

"Am I what?"

"Peckish."

"A bit, I guess."

"Don't you find that strange?" said Johanna. "I haven't felt hungry since we left the castle."

"Maybe. I'm more inclined toward a sip of something," said Eloise. "But I haven't seen even a spoonful since we started."

"Hmmm. No, I'm definitely more peckish than thirsty. But it's nothing I can't ignore. *Andiamo*, eh?"

"Yes, let's go."

They covered strong length after strong length. The further they went, the less ignorable the demands of their bodies became. Fatigue hit them faster and harder. Muscle soreness increased, and was particularly noticeable after they'd taken a break. "The mistake is stopping" became a phrase they said to each other whenever one of them suggested a rest break too soon after the previous one.

Whatever it was in the spell that had sustained them on their walk, it was most definitely lessening. There was still an astounding amount of residual magic around, though. Johanna could feel the land buzzing just as strongly as ever. But it was like Melveeta had said—aspects of the spell would wear off unevenly over time, some fast, some slow.

Hunger nibbled, then gnawed, then became all-consuming. They shared the tiny crust of bread Eloise had inadvertently left in her travel cloak. It hardly dented the feeling. If they saw a farmhouse or a hamlet, they'd poke around to see if there might be something left, but two centuries of the baleful spell had stripped the fog-bound realm of anything edible. There was neither skerrick nor morsel of sustenance anywhere.

And the thirst! Eloise decided it was far worse than the ache of hunger. Her mouth, nose, and even her eyes dried. Her skin felt like a reptile's. It became harder to speak, in part because her tongue seemed to be swelling.

It's not like neither of them had ever gone without food or drink. They had both taken part in fast days celebrating Çalaht, but this was different. A fast day did not involve endless walking and climbing, nor did it involve breathing dust in a landscape of hopelessness. Ritual fasting always held the promise of breaking that fast in just a short while, and rarely did one go without even a sip of water or a nip of Manny's

Shvitz, the excessively sweet devotional wine used by certain Çalahtist sects.

But here? Nothing. Wells were dry. Water pots in houses had long since yielded their moisture. Buckets, basins, and bathtubs were like bones in a desert.

Weakness crept over them, catching them unawares. Walking became increasingly difficult, and their progress slowed dramatically—not that either of them noticed. Eloise found her mind flitting from thought to thought, from how the dust swirled differently depending on how she put down her feet, to how nice clean stockings were, to how nice it might be nice to alphabetize the things in her room. Oh, her room. She missed her room, with its blankets and fireplace and all her things organized in even-numbered clusters and all in exactly the right place. Odmilla was in her room. Dear, sweet Odmilla. That platypus worked miracles with her hair. Her hair. It was all gone now. Her hair didn't need miracles anymore, and wouldn't for another year or two.

That rock looks like a woman's nose, she decided vaguely. That tree trunk looks like it might be named Ferdinand. How hard would it be to learn to juggle? By Çalaht's hair-encrusted elbow-wart, she was thirsty.

Eloise distantly noticed that Johanna was holding conversations with people who were not there. That struck her as odd, but not for long, and at least Johanna was still moving forward with her.

But then she wasn't.

Eloise had been making a list of words she didn't like, which so far included "candy," "moist," "ointment," "phlegm," "squirt," "jowls," and "protuberance," with "fog," "mist," and "haze" also on the shortlist. She roused herself enough to realize she was alone. She turned around, looking as far as the fog would let her, but she was most definitely by herself. Panic rising, Eloise followed her footsteps back the way she'd just come. "Jo? Johanna! You there?" No response.

Struggling for every step, Eloise covered 50 lengths before she found her sister sitting with her back against the trunk of a long-dead tree.

Its fallen, broken branches surrounded it, an echo of the life it once held. Johanna looked dully at her. "El. What doing here?"

"Came find you."

"S'nice. Needed rest."

"Mistake stopping."

"Know. Had to."

"Might need, too."

Johanna slowly patted the ground, sending a small cloud of dust flying. "Join."

Without another word, Eloise's knees gave out and she collapsed in a heap at the base of the tree. "Tired."

"Me too. Rest."

"Rest."

A few minutes later, Johanna cleared her throat. "Need say something."

"S'okay. Save strength."

"Need say something!"

Eloise looked at her? "Whuh?"

"S... Sorry." Johanna gave a weak wave. "Sorry. Now, have said it."

"Sorry?" Eloise shook her head. "For what?"

"For after Thorning Ceremony."

"Oh. Was nothing."

"Was not nothing," said Johanna. "Was stupid. Was angry. Was unnecessary. Was overreaction. Sorry."

"Sorry, too." Eloise reached for Johanna's hand, but was too tired to find it. She mimed squeezing it instead. "Made me sad."

"Made me sad, too."

Eloise felt tears welling, perhaps the last drops of liquid her body had to spare. "Missed you." She leaned in to Johanna.

"Missed you too." Johanna leaned back against Eloise. "Sorry took so long to say sorry."

"S'okay. Thanks for sorry."

Johanna closed her eyes. She'd said her piece, and Eloise thought she looked more content now.

They sat together a long time, dipping in and out of sleep. At one point, Eloise thought she heard Johanna mumble, "Still peckish."

"Sorry. No food," she managed.

"S'okay."

At some point, Eloise realized they would probably never stop resting here. She wondered if it had been forever since they'd sat down. It felt like it. There was enough going on in her head to realize that this was it. This was how the two princesses would end their days: sitting at the base of a dead tree, their clothes an embarrassment, their bodies desiccated. She felt bad she'd been unable to see her mission to its end and get Johanna home. She also felt bad that the Star of Whatever might fall into the wrong hands, if anyone ever found them. But there wasn't anything to be done about all that now. At least she'd ended that horrible spell. That was something. Probably no one would ever give her credit for it, since no one would know what had happened. Not even Johanna had been a witness, really. Oh well. No matter. *Nothing really matters*, she thought. *Nothing really matters to me.*

She decided to focus solely on resting well. Eloise wanted to get very, very good at just sitting there.

If she had been less delirious, she would have realized that, actually, what she was working on was getting very, very good at passing away.

❦ 31 ❦

SHATTERED TEACUPS

A strange calm settled over Jerome as he sat motionless in his dungeon cell. He'd faced death, and death had not claimed him. He hadn't exactly held his dignity, and if faced with the same situation again he'd like to think he might comport himself with more grace. But his encounter with the fogger, the guard, and the Purple Haze had done something to him. Something good, he thought. He may have failed as Eloise's champion. He may not have acted in ways that would make his mother proud. For that matter, he wasn't sure he'd made himself particularly proud. Even so, something inside him had shifted.

A line from a Lyndia Thrind song echoed in his head. In "Shards of a Teacup" (which he liked because of its poetic references to haggleberry tea), she sang:

After all the bombast, you're left with

Shards of a broken teacup

And shattered remnants of who you thought you were

But you're just the one throwing the cup.

He got that now. He'd been a teacup-thrower. He'd heaved a strong weight of them in his life. Maybe most of them had been thrown with a smile on his face, or a jest in his heart, but they were still teacups chucked, and the shards of his life were scattered everywhere.

Escaping the Purple Haze had focused his mind on what was important. Really important. His mother. Being a better person. Making a difference to the world. His service to Princess Eloise. He had no idea if Eloise still lived or not. Gääärvan, his lemur taunter, had said she'd disappeared into the fog, but it wasn't like he was a reliable source of information. If it was true, Jerome would be gutted, but he refused to believe she'd gone anywhere near the cursed mist until the information came from someone reputable.

Jerome touched the glass vial he wore around his neck, then gave it a little kiss. His mother had given it to him, and he chastised himself for not thinking about her more, for not giving her more to be proud of.

He considered how he'd been given a second chance, and resolved to make it count. He closed his eyes and pictured Çalaht. Obviously, he'd never seen her—it's not like anyone painted her when she was alive. At home, his mother had a bookend with an image of a woman carved into it. She wore a shawl, had long braided hair, and read a scroll by candlelight. When Jerome was a pup, he got it in his mind that the carving was of Çalaht, and whenever prayers to Çalaht were offered in his home, he imagined the scroll reader listening to them and smiling. This habit stayed with him even when he was old enough to know better. Sitting in his dungeon cell, mind cleared of extraneous junk, Jerome felt the urge to pray. In his mind, the shawl woman looked up from her scroll and into his eyes, and he said, "Thank you for giving me another chance. I promise to throw fewer teacups."

The dungeon door clanged open, interrupting his communion with the divine. Gääärvan poked his head into the cell. Jerome, tightening his grip on his composure, began to stand up, the way he'd been forced to in his previous taunting, but the lemur waved him off. "No, no, stay as you are. I'm just popping by to let you know they're going to try again tomorrow morning for your execution. Anyway, toodles."

The door clunked closed again, leaving Jerome in the dark gritting his teeth.

So much for a sanguine acceptance and promises to the divine. The familiar panic rose, and Jerome began to rock back and forth. He knew he wasn't far off running blindly around the cell, but he tried to hold it at bay as long as he could.

More than anything, Jerome wished he'd had a teacup to throw at Gääärvan's head. He imagined a fine porcelain cup hurtling through the air and clunking into the lemur's noggin. Then Eloise's champion devolved into panicked hyperventilation and uncontrolled fear.

HORSIES

Time passed, as it was wont to do—more so outside of the Purple Haze, but now, even there.

A NOISE REMINISCENT OF THUNDER SOUNDED IN THE DISTANCE. AS it grew closer, it resolved into the noise of eight hooves hitting the ground at a careful canter. They slowed to a trot, then stopped, when they reached the spot where the trail of human footprints went from two sets going in one direction to three sets, with one set coming toward them, then turning back around.

The horses studied the marks in the dirt, then continued walking forward. "Hello? Anyone there?" called one of them. The other said nothing.

There was no reply.

The limited visibility meant that the horses were almost on top of them when they found the two bodies. Scrawny, filthy, and unmoving, they looked like they were candidates for burial. Hector gasped. "Oh, no. No, no, no." He leaned down and tilted his head so he could look directly at them.

Not bodies—women. They still breathed, if only barely.

It was them, but not the "them" Hector remembered. They had the emaciated gauntness of alms-seekers. Their clothes were torn, faded, and grimy. But what was most striking was how old they looked. Gone was their youth. Their skin and faces looked much older. Johanna's hair was the color of birch bark at full moon. Eloise had almost no hair at all, and what remained looked like month-old snow. "It is as if almost a decade of birthdays has passed for them," said Hector.

"Princess Eloise? Princess Johanna? Hello?" Nothing. Hector raised his voice. "Princess! Can you hear me? What happened? Are you in pain?"

Again, no response.

Hector looked at the Nameless One. "What are we going to do?"

The Nameless One shuffled uncomfortably. He had an idea, but it was something he would never dream of doing if they were back at Court. Slowly, ever so gently, he stretched his neck toward Eloise, and blew a puff of warmth across her face. When she did not respond, he gave her a delicate nuzzle on the cheek. It was sweet and tender, but did nothing to bubble up her consciousness from its mind-numbness.

He tried again.

Nothing.

The Nameless One lifted his head, looked around as though checking that no one (besides Hector) was watching, and then caught Hector's eye with a look that said, "Tell no one."

And then he gave the Queen's first born, the Future Ruler and Heir to the Western Lands and All That Really Matters, a massive, slobbery lick across the face.

"Sweet Çalaht snorking oats from a nose bag!" cried Hector. "You licked the princess!"

When still she did not move, the Nameless One did it again. And again and again and again, like a mother dog with newborn pups, willing his vitality into her, calling her back from wherever she was.

Hector reluctantly and to his extreme discomfort, did the same with Johanna.

At last, there was a giggle, like a toddler tickled in her sleep. Eloise's eyes slotted open, and a drowsy smile crossed her face. "Look, Jo," she said. "Horsies. I love horsies. They're pretty."

Johanna also emerged into a dreamy near-wakefulness "I've never ridden a horse before. It's rude."

"Pretty."

"Rude."

"Pretty rude."

Then both women dropped back into what looked like slumber, but seemed much more dire.

"They're so weak," said Hector. "We have to get them back somehow. But there's no way they'll be riding anytime soon."

The Nameless One nodded his agreement. He nudged Eloise's shoulder, rolling her from her back to her side, and motioned for Hector to stand next to him. He took Eloise's collar firmly in his teeth and lifted, dangling her a full length from the ground, then laid her softly across Hector's back.

"Right. Got it." Hector hoisted up Johanna the same way and settled her carefully on the Nameless One. "OK, let's get them back."

Delicately balancing the limp bodies, the two rescuers looked carefully at the ground to pick up their trail of hoof prints, and took the first steps back toward the edge of the Purple Haze and whatever awaited them at Stained Rock.

A strong length later, Hector looked at the Nameless One and said curtly, "Let us never speak of the whole licking-the-face-of-royalty thing to anyone. Agreed?"

The Nameless One nodded.

The journey back was slow and precarious. Both horses had plenty of experience helping riders stay on, but this was like balancing untethered sacks of bony turnips—turnips with a propensity for giggling unexpectedly and slipping off. Hector worried for both princess' mental health. Yes, they were alive, but clarity of thought failed them.

Hector had a much harder time keeping Eloise on his back than the Nameless One was having with Johanna. His princess was prone to wriggling, and she'd lost any instinct for staying up. They stopped once again so the Nameless One could pick her up out of the dust and reposition her across Hector's back, and Hector asked, "Do you have any ideas where we can take them when we get back? We can't exactly wander up to Castle Blotch with them and ask for a spot of help."

The Nameless One shook his head.

"They need more care than an inn will provide. And who might be able to care for them? They will need more nursing than you or I can give them."

The questions hung in the air as they picked their way across broken fields and the ghosts of villages.

Steep hills were the most difficult. With no way to secure Eloise to him, Hector had to contort himself to keep her aloft. The Nameless One placed her in different positions after each fall, but the two horses rarely made it a full strong length without losing one of their passengers. Sometimes Eloise had enough presence of mind to say, "Oopsie," as she slipped, giving Hector the chance to aim her toward a soft landing spot. Johanna, on the other hand, just flopped.

Eventually, Hector and the Nameless One hit on the combination of Eloise sitting astride Hector, lying forward on his neck, with the Nameless One pressing his chin down on her back to keep her somewhat secure, while Johanna was draped crosswise across the Nameless One's flanks. It worked, sort of, but made for tedious going, Hector feared one of the princesses would break a leg or crack a skull, but they had the luck and manner of drunkards—they were so relaxed and unresisting that when they dropped, they simply landed in a floppy heap.

After what seemed like three lifetimes, they reached the spot where the bone slip had happened. "Not too much further now," said Hector.

They picked their way through the bone heaps and up the ridge, taking extra care so the princesses didn't slip off and plummet back down. Hector finally found the spot where they'd first come in, and he and the Nameless One stepped through the veil of the Purple Haze.

Hector turned his face to the wan, late afternoon sun and sighed. "Marvelous. Thank Çalaht, we made it." A chill wind slapped him—a rude welcome—but Hector didn't care. The horror of the Purple Haze was behind him.

They descended Fogging Hill into the lanes of Stained Rock, where they were met with bedlam. Townspeople rushed about—some crying, some hauling bodies on carts and drays, everyone looking stunned, confused, or frantic.

"What's happened?" said Hector.

The Nameless One shook his head slowly.

"Was there a fire?" asked Hector. "Has the town been attacked?"

The Nameless One shrugged, being careful not to drop Johanna.

Hector stepped slowly up the street, trying to sense if they were in danger. Despite the pandemonium, there didn't seem to be any coordinated emergency response, or troops being deployed.

He indicated Eloise and Johanna, and whispered, "We fit right in. I was worried we'd be conspicuous."

The Nameless One nodded.

The two horses watched the people. "It's not a riot," said Hector. "Too orderly. And there's a distinct lack of looting."

Another nod.

"Let's find the princesses suitable care. We can worry about whatever's going on here after they're being tended."

The Nameless One raised an eyebrow.

"I don't know where, yet. Any ideas?"

The Nameless One shook his head. They continued up the street.

Suddenly, Hector stopped. "Look!" He pointed to a warthog rushing past them on the other side of the road with a look of determined urgency. "Do you think that might be the person Eloise befriended at the Wart Cream Gala?" The horses had not met the head of the powerful Wart Creamers' Guild, but Eloise had said he dressed in "sober finery." That fit the look of this person, and Hector couldn't imagine that many people could afford to dress so richly. Plus, he was trailed by a nervous aardvark, clearly his junior, who wore the purple robes of the Wart Creamers' Guild and juggled an armful of scrolls as they hurried along.

"Princess Eloise said his name several times," said Hector. "What was it? 'Büüüttöööns,' maybe, or 'Buttons'? Something like that." He had no ear for dialects, and found it difficult to wrap his tongue around the oddness of all those foreign vowels. "Wait, no. She said he had a Southie name."

Risking Eloise falling yet again, Hector trotted to catch up with the warthog. "Excuse me, good sir," he called. "Sir? Mr Búüùttöööns." The warthog either did not hear, or chose to ignore him—perhaps because Hector had done such a bad job with his pronunciation.

Hector dodged through the crowd, circled around the aardvark, and skittered to a halt in front of Búüùttons, shifting his shoulder to ensure that Eloise did not flop off onto the cobblestones. The Nameless One clattered to a stop moments later. "Good sir," said Hector. "We are in need of assistance."

The warthog gave a peremptory wave of his hoof. "Apologies, good sirs, but I have not the time just now. I must attend to the urgencies that have suddenly sprung upon me. Upon all of us. I wish you both a good day." He moved to walk around them, but the two horses adjusted their stances, preventing his passing.

"Sir," tried Hector again. "Mr Büüüttóööns." The warthog winced at Hector's slaughtering of his name. "You were once kind to one I am charged with protecting. At the Wart Cream Gala. She spoke of your generosity. But, please, she is unwell. It is beyond what we can handle ourselves."

The warthog looked at Hector, curious. The unexpected delay disconcerted his attending aardvark, but she tried not to show it. "The princess?" he asked. "Princess Eloise?" Wáäàlter Áäàloysius Búüùttons moved to Hector's side and squinted into the face of the filth-encrusted woman sagging across his withers and back. "Why, this looks nothing like her. I'm sorry, but if you'll kindly—"

"I assure you, it is her," said Hector. "Her story is undoubtedly long, and I do not know a tenth of it yet. What I do know is that the two princesses require urgent care."

"That one is supposed to be Princess Johanna?" said Büüüttóööns, pointing at the skin-and-bones heap on the Nameless One's back. He gave an indignant stamp on the cobblestones, and his attending aardvark flinched. "I am busy," said Búüùttons. "There is no way that is Johanna Umgotteswillen Gumball. Look at her hair, her skin. Sir, I saw both of the young ladies at the Wart Cream Gala not three weeks ago. These two wretches look almost a decade older than the two I met. They resemble the princesses as much as I myself do. And I have tusks! Now, I've no time for jests, certainly not with everything that is happening. Again, please excuse me or I shall have to call the Evening Watch. I suggest you take them to an apothecary. Or maybe to the alms house."

At that moment, there was a giggle from the limp bundle dangling across Hector's back. Eloise opened her eyes, smiled, and in a dreamy voice said, "Why, Mr Búüùttons. Lovely to see you again. Why are you upside down?" She gave another weak giggle. "Look, Jo. Mr Búüùttons is upside down."

Johanna, who'd barely said, "Oof" since they'd been found, opened her eyes. "G'—" Her eyes darted, taking in the light and her surroundings. "G'afternoon, I believe. Are you well, Mr Búüùttons? Apologies that I don't seem able to curtsy as Protocol would encourage."

And then, as if on cue, the two sisters dropped simultaneously back into mind-numbness.

Búüùttons gawped at Hector. "By Çalaht's dislocated thumbs, what's happened to them?"

As if punctuating the question, Eloise slid off Hector and thwumped onto the street.

"Goodness!" Búüùttons scurried to prop her up. "Never mind what's happened. Let me call a sedan." He turned to the aardvark. "Leave the scrolls with me, Rëëëgïïïnäää, and call one of the Guild's chairs."

"But, sir," protested the aardvark. "We must—"

"It can wait, Rëëëgïïïnäää. I'll start without you." He took the stack of scrolls in one arm, handling them with practiced ease, while still supporting Eloise. "Take these two to my apartments, and make sure

Ëëëdnäää looks after them, not Bëëëääätrïïïx. And don't leave it to Ëëëdnäää to call the healer. You do that."

"Yes, sir. Of course, sir. I'll make sure Ëëëdnäää allows the healer inside this time."

"Very good. Meet me in the Guild Hall once they are settled. We are in for a long night, and strategy is called for. Now, go find a chair." Rëëëgïïïnäää bustled off to find a litter, and Búüùttons turned back to Hector and the Nameless One. "I shall do everything I can for them. But as you can guess, with the king incapacitated, turmoil is inevitable. I must play my part to settle matters."

"Incapacitated?"

"You have not heard? Yes. He lies on a bed in the Throne Room, inert, unable to be roused. I have seen him with my own eyes. He is in a most unnatural state, and was practically wasting away before me."

"I had no idea. Who keeps the kingdom from chaos?"

"Where have you been? His Jesterness Master Turpentine is regent."

"What?"

"I agree. An odd choice, for sure. I certainly doubt his ability to keep chaos at bay, but the Declaration of Regency is authentic, so the king's will be done."

The arrival of the sedan chair interrupted any further questions. The four women who carried it wore tunics and breeks in the purple of the Wart Creamers' Guild. Búüùttons and Rëëëgïïïnäää settled Eloise and Johanna into padded seats, and then the aardvark climbed in after them. On a count of four, the women picked up the litter and jogged off toward Búüùttons' home.

The head of the Wart Creamers' Guild adjusted the scrolls under his arm and turned to Hector and the Nameless One. "Ëëëdnäää will make sure the princesses are cared for. I look forward to hearing your tale, but I'm afraid that won't be possible for some time."

The horses bowed formally. "Thank you, good sir," said Hector. "Your kindness to the royal family shall be remembered to the queen."

"That is of no matter just now. But thank you all the same. Perhaps I'll be able to see you later, maybe for a late supper. For now, uncertainty awaits me at the Guild Hall."

❧ 34 ❧

STRANGE BED

A streak of noonday light barging through a closed curtain woke Eloise. She found herself in a strange bed in an unfamiliar room, with no memory of how she got there. The decorations screamed opulence, yet taste had clearly been applied to their choice and placement. The delicate vase of ceramic blossoms set off an ornate jar of Eastern Lands olives, whose silver and gold flecks caught the intruding sunlight and glinted brashly. A vanity made from ironwood that had been carved to look like it was covered in ivy picked up the rich, dark hues of an intricately embroidered tapestry depicting Çalaht at the edge of the Gőőődeling Sea, blessing the voles and sturgeons. The room had the feeling of a home rather than an inn, even as swanky an inn as, say, the Legs Not Arms, which had been so ridiculously expensive that Eloise's traveling companions had laughed when they'd heard the price.

Where was she?

Her eyes landed on a chair, where her clothes sat, folded and clean. Her travel cloak hung on a peg, and the strapped box with the Star of Whatever sat near it on a reading table. She wondered if anyone had tried to open it. She hoped not. Who knew what the thing would do?

So she wasn't wearing her own clothes. OK. Someone had done that for her. Or to her. Hard to say which yet. Her fingers felt the material of whatever it was she had on. Cotton. Soft. Good quality, which was consistent with the decor.

She tried to sit up, but quickly concluded that sitting was not a good idea. Her muscles protested like unionized stevedores on a hunger strike, and it felt like someone had picked her up and dropped her a hundred thousand times.

The latch turned, and a skunk shouldered open the door. She carried a tray of vials and a measuring beaker, and wore the blood-red cap and cape of the Consolidated Healers United Guild of the Generally Efficacious Remedy Systems. She stopped when she saw that Eloise's eyes were open. "Ah, thee be awake. A pleasant change to see." The skunk set the tray on the bedside table. "Can thee speak? How thee be feeling?"

"I'm not quite sure yet," said Eloise. Her voice grated its way out of her throat. "I'm sore everywhere. I suspect I have been playing left girder against an elephant hockey sacking team, although I can't recall doing so."

"Thee be summat bruised, that be for sure, but good to see thy sense of humor be present."

The skunk spread wide Eloise's left eye and peered into it. She did the same with her right eye, palpated her sternum in three different spots, then gripped Eloise's wrist with her paw and got a far-off look while she contemplated whatever it was that a pulse could tell her. "Hmmmm...." The skunk took another look at Eloise's left eye, then asked, "Will thee be taking a nip of the tonic on thy own this time, or will thee be needing persuading like thee did before?"

"I don't remember being persuaded previously."

"That be a blessing, then. Twas not pretty."

Eloise could imagine she had not been an ideal patient. Growing up, she had resisted the ministrations of all manner of healers. Herbalists, apothecaries, barbers, and chirurgeons had all met with stubborn opposition, whether she was bedridden with an ague or dealing with a bad splinter. Odmilla, her beloved platypus handmaid, was the only one who could persuade Eloise to take a medicament, and even that took inordinate negotiation and cajoling.

The skunk threw open the curtains, letting in the full shout of daylight. Bustling back to her tray, she unstoppered four vials and poured carefully considered amounts from each into the beaker. Eloise almost gagged at the smell. "By Çalaht's raked nostrils, what is that?" It was heinousness mixed with treacle, a small miracle of olfactory assault.

"Be thee a fully paid-up member of the Miscellaneous Modalities Conglomerated Healers Guild?" asked the skunk.

"No, sorry, I'm not."

"Then I can't really be saying more than it be a medicament, and that the impressive smell be part of its charm."

"Mistress... I'm sorry, I don't know your name."

The skunk clasped her claws in front of her and curtsied perfunctorily. "I be Chääärlöööttëëë Rëëëd. I be here at Mr Búüùttons' request to attend to thy healing."

"Pleased to meet you. I'm Eloise."

"Well I know who thee be. And princess or nay, thee'll be having a gill of this here medicament."

"I see."

"Please be sitting up."

Eloise ignored the screams of her muscles and slowly rucked her way upright. Chääärlöööttëëë handed her the beaker and said, "A dozen nips."

"A dozen!"

"Fine, then. Fifteen. Thee be needing it."

"A dozen, then."

The smell reminded Eloise of the rinse water from a tub of grubby soldiers' breeks. She steeled herself and sipped the concoction. The taste delivered on everything the smell had promised, an aggressive blend of cayenne, bilge sludge, and rice syrup. She quickly took a second nip, hoping to sneak it down with the first. "Blech."

"Ah, thee must be improved. Thee has modified thy word choice, bringing it back into the realm of things thee might say in front of thy grandmother."

"I don't remember any of that."

"Nay. Thee would not."

"No?" Eloise braved another sip.

"Nay. Twas the dryness." Chääärlöööttëëë reached over and pinched Eloise's cheek firmly.

"Hey!" Eloise tried to pull back, but couldn't, as the skunk held tight. Finally she let go, closely watching Eloise's face.

"Extreme dryness of thy body caused delirium in thy mind. Thy sister twere the same."

"Johanna! Is she OK?" Eloise's last remembered moments in the Purple Haze came rushing back. Johanna leaning against that dead tree. The bone-deep tiredness. The slipping off into mind-numbness. Next thing she knew, she was here, now.

"Aye, that she is. She be bouncing back faster than thee. And quite a nose for the medicaments has she. Sniffed out all the ingredients of that wee drink. Now, two more nips should do ye for the moment."

"Only two. Oh, thank you." Eloise choked down another sip. "Why did you pinch my cheek?"

"It tests thy heart and thy dryness," said Chääärlöööttëëë.

"My heart and dryness? How?"

"If thy heart be well and strong, thy cheek goes swiftly from pinched white to red. I can also check this by pressing thy gums, but the cheek pinch be good enough. As for dryness, if thee no longer be overly dry, thy skin smooths out from the pinch quickly." She pointed to a pitcher of water on the other bedside table. "Thee still be too dry. Thee be needing to drink a full eight pitchers of water."

"Eight! The pitcher holds, what, two volumes or so? That's 16 volumes!"

"Ach, aye. Good to see thee can once again do thy sums." The skunk moved to the other side of Eloise's bed and poured her a mug of water. "Eight pitchers. Thee be needing to chase away thy dryness. Thy waters need be clear and free of odors."

"Yes, Mistress Rëëëd." At least it wasn't 16 volumes of the medicament. Eloise could handle the water. She sipped from the mug, enjoying the cool wetness on her tongue.

Chääärlöööttëëë briefly explained where she was—which explained how nice the room was—but said she didn't know exactly how Eloise had arrived there. "They only be bringing me here to see to thy healing. I no be getting the story of thy transportation."

There was a knock at the door, and the healer pinched her face in annoyance. She walked to the door, pushed down the latch, and poked her head through. Whoever was outside spoke too quietly for Eloise to hear, but the skunk's side of the conversation was clear enough.

(Whisper.) "How did thee get past Ëëëdnäää?" (Whisper.) "Ach, well, Bëëëääätrïïïx would be letting thee through, would she nae." (Whisper) "No." (Whisper.) "I be saying no. Be that not clear?" (Whisper) "Because she be needing complete bed rest." (Whisper.) "I know there be chaos afoot. But it be no concern of hers." (Whisper.) "That can be waiting a few days. I don't want yon lass feeling like she be needing to get up." (Whisper.) (Whisper.) (Whisper.) "Oh." (Whisper.) "I see." (Whisper.) "I suppose thee may enter and deliver thy message."

Eloise had been growing increasingly concerned, and was glad when Chääärlöööttëëë relented, stood back, and made way for a disheveled and altogether unlikely-looking oryx wearing a page's tunic and breeks. She guessed from his stubby, ringed antlers that he was barely old enough to hold his position, and he carried the look of one who felt he was in way over his head. Carefully balancing a silver tray, the oryx delicately clopped into the room. He bowed and bobbled the tray, almost causing the note to slide off. Dramatically overbalancing to save the note from falling, he then recovered himself and, as though nothing was out of the ordinary, finished the bow.

"Message for you, Princess. I mean, mistress. No, he said 'princess.' Message for you, Princess." Color ran to his face, although it was hard to see because of his fur. "I'm sorry, yer majesterialness, I cannae remember if'n I'm supposed to know who you are or not."

"That's OK. You may know who I am. And thank you for my note. Do you mind?" The oryx realized he was holding the tray too far away and stretched it closer so Eloise could pluck the folded note from it.

The hemp parchment was crudely made and had an "E" written on the outside. She did not recognize the handwriting, but as soon as she read it, she understood why. It had been written by Hector. Or more accurately, it had been written for Hector. Holding a quill was difficult for horses—even though they could grip it in their mouths, their poor depth perception, especially at close range, along with the blind spot they had when looking down along their noses, made writing, especially legibly, arduous. Horses normally had notes quilled on their behalf. At Court, a cottage business of scribes had flourished, serving those without the physical means to easily write. If one was rich enough, one might retain a scribe exclusively, so that their "handwriting," if by proxy, was unique to them, just as it was for those who could write on their own.

Eloise read the note and nodded a thank you to the oryx. He retreated from the room with his silver tray, relieved to have discharged his task. Eloise finished her mug of water, then poured herself another, and another, drinking until the pitcher was gone. One down, seven to go.

Then without saying anything, she hauled her screaming muscles and joints from the bed.

The skunk was aghast. "Thee needs be recuperating. In bed!"

Eloise ignored her and staggered painfully toward the chair and table where her clothes were.

"Princess, please."

Eloise turned her back, let the oversized nightdress (where had that come from and whose was it?) slide off, and focused on the surprisingly difficult task of donning her breeks.

The skunk assumed her most matronly and imperious manner. "Princess, I give thee not leave to arise. Not for days, yet. I be worrying thee might damage thyself further."

"Thank you for your concern, Mistress Rëëëd." If Eloise thought the breeks were hard, putting on the tunic was worse, given the difficulty of raising her arms above shoulder height.

The skunk laid a soft paw on Eloise's arm. "Please, Princess. Don't be doing this. I be beseeching thee."

Eloise gave the healer's paw a gentle squeeze in return. "Mistress Rëëëd, there is nothing l would like to do more than lie in that bed and give myself over to recovery. Truly. I owe you seven more pitchers of water, and I will drink them as soon as I can, I promise, along with the missing eight nips of the tonic, if you insist. But for now, if you can please help me get dressed, I would be most grateful."

The skunk opened her mouth to protest again, but Eloise held up a hand to stop her—a commanding gesture she'd learned from her mother. She showed the skunk the note. "Please. Help me dress."

Chääärlöööttëëë read the note, then held up Eloise's tunic so she could slide into it. The healer kept up a steady trickle of admonition, which Eloise allowed to become a background buzzing . Her mind was on the content of the note, and the fact that she had no idea what she could possibly do.

Eloise donned her travel cloak, strapped the Star of Whatever safely to her hip, and tucked the note into her pocket. Then she limped out of the unfamiliar room and away from its strange, comfortable bed to go and find Hector. From the way the note had been written, Eloise could tell that Hector de Pferd had hired a pay-by-the-word scribe who threw in punctuation for free.

We must save Jerome & Lorch!!!!!
Their executions are tomorrow morning!!!!!

—

HdP!i!i!i!

❧ 35 ❧

MIRROR

Eloise struggled her way through the unfamiliar apartment looking for the exit. She found Johanna in a shady, heavily-canopied sitting garden pulling weeds with her bare hands. Near her on a table sat a pot of tea, a tea setting, and a hand mirror. Eloise almost walked right past her sister, because it took her a moment to recognize the woman who was attacking the stray plants. Cleaned of grime and in the full light of day, Eloise was stunned at just how much older Johanna looked. Not old-person-dribbling-in-her-soup old, and not old-as-their-parents old, but it was like eight or so birthdays had passed; a severe jump from teen to woman with no steps in between. The effect was made worse by the unexpected snow white of Johanna's hair.

The shock made Eloise look down at her own hands. She, too, was most definitely different. She hated to think how much.

Johanna barely glanced up from her weeds. "You've not looked in a mirror?" She'd been crying. Very recently, and very hard. There was a smudge of dirt on the side of her face, where she'd wiped away tears.

"No. There wasn't one in the room. I'm guessing that wasn't coincidence?"

Johanna fished an already well-used handkerchief from her sleeve, blew her nose, then took another swipe at her tears with the back of her hand. She nodded at the hand mirror that lay face-down on the table. "Feel free."

Eloise knew she shouldn't, certain that whatever she saw would upset her. What good could possibly come of it, especially with the urgent note burning away in her pocket?

But she couldn't help herself.

Eloise took a deep, steadying breath, then picked up the mirror and turned it toward herself.

Her first thought was that the mirror must be imbued with some sort of weak magic—maybe a farseeing weak magic that let her see into her home from a distance. Because the face looking back at her was very much that of her mother, if less wrinkled in the corners of the eyes. Uncanny.

But her mother did not have a stubble of white hair that looked like it had been styled using a dull axe, eyes ringed with the bruising of fatigue, nor a face pinched with the thinness of a crofter in drought. No, there was no weak magic at play here. She was looking at herself.

Even seeing Johanna had done little to prepare Eloise for seeing her own changed face. She watched her reflected image blur with her own tears. This was wrong. Very wrong.

Eloise wasn't even sure what she was crying about. Lost beauty? Maybe, but that seemed awfully vain. The fact that it seemed like someone else was there? Concern about what others might think? Worry about what this, this—alteration, this jump in years—meant for the rest of her life?

All of it? None of it?

No. It was simple devastation. Something had been taken from her unexpectedly and without permission, which could never be returned. It's not like she was suddenly an old hag, but still, the change was significant, indelible, and down to the bones. She didn't like it one bit.

Eloise wanted to hurl blame at whoever had done this. But who? Her uncle, King Doncaster for taking Johanna from their home—kidnapping her and feeding her prattleweed? Seer Maybelle de Chipmunk, for having the vision that triggered Eloise's journey? Melveeta for casting the spell? The long-dead Gwendolyn for the jealousy that sent Melveeta on her mission? The longer-dead King Brüüütus for his faithlessness? The unremembered woman who had "ensorcelled" Brüüütus?

There were plenty of people she could point a finger at.

But what good would that do?

Eloise stared at her face in dismay and realized there was one person responsible for what had happened to her.

She was.

She had made choice after choice that had brought her to this moment. She had volunteered to go after Johanna, had persisted even as they went in completely the wrong direction, had gone back into the Purple Haze after getting Gouache out, and had chosen to find the source of the spell.

Growing up, Eloise often felt she'd had little control or agency over her life. She'd been at the mercy of Protocol, of Court, of her mother the queen, of expectations, of generations of Gumballs before her. But this was different. It was her actions and decisions that had led her to this moment. This was all on her.

All of it.

And somehow, that felt good. Eloise could hold on to that realization, which let her take responsibility for her choices, which let her accept agency in the face of undesirable consequences.

Eloise put the mirror back on the table, pulled a freshly laundered handkerchief from her breeks pocket, wiped away her tears, and blew her nose. "I have to go."

"Where? Where could you possibly need to go?" Johanna had pulled an impressive pile of Johnson grass from a less-tended part of the garden. There was plenty more to go.

Eloise showed Johanna the note. "I have to find Hector and work out what's going on."

"Right." Johanna stood and looked for a rag to wipe the dirt from her hands. Not finding one, she used a bleached linen napkin from the tea setting instead. Once the worst of it was off, she poured herself half a cup of tea and took a long, savoring sip. "A superb cuppa. Just stellar. Have you eaten?"

"No, thanks. I'm not hungry," said Eloise.

"We'll grab a roll or something on the way out."

"You're coming with me?"

"Of course I'm going with you. What do you expect me to do, sit here crying for the rest of my life?"

"I'm not... I..." Eloise swallowed. "Thank you."

❧ 36 ❧

"APARTMENT"

That Wáäälter Búüùttons called his home an "apartment" was a modesty. The dwelling stretched length after length, one sumptuous room leading to the next. Living at Castle de Brague meant Eloise was used to being surrounded by finery, but this was different. The richness of their castle was historical, accumulated over centuries. It reflected the tide of tastes that washed in and out with the different eras and occupants of the queen's throne. Búüùttons's home had a more unified style, a decor that suited a singular taste with a particular eye.

For example, she and Johanna passed a collection of tea caddies laid out on a sideboard. Their quality ranged from the finest, most delicate ceramic craftsmanship to one that looked like it might have been carved from scavenged materials by a convict in a penal colony. Eloise imagined each caddy filled with a different sort of exquisite haggleberry tea, and Wáäälter Búüùttons looking at them in the evening, and choosing one based on his mood and the kind of day he'd had.

Overall, there was an order and precision to the interior's design, selection, and placement that reflected a surety in the person making the choices. The taste on display was also distinctly masculine, without being blokey—the expression of a long-time bachelor who was happy to remain exactly that.

"What are you doing?"

The clipped, hissed words halted the sisters' search for an exit. Eloise spun and saw huge, piercing eyes staring at her, unblinking—eyes that seemed too large for the round head and narrow snout below them. The person wore a plain, practical outfit of black, which covered her from neck to wrists and ankles, and an equally severe cap. This was, by far, the fiercest slow loris Eloise had ever seen.

"Oh, pardon me. My name is—"

"I know who you are," the slow loris hissed again. "What are you doing skulking about?"

"Skulking?"

Johanna stepped forward and bowed slightly to the slow loris. "Mistress Ëëëdnäää, may I formally present to you my sister, Eloise Hydra Gumball III. Eloise, allow me to introduce you to Ëëëdnäää de Löööri, the head of Master Búüüttons' household, and if I'm not mistaken, the masterful brewer of the exquisite haggleberry tea I just enjoyed."

"Pleasure to—" started Eloise.

"'Guild Master Búüüttons,' if you please," corrected Ëëëdnäää. "And you have not answered my question. Why are you skulking through the apartment?" She pointed at Eloise. "Are you not supposed to be confined to your bed? That was the instruction I had from Mistress Rëëëd. Skulking was most certainly not on the extensive list of 'do's' and 'don't's' she regaled me with last time we spoke, which was but a few minutes ago." She nodded at Johanna. "I'm glad you liked the tea."

The slow loris's intense way of speaking gave the statement the feeling of a challenge, rather than thanks for a compliment. Turning back to Eloise, she said, "You are in no fit state to be up and about. Look at you. You can barely stand."

It was true. Eloise's legs wobbled noticeably when she walked. She didn't know what to do, so she simply handed the slow loris Hector's note to read.

Ëëëdnäää carefully unfolded the parchment and read it. It did not seem to make an impression. "And?"

"The 'Jerome' in there is Jerome Abernatheen de Chipmunk, my champion. 'Lorch' is Guard Lorch Lacksneck of Lower Glenth, charged with my protection. I must help them, somehow."

This seemed to work. Ëëëdnäää carefully refolded the note and gave it back. "I shall hail you a sedan."

Her sudden change of manner surprised Eloise. "Oh, thank you Mistress Ëëëdnäää."

Ëëëdnäää led them to a dining room to wait while she arranged things, after first providing some simple foods. Eloise nibbled some dry rye toast and managed to keep it down. While they waited, Chääärlöööttëëë Rëëëd, her blood-red cloak flapping behind her, hurried into the dining room for one last look at the twins. "I'll be checking in on thee this evening. Both of ye. And you..." She looked at Eloise, then pointed at the pitcher that sat on the table. "Drink."

Eloise put down her toast, poured a generous goblet of water, and sipped. The skunk, satisfied for the moment, bid them goodbye.

Ëëëdnäää reappeared. "Your sedan chair has arrived. Do you require anything else?"

"No, thank you, Mistress de Löööri," said Johanna. "We're good."

They stood, and Eloise downed the last two mugfuls from the pitcher. "Six more to go."

"You're going to slosh when you walk," said Johanna.

"Didn't the healer ask you to drink eight pitchers full?"

"Goodness, no. Just, 'Get some fluids.' Eight! Not eight mugs? Or cups?"

"Pitchers."

Johanna chuckled. "Lucky you."

Ëëëdnäää led them to the entryway, and with a polite nod, opened the front door. Eloise said a final thank you and walked out into the sunshine for the first time in—she had no idea how long. Eloise looked up. "Look, Jo. Blue sky."

"I know. What a relief."

"Excuse me while I kiss it."

A sedan chair large enough for two passengers, along with four fit-looking young women, stood waiting outside an intricately made wrought-iron gate at the end of the pathway. Just beyond the chair, Hector and the Nameless One craned their necks.

"Princess! And Princess! It's you!" called Hector.

"Hector! Nameless One!" Eloise hastened forward as best she could. One of the litter carriers opened the gate, and she rushed through and, in a most unprincessly way, threw her arms around Hector's neck. Seeing him triggered memories—vague mental images of horses in the deathly hellscape of the Purple Haze. "It was you, wasn't it? It was you two who found us."

"Why, Princess, yes," said Hector, flustered by the unexpected greeting. "It was us. What a relief to see you up and walking."

Eloise let go of Hector, hobbled over to the Nameless One, and gave him a hug as well. "Thank you." She let go, and he nodded his acknowledgment.

"What happened to Jerome and Lorch? Are they really to be executed?"

"That is what the royal herald proclaimed two hours ago, as well as an official announcement of a day of prayer for the king."

"A day of prayer?" asked Johanna. "For Uncle D? Why?"

"You haven't heard? King Doncaster suffers complications from injuries he received when the Purple Haze attacked the castle," said Hector. "I'm... I'm sorry, but he's apparently most unwell."

Johanna blanched, and tears again filled her eyes. "Excuse me," she said, and stepped into the sedan chair, closing its door behind her to take advantage of the small privacy its confines allowed. Moments later, sobs came from within. This surprised Eloise. The king had kidnapped and drugged her sister, and tried to forcibly marry her, yet Johanna still had enough feeling for him to cry at his suffering. Deep down, he was still her "Uncle D," clearly.

Eloise decided to give her sister a few moments alone. "What do you mean the Purple Haze attacked the castle?" she asked Hector.

"It moved forward unexpectedly, causing massive loss of life to a significant section of Stained Rock. You were not told?"

"No. It seems there's a lot for us to discuss. Perhaps instead of rushing to the castle, we should find somewhere private to talk, get ourselves oriented, and come up with a plan."

"Yes, Princess. I know just the place."

$$\mathscr{H} \quad 37 \quad \mathscr{E}$$

THE SPLINTERED DRAY

Eloise left Hector to give the sedan chair carriers directions, knocked gently on the door to the passenger chamber, and cracked it open. "Jo? Can I come in?"

Johanna wiped away tears with her already-sodden handkerchief and nodded, scooting over to make room. Eloise stepped in and closed the door behind her. Moments later, the sedan jostled and they were on their way.

They rode in silence, looking out opposite windows, each lost in thoughts that were strong lengths apart. While Eloise tried to conjure up a set of circumstances that might lead to a judgment of execution for Jerome and Lorch, Johanna contemplated the incapacitation of the Half Kingdom throne. Their only common thought was, "What now for the Half Kingdom?"

Eventually, Eloise reached over and gave Johanna's hand a gentle squeeze. "Are you OK?"

Johanna sniffed and wiped her nose with a handkerchief. "No. No, I'm not."

"Talk to me."

"What's there to say that you would understand? For whatever reason, you don't get along with him. I get that. But he's been my Uncle D since I can remember. He's funny. He's odd. He's not Mother and not Father, but he's family. His taste in gifts is sometimes bizarre. I mean, who gives a little girl a stuffed rutabaga?" Johanna chuckled as she wiped her eye with the back of her hand. "But he paid attention to me and let me ride on his shoulders. I liked that. I liked him. I *like* him. Not enough to marry him, but enough to be glad he's part of my life. And now..." She trailed off with a sniff.

"I understand," said Eloise. She leaned in to Johanna so their arms touched.

"Do you?"

"Yeah, I do. I may not feel it, but I get it."

Johanna nodded.

A sudden halt told them they'd arrived.

"A stable?" asked Johanna, staring at the decrepit building where they'd stopped.

"We need somewhere private to talk so we can find out what Hector and the Nameless One know, and work out what to do."

"Yes, but at a stable?"

One of the carriers opened the door for them. "If the mistresses will stay on the planks, they will avoid the worst of the mud."

It was not just any stable. The Splintered Dray was the most disreputable public inn that Eloise had ever seen, far worse than anything they'd encountered in Port Port or Haze Town. No tidy stalls, clean mangers, or gleaming troughs here. Instead, sawdust covered the floor, along with crusty barrel halves filled with allegedly drinkable fluids and a selection of strongly flavored hays and mashes. The oversized bar was surrounded by a sordid clutch of reprobate horses, donkeys, and mules who looked like they'd given up on both sobriety and personal hygiene. Tarted-up mares and geldings dotted the room, adding ambience, a whiff of pheromones, prattleweed smoke, and the opportunity for all manner of entertainments.

So, not the kind of place accustomed to entertaining royalty.

The innkeeper was a bald, shirtless, gargantuan human covered in tattoos and scars, some of which were hidden beneath the bar towel he wore over his shoulder. A massive carpet of hair covered his torso (both front and back), he had six fingers on each hand, and a horseshoe-shaped divot in his forehead.

"This way, Princesses," said Hector. They followed the Nameless One through the inn and its overpowering fug of horse odors, alcohol, and wood smoke.

The Nameless One led them through a saloon door toward the side. It looked comically large to Eloise until she realized it was scaled to fit a horse. They walked down a dimly lit hallway until they came to a door leading into a private stable, the cleanliness of which was in sharp contrast to the grime they'd just walked through. The enclosed room was large enough to accommodate two horses, and clean, loose straw was heaped along two walls as bedding. Both spots had been flattened from use.

"This is where you've been sleeping?" asked Eloise.

"Yes, Princess," said Hector.

"Why?"

"It is inexpensive, we are unlikely to be spied upon, and the gentleman at the bar is the Nameless One's friend."

"The six-fingered giant?" asked Johanna. "Really?"

"Indeed. They apparently grew up in the same village. They share a peculiar sense of humor. One that escapes me. A lot of rhyming slang and puns."

"How can the Nameless One pun?" asked Eloise. "He does not speak."

"True. And yet, he manages. Keeps Ëëëlmööö—that's the gentleman with extra digits—in stitches."

The Nameless One indicated two unopened hay bales, inviting Eloise and Johanna to sit. But before they could, there was a thudding knock at the door. At Hector's "Yes," Ëëëlmööö elbowed his way into the room holding a couple of stubby, three-legged stools. "I brung county fairs fer yer loyal quinces."

There was an awkward silence while everyone tried to work out what he'd just said. Eloise noticed that the Nameless One was chuckling, but it was Johanna who parsed the first part. "'County fairs' must mean 'chairs.'"

"But 'loyal quinces'?" asked Hector.

"Loyal quinces," said Ëëëlmööö again, as if repeating it would explain everything. "Yer know, soil blintzes. Boil rinses. Are yer all daft?"

Another puzzled silence.

Ëëëlmööö pointed. "Her and her. Coil chintzes."

"Oh!" said Johanna. "Royal princess."

"Ah, she speaks the sting's bung."

"King's tongue?"

"Too right." Ëëëlmööö set down the two dust-covered stools and slapped his bar towel across their seats several times to dislodge the worst of the grime, leaving them nowhere near clean and his towel that bit less hygienic. From their disuse, Eloise guessed there was not a lot of call for human-oriented accoutrements at the Splintered Dray. "Now, do yer want a fink and a steal?"

More puzzling. Eloise ventured, "A drink and a meal?"

Ëëëlmööö gave her a thumbs-up. "Give her a prize."

Once again, they went quiet, trying to figure out the slang. "Forgive her surprise?" suggested Hector.

"Shiv her disguise?" asked Johanna.

The Nameless One chortled, as Eloise said, "Actually, I think that time he actually meant 'Give her a prize.'"

Ëëëlmööö gave her another thumbs-up. "Too right."

"I don't think I could eat anything, but perhaps I could have a pitcher of water," said Eloise.

The Nameless One shook his head "no".

"I have to agree," said Hector. "The water here takes a strong stomach. But if you have tea, at least it will have been boiled."

"Tea, then."

"Two troughs of tea for us as well, please," said Hector.

"I'll have tea, too," said Johanna. "And thank you for the county fairs."

Ëëëlmööö smiled. "Too right, love."

✢ 38 ✣

THAT SOUNDS LIKE A PLAN

Eloise, sore and exhausted to the bone, shifted the Star of Whatever's box on her hip and eased gingerly onto one of the stools. She and Johanna immediately peppered Hector with questions.

"Is Uncle D going to die?" asked Johanna.

"Why did the Purple Haze attack?" asked Eloise.

"Who is ruling the kingdom?"

"Why are Jerome and Lorch being executed?"

"How did you find us? How did you know where to look?"

"How did you know you could enter the fog?"

"How many months—or years—were we gone? It felt like forever."

Hector held up a hoof to stop them. "Whoa, there, Princess, Princess. One at a time. Let me see..." He paced across the stable, trying to figure out how to start. "I'll answer the last one first," he said. "It has been three weeks to the day since you disappeared, including the two days you were in Mr Búüùttons's home. But let me back up from there."

Hector explained how they had followed the princesses out of the castle and up Fogging Hill. He described their disappearance, seeing Eloise reappear, and his initial attempt to go into the fog after her. Then he explained the difficulties they'd had getting information on Lorch and Jerome, the failed fogging and how that had given them the idea of trying to go into the fog, and finished with how the horses had found the young women in such a dire state.

At some point during the story, Ëëëlmööö wheeled in a cart with a porcelain tea set patterned with horseshoes, and two laterally cut barrels. He poured out dainty cups for Eloise and Johanna, and bucketed tea into the troughs, so that all four containers brimmed with the same steaming, dark liquid. Then he set out scones and haggleberry jam for the humans and appetizer-sized hay nets for the others.

When Hector had finished, Eloise and Johanna shared their tale—why they left the castle and went up Fogging Hill, how Turpy had held Eloise and told Gouache to fog Johanna, how Eloise broke free and slammed into Gouache too late to stop him, then rolling into the fog with Gouache, and finally saving him. She didn't realize Hector had seen her go back into the Purple Haze. That explained how he'd known to come looking for them. She outlined why she thought the mist did not affect them, and the inner tug that had led them to Melveeta. Hector asked a lot of questions about Gwendolyn's champion, and especially about the Star of Whatever, and Eloise described both with as much detail as she could. If she was going to carry the Star on his back, she thought he ought to know as much about it as she did.

The discussion turned to Lorch and Jerome. "Isn't there something to be done legally?" asked Eloise.

"We've covered this so often with the Speaker for the Indigent that his tentacles twitch when he sees us. As he puts it, the ruling was laid down by the king, and would have to be countermanded by him, especially since the regent has affirmed the king's will."

"How is it possible for a jester to be regent?" asked Johanna. "Can you imagine old Stoofy being named regent for Mother?"

"Your mother has legal successors and a king. Who does Doncaster have? We raised this with the Speaker for the Indigent, thinking that might be an out or a route of appeal. Apparently the First, Second, and Third Advisors all verified the authenticity of the Declaration. So long as the king breathes and there's a chance he'll recover, the regent is within his rights."

"There's no way I will let my champion and my guard come to harm. We have to save them," said Eloise.

"The question is how," said Hector. "It's not like we can wander up to the castle and trade for them. Or steal them."

"What about Fogging Hill?" asked Johanna. "Could we do something there?"

"They have all kinds of guards at the foggings," said Hector.

"They didn't exactly strike me as elite units," said Eloise. "Could we swoop in and snag Jerome and Lorch?"

Hector thought about this for a moment. "If they still send the prisoners into the fog—and at this point, that's a big if, given they know the behavior of the fog has changed—it might be possible to grab one as they make their way into the Purple Haze. But there are problems." He took a slurp of tea. "For one, they're sent down one at a time. Let's say we grab one. You'd still have the other one stuck up at the top with all the guards. Plus, what would you do with the one you had? You'd have to bolt away, escape the town walls, and get as far away from Stained Rock as possible, as fast as possible, to avoid recapture. Messy."

"Messy, yes." Eloise ran a hand across the stubble of her hair. "Could we get a message to them?"

"With time, probably," said Hector. "The Speaker for the Indigent could visit them with enough notice. But he can't just waltz in unannounced. They have procedures in place. It is, after all, prison."

"Since the fog is no longer a danger, they could hide in it. Or we could," said Eloise. "If we could get a message to them, then they could just go ahead into the mist when the fogger tells them to, and wait there for us, or meet us there, depending on circumstances. And assuming they're still sent into the fog, which, as you said, is a big 'if.'"

"Time is the problem. I'll see if I can get to the Speaker for the Indigent, but it's already getting late, and the event is tomorrow morning. The Speaker for the Indigent would have to get into the dungeons between now and then. I don't like our chances."

"What about forging something? Could we forge a pardon?" asked Johanna.

"Again, all of those things take time, and time is not our friend," said Hector.

Eloise sat her spoon on its saucer. "I quite like the direct approach. We need to be ready to just charge in there, grab them, and get out of here. We can swoop down when one or both is away from the guards... I don't know. This is straw-clutching."

"We have been trying to puzzle this one out for days, Princess. Days and days."

"We have to do something," insisted Eloise.

The four of them fell into a contemplative silence. It seemed like the conversation had gone as far as it could. They sat quietly in the darkening stable, letting the uncertainty swirl around them.

In the dimming light, they didn't see the cockroach—the one who'd been spying on them the whole time—scurry away to file his report with the regent.

PLAN BS

Fogger Abigail Bronzer Splintfinger plucked at the sleeve of her purple robe and tried to ignore the wintry wind whipping across Fogging Hill. Thirteen sentenced prisoners stood bound, gagged and shivering in the pale morning sun, ready for another attempt at being fogged.

Abigail had her doubts.

She had nothing but doubts.

Abigail looked down to the bottom of Fogging Hill where it met the Purple Haze, and sighed. The gold embroidery on Guild Master Frÿÿÿ-denburg's purple robe glinted in the mid-morning sun when the wind snapped it to just the right angle. They had that rat—no, not a rat, a chipmunk—tied up and tethered to a rope, and were testing different ways to propel him into the Purple Haze to see if anything might work.

Nope.

From the way the Guild Master shook his head, she could tell the Purple Haze was still broken. Not good. If the fog stopped working permanently, there'd be no need for foggers like her. And then what?

She'd been with the Foggers' Guild since she'd apprenticed as a teen, and had spent her life sending people into the "uncertainty" of the fog. She was good at her trade, enjoyed its benefits, and knew how to manage both those sentenced to foggings and their family and friends, especially the latter, since they were the ones who had to pay up. That's why she tried to keep the tone of her foggings light-hearted, quick, and professional. It was best for all involved.

Abigail brought in more money than other foggers who were somber, judgmental, or tried to convey the weight of the king's justice in their approach to the ceremonies. She wasn't supposed to know she netted more dosh, but she'd snuck a look at a few of Guild Master Frÿÿÿden-burg's ledgers, and discovered that she brought in 15 percent, maybe even 17 percent, more than her fellow guild members. That wasn't nothing.

If she couldn't be a fogger, what was she supposed to do? How could she keep up her payments on her cottage, or the installment arrange-ment she had with the apothecary to cover her mother's prattleweed needs? If the Purple Haze was permanently kaput, she was screwed. Royally, thoroughly, permanently, righteously stuffed.

"Fogger Splintfinger?" Her apprentice's voice broke through her thoughts.

"What?!" she yelled, startled. Öööscar blanched and took a step back, and Abigail immediately felt bad. It wasn't this goofball's fault she'd over-leveraged herself to get the loan for her medium-sized pink cottage in the nicer part of town. She could hardly afford it with her current fogger's rank, but she'd expected to rise within the guild's hier-archy. Plus, she'd fallen in love with its cute little gingerbread windows, its exposed beams, its thatched roof (*that* was a mistake), its curlicues, and its out-of-plumb walls. It wasn't his fault that her mother had grad-uated from prattleweed to prattleseeds to prattleweed tincture.

"Sorry. What did you want?"

"I wondered if it was time to try other options." The broken fog had given Öööscar a chance to display ingenuity, creativity, and initiative. It would be years before he qualified for full Foggers' Guild robes, but it was never too early to make oneself noticed and indispensable. Attitude was everything.

His attitude drove Abigail spare. His attitude, and the fact that he reminded her of herself as an overly eager apprentice. She could have chucked herself into the fog at the memory, except the mist was broken. She sighed again. "I suppose it is. You have your Plan B?"

"Yep, three Plan Bs, all together."

"Off you go then. Get them ready."

Öööscar scooted to the small cluster of onlookers and motioned for three people to come forward from the crowd—two humans and something small—and lined them up for her to consider. "Prepare to be astounded!"

It was not the most impressive collection of Plan Bs she could imagine, so being astounded struck her as unlikely. "I suggest we wait for the Guild Master to join us. He has approval rights."

"Oh, I think he will approve," jigged Öööscar.

They watched Guild Master Frÿÿÿdenburg trudge up the hill with Geoffrey the guard. Geoffrey held the chipmunk by the scruff, waving him around as he punctuated their animated conversation with gestures. The chipmunk looked nauseous, not that he could toss his gruel with his snout tied shut. The wind blew up snatches of their conversation: "... ruin...", "central to the king's justice...", "... best not tell...", "... broccoli dumplings..." They covered the last ten lengths to the top of the hill in silence.

"Well, Abigail. It looks like we're going to need those Plan Bs you mentioned."

"Credit where it's due, Guild Master. I let Öööscar take the lead on the Plan B," she said. "I thought it would be a good opportunity for him." And it meant she could avoid blame when it failed.

"Öööscar?" The Guild Master looked surprised. "Most generous of you to give a new one a chance. But just because he's my nephew doesn't mean he deserves preference." He turned to the apprentice. "Well, boy, you've been given a tremendous opportunity by Fogger Splintfinger. What do you have?"

Öööscar swallowed his nerves, smoothed down the front of his purple tunic, and launched in. "We have three good possibilities, Guild Master and Madame Fogger." He waved forward the first of the two humans like a visiting diplomat. One was a shriveled old man who looked and smelled like his field of expertise was the interior land-scapes of the realm's public inns. "This is Peter," said Öööscar. The old man bobbed a hello that could also have meant, "Do you have any beer?" "Peter has a weak magic for making things near him wither. You know, like plums withering to prunes, or grapes withering to raisins. I thought he could wither the condemned."

The Guild Master wrinkled his nose. "You want him to turn the condemned into prunes?"

"Something like that, yes."

"How would that work?"

"Simple. He would just sit next to them, and they'd wither."

The Guild Master considered this. "How long would that take?"

Öööscar had not expected this question, so he deferred to Peter. "No more than a week or two each," rasped the old man. He pointed at Lorch. "Maybe three weeks for him."

"You've done this before?" asked Frÿÿÿdenburg.

"No, of course not. Don't be daft. I'm simply calculating how long it takes me to turn a bushel of plums into prunes, and extrapolating from there, allowing for size, density, weight, and water content."

A few moments of silence passed while that sank in. The Guild Master didn't look overly impressed, so Abigail jumped in. "What else do you have, Apprentice Öööscar?"

"Right. OK. The second Plan B." The apprentice picked up someone from the grass and held it in his palm—a leech. It was the scruffiest leech Abigail had ever seen. "This is Hüüübert." He said it as though that was all the explanation needed.

"And?" asked the Guild Master. "How does Master Hüüübert come into play?"

"Well, he's a leech. He can suck out their blood."

"Is he out of his mind?" said Frÿÿÿdenburg. "He'd be thrown out of the Leechers' and Bloodletters' Guild."

"No, no, that's not a problem," protested Öööscar. "He's already gone rogue. He's happy to help us out."

"A rogue leech? I can't engage a rogue leech. The Leechers and Bloodletters would come down on my head like a strong weight of cobblestones."

Abigail did not like the way this was going. The odds of the Guild Master blaming her were rocketing skyward. "If we engaged Master Hüüübert's assistance, how would it work?"

Öööscar looked flustered. "He's a leech. He sucks blood. How much more do we need to know?"

"Well, how long would it take for him to, you know...?"

Again, Öööscar was unprepared for this question, so they all turned to the leech.

Hüüübert bobbed his head, thinking, then squeaked, "I'm big, for a leech. I could probably handle the rat—"

"Chipmunk," corrected Abigail.

"Chipmunk, then, in a week, maybe ten days. The big guy..." He moved his head, indicating Lorch. "Half a year, plus or minus. Depends on whether you feed him along the way. If you do, he makes more blood, which slows me down. If you don't, he starts to taste sour, which also slows me down. So, yeah, half a year."

The Guild Master straightened. "Thank you, Master Hüüübert for your time. And good luck with your roguish future."

"No problem." The leech dropped off Öööscar's palm and inched his way back toward the onlookers.

Frÿÿÿdenburg cleared his throat to get the focus back to the matter at hand. "Any other Plan Bs, Öööscar?" The Guild Master looked like he hoped there wouldn't be.

"There's Wääälton." Öööscar waved forward a tall, thin man wearing a crofter's breeks and tunic, with a tangled bird's nest of hair, and no hat. His rough, leathery skin looked like it had seen every ray of sun to ever make it through the clouds. The crofter carried a mixed sheaf of barley, wheat, and oats, as well as a flail.

"And?" prompted Abigail.

"He's the one you suggested."

"I suggested? I didn't suggest anything."

"Sure you did. Wääälton is a thresher." Öööscar's frustration rose, along with the pitch of his voice.

"Thresher? What does that have to do with anything?"

"You clearly said, and I quote, 'We should find ourselves a cereal killer.' Well, here he is. Wääälton is the finest thresher in the realm."

The ensuing pause was as long as it was awkward.

"I joked—*joked*—that we needed to find a 'serial killer,' not a 'cereal killer.' With an 's,' not a 'c.' 'Serial.'"

Abigail watched Öööscar's face, seeing the gears of his mind seize up for a few moments, then unjam. "Oh," he said. "I get it. That makes much more sense. I don't know any of those. Do you?"

"No. I don't."

The Guild Master gave Öööscar a disappointed shake of his head, another in a long line of them, then turned to face the shivering prisoners. "Apologies, everyone, but it looks like we're going to have to suspend ceremonies again, until we either find a suitable alternative or the research mages figure out how to fix the fog. As Guild Master, please accept my apologies for the delay. The guards will return you to the dungeons where your regular routine of torment and unpleasantness can resume. Thanks for your understanding. Please know we take your sentence of execution seriously, and will do everything in our power to rectify this unexpected, and unfortunate, situation."

Abigail watched the Guild Master stride back toward town, and thought, "I really am stuffed."

❦

ACROSS FOGGING HILL, ELOISE SAT ON HECTOR, AND JOHANNA ON the Nameless One. They watched the prisoners turn away from the fog and shuffle back toward the castle.

"We could just swoop in there," said Eloise. "Full frontal attack. Scoop them up and carry them off to safety."

"Sadly, Princess, they're too heavily guarded," said Hector.

"I know. I just like the idea of doing something, rather than nothing."

"Did the Speaker for the Indigent get anywhere close to delivering a message to them?" asked Johanna.

"No, I don't think so," said Hector. "He couldn't get to the correct wing in the dungeons."

"At least they're still alive," said Eloise. Then, without warning, she waved her arms over her head. "Hey! We're here," she yelled. When the prisoners didn't respond, she cupped her hands to the sides of her mouth. "Lorch! Jerome! We're here!" Her voice echoed across the hillside.

The two of them, gagged and tied, stopped and looked around.

Eloise kept waving, and yelled, "Don't give up! Don't give up!"

Jerome's eyes went wide when he saw her, and he immediately tried to run toward her. He got four steps before the rope on his legs tripped him. A guard reached down and picked him up by the scruff.

Lorch turned to face Eloise across the hill. He flattened his tied hands palm to palm and gave as deep a bow as his restraints would allow.

"Oy, you," snarled the guard holding Jerome. "Eyes forward and get moving." He poked Lorch with a wooden staff for emphasis.

The prisoners resumed their trudging.

Eloise and the others held vigil until the prisoners were out of sight.

"I can't say it was good to see them like that," said Eloise. "But by Çalaht's webbed toes, it was good to see them."

"I know what you mean," said Hector.

They stood looking in the direction the prisoners had gone, watching in silence long after they had disappeared.

"You know what?" said Eloise.

"What?" said Johanna.

"I think we should pay a surprise visit to the castle. Let's get them back."

❧ 40 ❧

MERFFERNS

"I look ridiculous," said Hector. "There's no way the castle guards will be fooled by this."

"You'll be fine," said Eloise. "Just try to look like your life has been an endless sting of burdens. Try to get into the role."

They walked toward the Castle Blotch delivery entrance in the fading afternoon light. A line of delivery carts waited to get through security. Hector and the Nameless One were pulling a cart laden with old cloth and baked goods. They were supposed to look disheveled and down-trodden, but Hector was having a hard time with it.

"Think of it as spycraft," said Johanna.

"I was never very good with disguises. People always seemed to be able to pick me out. I'm not sure why."

Eloise knew why. The sheer physical magnificence that served Hector so well as a ceremonial Horse Guard made a mockery of their attempts to transform him into a convincing carthorse. Even having his mane rubbed into matted knots and his luminous coat smeared with muck could hardly hide his regal manner. The Nameless One had coached him on how to walk with a shuffle and a limp, which helped a little, but Eloise was far from certain this would work.

The problem was castle security. They had to assume that Hector and the Nameless One were still on the Nope Don't Let In No Matter What's Going On list and that Eloise was on the List of People to Arrest on Sight list. Hence the disguises.

"At least we have proper paperwork," said Johanna, adjusting her kerchief so it covered more of her white hair. The Nameless One had convinced Kïïït, the scullery mare, to place an official order with a fake enterprise called Ragamuffins to supply the castle with rags and muffins. In the cart, the smell of the fresh baked goods competed with the moldy, dank smell of rags. Kïïït had to fudge the kitchen's processes somewhat to get the order placed without Cook's notice, but had managed to sweet-talk the head cook's Second Cook into doing it.

It had taken hours to assemble their ragpickers disguises. Eloise and Johanna looked thin enough to be almshouse poor, so it was just a matter of dressing badly enough. Wáäàlter Búüùttons did not have a lot of rags hanging around, but Ëëëlmööö had come to their rescue, providing a bedraggled cart, a load of tattered dust cloths, cast-off outfits, and half a dozen baskets of raspberry muffins that smelled of heaven.

"Jerome would have enjoyed trying to pull this off," said Eloise. "This sort of shenanigan is right up his alley."

"He'd have come up with an entire history for each of us," said Johanna.

"I can imagine him spending days scratching out scroll after scroll of backstory," Eloise agreed.

"He'd give you the good role, of course. You'd be the plucky, enterprising, entrepreneurial ragpicker destined to rise above her miserable station."

"Naw," said Eloise. "That'd be you, because he'd be too scared to make you a have-not character. I'd be the half-witted sister who knew how to bake incredible raspberry muffins, but nothing else, since that was all our parents managed to teach me before they were tragically killed in a freak muffin-batter mishap."

"And it would be up to me, as the plucky, enterprising, entrepreneurial sister to provide for our pathetic, broken family. You, of course, would be a magician with a raspberry muffin, but I would have a horrible blind spot when it came to blueberry ones, and the market would leave us behind."

"Jerome was certainly fond of minor character flaws."

"Excuse me, Princess, Princess. Would it be possible not to refer to Champion Abernatheen de Chipmunk in the past tense? I've not given up on him yet, nor Guard Lacksneck."

"Sorry, Equine Designate de Pferd. Of course, you are right."

They walked the rest of the way in silence.

Eventually, they got in line for the guards to check them through the gate. Eloise's jaw tightened when she saw it was Mööööëë, along with Lääärry and Cüüürly. "I thought they guarded the main gate, not this one. They met me from before. What if they recognize me? They'll know I'm lying."

"Stick with the plan," whispered Hector, increasing the severity of his fake limp. "You are well disguised. Plus..." His words faltered, but he pointed his chin indicating Eloise and Johanna's hair. "There are some differences to the last time you met them. Apologies for having to say it, Princess, Princess."

Both Eloise and Johanna nodded and lowered gazes to avoid eye contact with the guards.

"Papers, please," said Mööööëë when it was finally their turn. Johanna handed over Kïïït's scroll. Mööööëë looked it over and glanced at the cart. "I see you're a new supplier. 'Ragamuffins'? Huh. There are forms you need to fill in. Can you write?"

"Nerp." Johanna shook her head and smiled sweetly.

"Never mind. Cüüürly knows most of his letters. He can fill in the scroll for you."

"Yerp."

"Have you received your security orientation yet?"

"Nerp."

"New procedures put in place the last few days. I'll need all four of you to just step into the small auditorium over there, and Lääärry will enact the security theater, wherein he'll cover your roles and responsibilities as a crown-approved supplier of goods. After that, Cüüürly will sketch you for your security badge, which must be kept on you and visible at all times. Understand?"

"Yerp."

Möööëëë looked at Eloise and furrowed his brow. "Mistress Ëëēlöööïïïsëëë? Is that you?"

"Nerp," blurted Eloise, imitating her sister's bizarre accent. "Nerp, nerp, nerp."

"Are you sure? What is your name good woman?"

Eloise froze. In all their preparations, fake names hadn't occurred to any of them.

Hector jumped in. "Her nerm erse Éëërléëèrise. Yer merst perdern therm berth. Thery're berth er bert sermple ernd derft."

It was the worst pretend accent Eloise had ever heard. Hector may as well have worn a sign saying, "I am a fakety fake fake faker faking fake stuff."

But Möööëëë merely nodded, dipped his quill in an ink pot, and jotted a couple of words. "Simple and daft. Got it. Well, good for them for showing initiative and taking on the big wide world."

"Werld yer lerk er merffern?"

Möööëëë looked around to see who might be watching, then leaned in close to Hector. "Actually, I would love a muffin."

"Éëërléëërise, plerse gerve ther nerce mern er merffern."

"Yerp," Eloise said. She grabbed one of the muffin baskets from the cart, lifted the serviette covering them, and held out the basket.

Möööëëë scooped the air above the muffins with his hand, wafting the aroma toward him like a perfumer, and breathed deeply. A smile of joy lit his face. "Çalaht searing a saucepan, that is divine!" He wiped his hand on his tunic, plucked the topmost muffin, and took a delicate nibble. "Oh! Oh, my! That's remarkable." He took another bite, melting into muffin-induced bliss. "Incredible. Did you bake these?"

Eloise shook her head quickly. "Nerp." She pointed at Johanna. "Herp."

Möööëëë bowed to Johanna. "Good woman, that is the most scrumptious muffin I have ever had the pleasure of tasting. And I've tasted a lot of them."

"Werld yer lerk er wherle berskert?" asked Hector.

"A whole basket? Really? No, I shouldn't, absolutely shouldn't," he said taking the basket from Eloise and tossing the scroll on a pile behind him. "Everything seems in order. Now, if you could please follow Lääärry to the theaterette."

Lääärry's security theater enactment was as riveting as one would expect, although the interpretive dance about preventative surveillance and proactively reporting suspicious behavior was surprisingly moving. Cüüürly had no talent at all for drawing. His rendition of Eloise for her security badge was a stick figure with no hair, which Eloise had to admit was probably fairly accurate. He did a little better with Johanna —her stick figure had several long lines representing hair. Cüüürly then sketched their fingerprints and traced around the horses' hooves.

Mouths full of muffins, the three guards made sure the security badges were properly displayed, then waved them through to the castle grounds.

❧ 41 ❧

COOK

The four of them picked their way across the castle grounds to where Kïïït had said they'd find her. The mood around them was very different to the last time Eloise was there. Servants moved faster, and they looked nervous, strained, or exhausted. The few conversations held were hushed, almost conspiratorial.

The plan was to have Kïïït sneak them into the castle through the kitchen, but it would only work if Cook could be distracted enough not to notice them. This was a weak part of their plan—one of many— as she was notorious for ruling with an iron hand and seeing (or smelling) everything in her domain.

They found the scullery mare unloading the last sacks of grain from a rye monger's cart. Kïïït nodded at Hector, and gave the Nameless One a sly smile, but clearly did not want to converse. The mare picked up a sack by the corner using her teeth, and with a practiced toss, flipped it over her head and caught it on her back. She unloaded half a dozen that way, then walked through the kitchen doorway and into a pantry.

The rye monger nodded to Eloise and Johanna, but said nothing. He didn't help unload—apparently it wasn't his job—nor did he seem to appreciate the skill that Kiïït brought to the task. "I'm trying to get home before dark, love, and I've got strong lengths to go before I sleep," he said when she came back out. "If you could pick up the pace there, I'd be most obliged."

"Of course, good sir. I'll have it done as soon as possible." She didn't seem to take offense at being hurried along, nor did she change the pace at which she worked. Another two trips and she was almost done.

"Bring three sacks to the grinding table," barked a voice from the kitchen. "Now!"

"Yes, Cook," called the mare. "Right away." She chucked the remaining sacks onto her back and said, "Lovely to see you again, Good Sir Barley. I look forward to tomorrow's conversation."

"Don't be impudent, young lady," grunted the rye monger. Then, inexplicably, he leaned in, kissed her on the cheek, and said, "See you tomorrow."

"Tell Iïïrma and the sprogs I said hello."

"Say hello to your mother for me. I'll see her at the devotional house on Sunday."

"She'll like that."

Kiïït went to deliver the sacks, and the rye monger stepped into his empty cart and left.

The mare returned moments later. "Hi, Sweetie Pie," she said, giving the Nameless One a quick nuzzle. "Hello, Hector, ladies. I'm Kiïït." She paused, sniffing, and turned her head so she could see the baskets in the cart. "Those smell amazing! You'd better get rid of them, quick!"

"I beg your pardon?" said Eloise.

"If Cook finds out that someone brought baked goods into her kitchen, she'll be looking for someone's head to remove, and I'd rather it wasn't mine. No one, but no one, dares bring baked foods anywhere near her, if they value their lives."

"Surely that's an exaggeration."

"I wouldn't want to be the one testing the boundaries when it comes to Cook. I've been here long enough to know a happy Cook is a happy castle, and an unhappy Cook is a misery. I once saw her chew someone out for—"

"What. Is. That. I. Smell?"

They all froze, and Kïïit looked like she might lose her lunch, as Cook stormed out of the kitchen. She was a gaunt giant of a woman in a black cook's outfit with a starched white apron and a set of knives holstered around her waist. Her nose was the most disproportionate protuberance Eloise had ever seen—a giant spud of a honker that commanded attention and dominated her face. Her hair was tied back in a severe bun, its bright red competing with the red of her cheeks (too much proximity to cooking heat) and hands (too much time in washing water). Eloise was used to Chef, who was warm, round, and welcoming. How a woman could work so close to so much food and not look like she ate any of it confounded Eloise.

"I smell something I did not bake," she said, her nose twitching as it tracked down the foreign cooking. "A muffin, I say. A muffin! Who was stupid enough to bring a muffin near my kitchen? I'll slice your—" All of a sudden, Cook stopped cold. She sniffed the air, licked her lips once, opened her mouth and sucked in a lungful of air. Her nose was like a detective, collecting, sorting, and analyzing the invisible clues that wafted on the light, early evening breeze.

"How could it be?" she murmured, confused. Cook snapped her fingers and pointed at Eloise. "You there. Bring me one of the baskets."

"I..."

"Now."

Eloise lifted a basket from the cart and brought it to Cook, who peeked under the serviette like she was checking out a basket of baby cobras. She took the basket with both hands, and with short, sharp sniffs, she smelled it and its contents from every angle. "Bring me a plate," she barked into the doorway. "And tongs." Within moments, a kitchen maid rushed out and handed her a fine china dessert plate, and a pair of heavy iron tongs for grabbing firewood in a fireplace. "Dessert tongs, you ninny," she snapped at the maid, who rushed away to fix her error.

Cook put the plate on an upturned barrel, looped the basket over her arm, closed her eyes, and held out her hand, waiting for the tongs, which seconds later were delicately placed into her open palm. Eyes still closed, she used the tongs to pull a random muffin from the basket and put it on the plate. "Knife. Fork." In a flurry of apron and skirts, the kitchen maid produced cutlery that matched the pattern of the tongs.

Eloise watched, fascinated at the way Cook dissected the muffin, slicing into it with delicate, practiced movements, laying open the mysteries within. She cut a parchment-thin slice, pierced it with the fork, and held it up to the fading light. Again, she smelled it, eyes calculating. Then she put the morsel in her mouth, and instead of chewing, worked it with her tongue to wring out every nuance of flavor.

Then Cook did something Eloise hadn't thought possible—she smiled. Not a little grin, but a massive, beaming, face-splitting smile that erupted unexpectedly from her. "Oh, my sweet boy. You've returned to me." Cook picked up the muffin and, eyes closed, ate it like it was the most precious food in all the realms.

And then she ate another.

And then another, her joy growing with every bite.

Cook opened her eyes, looking like a new woman. "It has been two decades since I've tasted his muffins." Red blushed her cheeks, and a coquettish delight took over her. "But I'd recognize his signature spice and sugar anywhere. Are you telling me that Ëëëlmööö Göööber-mouch is near enough to here for you to deliver a basket of his muffins warm? Where? Where is that six-fingered heartbreaker?"

"He runs an inn catering to equines. The Splintered Dray. Across town," said Eloise.

"Well, well, well. Well, well, well." Cook stepped over to the cart and gently picked up the other four baskets. "The Splintered Dray, huh? Well, well, well." Cook turned to the kitchen doorway, her thoughts lost to a past she never thought she'd revisit. "Kiïit, why don't you give your friends a cup of haggleberry tea and a spot of dinner? I'll be in my office." She softly hummed a sweetheart's melody as she walked through the kitchen and closed the office door behind her.

Kiïit looked at the closed door and gave a wistful sigh. "I wish someone loved me that much," she whispered. "Maybe someday." The scullery mare sighed again and turned to the others. "I didn't expect that. Anyone care for tea and dinner?"

"I would love to," said Eloise. "But we have some friends to rescue."

✤ 42 ✤

SPLITTING UP

Abandoning their cart, Eloise and Johanna grabbed one of the rag bundles each, then the four of them followed Kïïït through the kitchen and into the castle proper. Their plan was simple and inelegant: Eloise and Johanna would sneak down into the dungeons, find Jerome and Lorch, and break them out. Hector and the Nameless One would cause a distraction to draw off the guards so the twins had time to act. The holes in the plan were large enough to drive a fully laden tinker's wagon through, but it was the best they had.

They huddled in an out-of-the-way corner of a side hallway. Eloise and Johanna both untied their bundles. Eloise's was her travel cloak wrapped around the Star of Whatever box. She strapped the Star's box to her hip and concealed it by putting on her cloak. Despite its road weariness, the cloak had held up well, and wearing it made her look a lot less ragpicker-y, which would have make her conspicuous inside the castle.

Johanna's bundle was also a cloak, a ridiculous concoction of flounce, frills and lace, which ËëëlmÖÖÖ had dug out of a lost-and-found box. It smelled of the perfume worn by its previous owner, and despite looking like it had been made by someone trying to cram two centuries of styles into the garment, it sort of looked like it belonged at Court. When Johanna put it on, the hodgepodge of bad design choices transformed into a fashion statement. Eloise marveled at how her sister could do that.

"I still don't like the idea of splitting up," said Hector. "That's how we got into this mess in the first place."

"What choice do we have?" said Eloise.

"If Kïïït can get down into the dungeons to 'slop' the prisoners, then we can get down there too," said Hector.

"There's a difference," said Johanna.

"Oh?"

"She's a very large, four-legged person in a dark, narrow space wearing familiar clothing, with the manner and intention of doing her job. In other words, she's supposed to be there. You are a large, four-legged person in a dark, narrow space wearing unfamiliar clothing, with the manner and intention of doing mischief. In other words, you're not supposed to be there. I'm sure the people down there will cotton on to the difference, even if they only have sufficient mental agility to garner work as a dungeon guard."

"Oh."

"Johanna's right," said Eloise. "We're more likely to be able to sneak around down there, or to fake a purpose."

"Fine. The Nameless One and I will stay up here to create the diversion," said Hector.

"Have you worked out what you're going to do?"

The Nameless One shook his head. It had been a point of contention. Hector argued that the best diversions included blowing things up, burning them, or preferably both, and the Nameless One had agreed. But Eloise insisted that the diversion be something where no one would get hurt, nothing of substance would be destroyed, and minimize the likelihood of Hector and the Nameless One ending up incarcerated. They'd argued about it while they'd hauled the rags and muffins toward the castle, but had not come to an agreement.

Now the moment was here, and none of them knew what to do. It was just another hole in their planning.

"We'll work something out, Princess," said Hector.

"And?" said Eloise.

"And we will neither burn nor break anything."

"Good." Eloise looked at Johanna. "Ready?"

"Are you sure this is the way to do this?" Johanna asked.

"No. I'm not. Got a better idea?"

"Other than just wandering around to see what else is possible, no."

"We can do that if you think it will work," said Eloise.

"I don't think it will work." Johanna picked a fleck of nothing from the hem of her coat, thinking. "From what we've gathered, 'His Jesterness and Regent' is erratic. Even if we confronted him, there's no way of knowing we'd get anywhere."

"Right," said Eloise. "Then we'll stick to the plan, such as it is."

"Agreed," said Hector. "Good luck, Princess, Princess."

"Thank you," said Eloise, then she and Johanna turned and made their way to the dungeons, armed only with a forged note from the Speaker for the Indigent and a vague notion from Kïïït about where Lorch and Jerome might be.

Hector watched them go, then said, "Nameless One, are you ready to draw the attention of our hosts?"

DIVERSION

Hector followed the Nameless One through hallways that grew wider as they approached the center of the castle. They moved with purpose and speed, figuring that was the best way to make it look like they belonged there. Finally, they made it to the entrance of a large courtyard. It was surrounded by important-looking buildings that reached a massive four, even five stories into the sky. The courtyard's architecture was impressive largely due to how unimpressive it was—a space designed with the flair of a yawn and the panache of a ditch filled with oatmeal. Gray cobblestones paved the piazza, which blended perfectly with the gray stone walls. The open space was unmarred by such eyesores as fountains, plants, statues, or other frippery and flounces. It was, without doubt, the most utilitarian public area Hector had ever seen.

Yet it hummed with people and activity. There was a steady flow of servants, merchants, tradespeople, plus a smattering of nobles. These were not the people Hector was trying to distract, though; he was after the guards. Maybe the crowd could somehow prove useful.

The two horses looked around for something they could use to draw attention. Hector felt hampered by Eloise forbidding destruction.

Explosives were the perfect way to get noticed. Granted, there was the small matter of not having any. Plus, he'd have to use his mouth to work with them, which was always tricky for someone with bad depth perception and a severe blind spot at close range. He'd need time, which was also something he didn't have. Hector pushed thoughts of explosives out of his mind, humphed, and said, "I don't see anything useful to us. Nothing."

The Nameless One pointed his nose toward a stack of barrels, a market stall of vegetables, a flower monger next to a flour monger, and a washerman carrying a large basket of dirty laundry. Then he shook his head, agreeing there wasn't much around them to draw on.

"I'll try speaking to them." Hector cleared his throat. "Excuse me! Excuse me, good people! Your attention please!"

No one even looked at him, save Dirty Laundry Man, who glanced up on his way into a side walkway.

"Maybe it's my accent," said Hector. He tried again. "Excüüse më! Excüüüüse më, gööööd peööple! Yööur attëëëntion plëëasë!"

The flower monger glared at him. "Oi. Quit takin' the piss, mate."

Hector looked at the Nameless One. "Was my accent that bad?" The guard horse gave a noncommittal head shake, trying to spare Hector's feelings.

"Right. Well, crummy accent or not, this isn't helping us stage a distraction. But what can we do? We could set up a traveling circus and a supporting quartet in the middle and they'd still ignore us. There'd have to be a full-blown spectacle to get them to crane their necks even slightly."

The Nameless One got a that-gives-me-an-idea look. He turned his back on Hector, strode to the center of the courtyard, and turned to face what looked to be the most important building. Suddenly—*clop!* His left front hoof slapped the paving stones. *Clop-clop!* His right forefoot and left hind smacked down, one after the other. The Nameless One stretched his neck as high as possible, and held his head unnatu-

rally still, which down below, his feet beat out a rhythmic pattern
—*clop, clop-clop, clop-clop-cloppity-clop.*

"Çalaht clogging on a crumbling clapboard," muttered Hector. "He's
going to make a spectacle of himself."

Slowly at first, then with ever-increasing speed, the Nameless One
tapped and clopped his way into a four-legged version of a Half
Kingdom favorite, the Dance of the River. The Dance of the River
was known for its strict rules of movement and fast, complicated foot-
work. When humans did it, they performed with their arms held
unnaturally straight and close to their sides, dancing shoulder to
shoulder with their feet tapping, shuffling, and crossing in front and
behind each other. The Nameless One had no arms to keep by his
sides, but he had four feet where humans only had two, and the hard-
ness of his hooves made a natural tapping sound as he sped up the
dance. Even without musical accompaniment, it was impressive. The
complexity of rhythm and the variety of movement that the Nameless
One's four feet provided was beautiful and fascinating. Like a busker at
a local fair, the Nameless One entertained for whoever cared to stop
and watch.

And stop they did. One by one, then in groups of twos, threes, and
fours, the people in the courtyard drifted over to watch this unexpected display of agility and skill. Hector saw that his friend had also
drawn the attention of people in the rooms around the courtyard as
they poked out their heads to see what was going on. Five minutes
passed, becoming ten, then fifteen. The Nameless One danced like his
life depended on it, a graceful display of sweeping legs and blurring
hooves. Faster and faster, the Nameless One danced and danced, full-
bodied, joyous, spinning and flying. Then, with a loud *cloppity-cloppity-
cloppity-clop-clop-clop*, he froze, suddenly motionless—his routine
finished.

To Hector's surprise, there was a raucous round of applause, hoots, and
cheers, and a rain of tossed coins.

The Nameless One had, indeed, caused a diversion. But it was not big
enough, nor had it lasted long enough. Hector knew they needed even

more spectacle, especially if they were going to draw out the guards from their posts.

When the applause stopped, the Nameless One started another rhythmic stomp—a simple, repeated clop of his right fore hoof that echoed across the courtyard. *Clop! Clop! Clop! Clop!* He hammered out a four-beat rhythm, and caught Hector's eye with a look that pleaded, "Help me."

Hector had no idea what to do. He had a natural grace and had learned a dance or two at Court, but he was used to a particular kind of performing—precision group movement, with his Horse Guard. He was no stranger to being on display, but this was different.

The crowd, won over by the Nameless One's dance, clapped along with the beat of his hoof. "Right then," Hector said, and stepped carefully through the crowd to the middle of the piazza. He stood next to the Nameless One, facing the same direction, head tilted slightly toward him so he could see what he was doing. Hector watched the *clop-clop-clopping* beat and realized that the Nameless One had changed what he was doing, adding additional beats with his other feet, forming something familiar, a pattern that scratched at the back of Hector's head. A chant? A parade ground call and response?

No. A song.

Suddenly Hector knew exactly what the sound was. It was the beat to a very, very familiar song. For weeks, he'd tried to escape it, ignore it, and block it away. But the song had seeped deep into his bones. So much so, Hector had no choice but to open his throat and heart, and let That Song fly in a deep *basso profondo*.

There's a lady who knows all that that glitters is groats...

Hector poured his soul into performing "Three Bags of Groats for My Sweetheart." He drew on his every memory of Jaminity Delgado Blister and Alejandro Diego Ferdinando Felipe Esteban Iglesias Desoto de Lugo, on Lyndia Thrind, on Gouache Snotearrow McCcoonnch, and even on Jerome's maddening humming. In a detached corner of his mind, he thought, *Jerome, this is for you.* The lyrics and melody poured forth, and everyone—absolutely every merchant, mendicant, and guard was drawn to the singing, and was transfixed.

Hector lost himself to the simplicity of the song and the Nameless One's clopping accompaniment. And when the last word rang out, the audience was silent. The silence lasted five, then ten seconds while the echoes of what they'd just seen reverberated from wall to wall.

And then they cheered in a hail of "bravos," whistles, and clapping.

While that was going on, Hector noticed that Half Kingdom guards surrounded them, a three-deep ring of pike-wielding soldiers blocking any escape.

The largest of them stepped forward. "On behalf of His Jesterness and Confirmed Regent Turpentine Snotearrow McCcoonnch, you are under arrest."

❧ 44 ❧

SUPER, SUPER AWESOMELY
EXCELLENT

Eloise and Johanna walked down the hall leading away from the kitchen. Kïïït had told them where they needed to go, and Eloise held the mud map that Johanna had scratched on a scrap of parchment using a chunk of coal.

The twins had four main problems: finding the dungeons, getting past the guards, finding Jerome and Lorch, and getting them out. So, basically, the whole thing was a problem, and it was bound to get worse the further they got.

They had two options for getting in. One was to go through a service tunnel, the way Kïïït would when it was time to slop the prisoners. This was a well-used pathway protected by an enormous number of guards who all knew exactly who was and was not supposed to be there. The scullery mare said getting through there required a security badge and documentation, which the guards didn't always check, but would if they didn't know your face or purpose.

The other choice was something that Kïïït called The Hole. This was more of a pedestrian entrance. It was still guarded, but because it was smaller, less convenient, and less used, they were more likely to find a way, somehow, to get in.

Eloise pointed. "Look. There's the marble statue of a nematode perched on a lily. This must be our last turn."

"I don't think the realms have enough nematode statuary. We should suggest that Mother commission some."

"Nematodes are people, too."

"I know," said Johanna. "But I can see why this statue is not in the most prominent place. Look how the artist has captured the flow and motion of its bristles, and the grand ornamentation of its ridges and rings."

"You're not being statue-ist, are you?"

"Let's just say it does not pass the 'Is this art I'd like in my bedroom?' test."

"Come on, we need to get going."

"Hector and the Nameless One must be doing something right. From what I remember, there are usually a lot more guards around."

"Çalaht, I hope they're OK."

They walked to the end of the hallway, which stopped abruptly in a poorly lit dead end.

"This can't be right," said Johanna. "There aren't any doors. Maybe that wasn't a nematode."

"It was a nematode. This has to be it."

They squinted at the walls to see if there was a hidden doorway, or something else they'd missed.

Nothing.

They stood in the middle of the hallway, looking around. "This doesn't make sense," said Johanna.

Nearby, something squeaked—the sound of metal against metal lasting about a second. Eloise looked at Johanna, who shrugged. It happened again. Then again. Squeak, pause, squeak, pause, squeak.

Suddenly, the floor beneath them jostled. Once, twice it moved, then nothing.

"Oi! Someone up there on the door?" The deep, muffled voice sounded like boulders rubbing against each other.

"Sorry," said Johanna. The twins jumped back several lengths, and a trapdoor began to creak upward from the floor.

"Oh, 'The Hole,'" said Eloise. "I get it."

"Kïïït might have mentioned the door was in the floor."

The trapdoor was huge—three lengths by three lengths, easy—and was slammed opened by a massive, hairy man who wore the helmet and breeks of a guard, but no shirt. He was twice Eloise's height, and easily four times her weight.

An unholy smell rose up, a stench of sulfur, sweat, and rot that screamed, "Release thy breakfast from thy guts!"

"By Çalaht's blessed bile duct, what do they keep down there?" whispered Eloise. She clapped her hand over her mouth and nose.

Johanna also pinched her nose shut. "Desperation and misery, but apparently not much soap."

The thought of going anywhere near that horrible smell, much less down into it, made Eloise's skin twitch. Her habits, pushed aside for what must have been days, set off alarm gongs in her head and clutched at her throat. She wanted to sprint away from this place, leaving whatever horrors waited below undiscovered. Instead, she grabbed Johanna's elbow to steady herself, and turned her mind to figuring out a way to convince the guard to let them in.

The squeak, pause, squeak resumed. It was a hidden rope and pulley system, which the guard hauled on to raise the platform he stood on. He tied it off at floor level and stepped aside to let pass a one-armed capuchin carrying a decorated fishbowl with a blue-gray jellyfish in it.

"Thank you, Kёёёrmïïït," bubbled the jellyfish. "See you soon."

"See you."

The capuchin nodded at the girls as he rushed past with the jellyfish.

The guard rubbed a hand over his face like he needed a nap but had to stay awake, then reached to untie the rope from its tether.

"El, look," whispered Johanna, pointing surreptitiously. "Look at him. You see that?"

"I see someone who looks like he could moonlight as a continent."

"His hands. Look at his hands."

Eloise shifted to see the guard more clearly. "Oh, wow. He has six fingers," said Eloise, counting them again to make sure. "How likely is that?"

"Not likely at all."

The guard readied the ropes to lower the platform, then grabbed another that would shut the trap door.

"We have to do something," whispered Johanna. "What are we going to do?"

"Right. Do something." Eloise stepped forward. "Hi there!" she said in a hyper-cheery voice. "G'evening. Kёёёrmїїїt, is it?"

The guard stopped fiddling with the ropes. "What do you want?"

Eloise laughed. "Oh, it is most awesomely excellent that it's you. Ёёёlmӧӧӧ said we'd find you here, and here you are!"

"You know my brother? I told him not to send people to bother me at work."

"Your brother is most awesomely excellent, and he told us you were super, super kind and might help us out. My name is Gїїїllian, and this is Fräääncine."

"Hi, I'm Fräääncine." Johanna waved, matching Eloise's excessive cheeriness. "Awesomely excellent to meet you."

"We're starting up a new venture," said Eloise, mind scrambling. "A new 'ad-venture,' you might say."

"We're super, super excited about it," said Johanna. "It's going to be awesomely excellent. Tell him about it, El—, er, Giïïllian."

"I'd love to, Fräääncine." Eloise gestured like she was pointing to words on a sign. "Dungeon Tours."

"What?" said Këëërmiïïit and Johanna at the same time.

"Isn't that awesomely excellent? And we have a slogan. 'Dungeon Tours — A Hole Lot of Fun!'"

"We're super, super excited," said Johanna. "And since we have permission from the king and the regent and everyone else…"

"Soooo much permission we have. Strong weights of permission."

"Scrolls and scrolls of permission. Every permission you could ever want. And Ëëëlmööö said you were the most awesomely excellent person to help us."

"Help with what?"

"Oh, Këëërmiïïit, you're super, super the right person to give us an up-close look at the dungeons," said Eloise. "How can we plan a 'hole lot of fun' for our hundreds of Dungeon Tours fans if we don't know where the fun, the exciting, and the scary bits of the dungeons are?"

"We are all about the authenticity, Këëërmiïïit," added Johanna. "Awesomely, excellent authenticity. We want our thousands of fans to know what it's really like down there, especially to be someone with the kind of responsibilities you have. What you do is super, super important, and we think more people need to know that."

"Oh," said Këëërmiïïit. "Do you really think so?"

"Absolutely!" said Eloise. "Like, here you are responsible for the entrance to the dungeon. And for this device."

"All I do is pull the rope to go up, and ease the rope out to go down."

"See what I mean? That is super, super fascinating. Our tens of thousands of fans will be enthralled. But if you think about it, they're actually your fans, Këëërmïïit, because you are crucial to this whole enterprise."

"I like the idea of having fans. You said Ëëëlmööö sent you?" Këëërmïïit rubbed the top of his head, like it might help his brain work a little better. "Well, then, I guess."

"Oh, that is super, super awesomely excellent! Come on, Fräääncine." Eloise looped her arm in Johanna's and they stepped onto the platform. "Ready when you are, Këëërmïïit."

"I, uh, I didn't realize you meant today."

"You wouldn't want our fans to wait, would you?" said Johanna.

"I guess not."

Eloise gave him a big thumbs-up. "Let's do this! Dungeon Tours, ho!"

45

TOURISTS

Këëërmiïïit turned away from them to resume fussing with the ropes. Eloise dropped her chipper manner for a moment, covered her mouth and nose with her hand, and whispered, "I guess we're going to do this."

"It would appear so," said Johanna.

With his back to them, Këëërmiïïit said, "As required by the Bureau of Moving Platform Regulation, I must inform you it's important you stay in the center of the platform and not touch the sides as we move. The Bureau hopes you enjoy your journey insert either up or down." His rote recitation of bureaucratese showed he'd not put a lot of thought into what the words actually meant. Këëërmiïïit released a lever, and with a small lurch, the platform descended, accompanied by the squeak-pause-squeak of him letting the ropes feed out their slack. When they were well below head height, he wrapped a rope around an iron ring set in the stone wall, and grabbed a different rope. With a rusty creak, he hauled the trapdoor up until its weight whomped down on top of them, hurting their ears with a jolt of air pressure and plunging them into darkness. Claustrophobic darkness, mixed with the stench. Eloise felt panic form in her guts, and her breathing raced.

"Easy there, Gı̈ı̈ı̈llian," said her sister. "Këëërmı̈ı̈ı̈t here has everything under control. Don't you, Këëërmı̈ı̈ı̈t? We're going to be fine, right?"

"Yes. Usually everything's fine."

"See," said Johanna.

"What does he mean, 'usually?' Why 'usually?' What happened when it wasn't fine?"

She couldn't see it, but it sounded like Këëërmı̈ı̈ı̈t rubbed his head again. "One time, someone had a bucket of soup, which got spilled. It was cream of broccoli, I think. Got everywhere. A real waste of soup. Another time, someone didn't pay attention to the rules, and they got a little scrape when they touched the wall on the way down. That would have hurt."

"Spilled soup and a scrape. Think you could handle that, Gı̈ı̈ı̈llian?"

"Another time, one of the ropes slipped, and the platform plunged to the bottom, smashed to pieces, and killed everyone on it. That wasn't so great."

Eloise moaned.

"I wasn't working that day. I think a box of crackerbread got damaged that time too. Anyway, the Bureau of Moving Platform Regulation came in and made a bunch of changes. It's been much better since then, just the soup and the scrape."

Eloise found Johanna's hand and held it. She forced herself to slow her breaths, which helped steady her. "Awesomely excellent," she managed. "I'll be fine."

Këëërmı̈ı̈ı̈t untied the rope from the ring and lowered them squeaking all the way to the bottom. It felt like it took forever, but Eloise guessed that if each squeak was about a length of rope, then The Hole must have been 20 lengths deep at most. When the platform thunked to a solid stop, he coiled the ropes neatly and took a lit torch from its sconce. "What do you ladies want me to show you?"

Sensing that Eloise was still recovering, Johanna took the lead. "We were thinking something creepy, something spooky, something secret, something memorable—that kind of thing. We thought that might make for an awesomely, excellent dungeon tour. You're the expert, Këëërmïïït. If you were one of our many, many fans, is that what you would want?"

"Uh... I guess." Këëërmïïït was unused to going off script, and looked like he was thinking hard about what might fit. "What's the difference between creepy and spooky?"

"I think of creepy heading in the direction of disgusting or eerie. Spooky is more ghostly or ghoulish."

"I guess." More head rubbing. "I—I think I might have something. Follow me."

He walked them down a hallway toward a guard station manned by a hamster, a macaw, and a marmoset playing a tense card game by torch-light. All wore the same guard helmet and breeks as Këëërmïïït, but were armed with an impressive collection of knives, knuckledusters, and cudgels.

The hamster put her cards face-down and swaggered to the edge of the table. "What have we here?"

"Dungeon Tours. That's Gïïïllian, and that's Fräääncine," said Këëër-mïïït. "I'm supposed to show them around." The twins gave cheery waves from behind Këëërmïïït.

"Dungeon Tours, huh? Who'd want to tour a dungeon?" asked the hamster. "Doesn't that strike you as a bit odd?" She tilted her head and scrutinized the girls.

"They have a lot of fans. Thousands," said Këëërmïïït.

"And they've got permission for this?" asked the hamster.

Këëërmïïït nodded. "Yeah. Lots and lots of permission. So much permission."

The hamster shrugged. "Off you go, then." The hamster swaggered back to her spot on the table, picked up her cards, and fixed the marmoset with a deathly stare. "Got any threes?"

Këëërmïïït shouldered open the door, which swung open to emit a fetid funk that made the previous unbearable stench seem like a bouquet of gardenias. Eloise swallowed down the acid reflux that found its way to the back of her throat and put her hands on either side of her head to keep from swooning.

"By Çalaht's suppurating psoriasis sores, that is vile," said Johanna. "How can you stand that?"

Këëërmïïït looked at her, puzzled. "Stand what?"

"That smell."

"What smell?"

"You don't smell anything?"

"Nope."

"You, sir, are particularly well-suited for this work."

"Thank you?" Këëërmïïït pointed at two torches burning on the wall. "You should take one of those. It's dark."

Eloise and Johanna took a torch each, and followed Këëërmïïït, who lumbered ahead.

The dungeon air was chilled, interrupted by pockets of unexpectedly warm air that unnerved rather than provided relief. They traveled through hallways slick with seepage that oozed down through cracks in the stone walls, leaking into puddles that their host splashed through, but which Eloise and Johanna stepped around as best they could. Even so, their feet were soon soaked. Eloise's habits clawed at her to do something about it. Their screaming made it difficult for Eloise to memorize the path they were taking for when she had to go back the other way with Lorch and Jerome. They turned randomly down hallways that had few landmarks to latch onto. Within five minutes, Eloise was lost.

Suddenly, Këëërmïïït held up a hand to stop them. He faced a wall and held up his torch to shine light on it. "There."

Eloise and Johanna stopped and looked at the wall. "Yes?" said Johanna.

"Pretty creepy, isn't it?" said Këëërmïïït.

Eloise had no idea what he was talking about. She and Johanna leaned in, trying to get a better look at whatever it was he was showing them.

"You're too close. You can see it better when you stand back a bit."

They backed up a few steps and looked again. But even with the three torch lights and the greater distance, they still had no idea.

"This is super, super, awesomely excellent," said Eloise. "What is it exactly?"

"Yes. I'm a little in the dark here, too," added Johanna.

"You don't see it?" Këëërmïïït looked disappointed, but tried again. "Look—there, there, and there, plus the squiggle here and those oval bits."

Eloise looked hard at where he pointed. "Sorry. I'm just going to need a little more help."

Këëërmïïït looked at them like they were simple. "It's so obvious, but OK. The cracks look like a durian that's been cut in half across the middle. There's a worm coming out of it, and the worm has three eyes. Plus, the seepage makes it look like the worm has conjunctivitis."

The two sisters tilted their heads. "I can see that," said Johanna. "Those are the eyes, and that's the worm's body emerging from the durian."

Këëërmïïït smiled, pleased. "The dungeon is full of creepy stuff like this."

"That is super, super creepy, for sure."

"What other awesomely excellent dungeon stuff do you have for us?" asked Eloise.

"This way."

Deeper and deeper they went. Këëërmïïït showed them a crack where, if you put your ear to it, it sounded like someone whispered "Paul is dead" (spooky), a place where he had once found a pile of rags, and no one knew where they'd come from (creepy), a spot where he sometimes hid his lunch (secret), a mug where someone decades before had left their false teeth (creepy), and a scroll where a prisoner once drew and numbered the various pustules that pocked his body, and what came out of them when they popped (creepy, spooky, and secret).

At some point, Eloise realized that she'd become accustomed to the smell. Thank Çalaht for small mercies.

The dungeon complex was huge, cell after cell dug into the ground. The stone-lined walkways twisted and turned with little observable order. "Just how many dungeon cells are there?" asked Johanna.

"More than this many, at least." He held up his twelve fingers. "But I don't count so good. You'd be better off getting a counter-type person to count them for you."

"Well, let me ask it differently. Is there any sort of organization to where people are?"

"Organization?"

"How they're arranged. Grouped."

"Oh. The prisoners are... wait, I'm sorry. I'm not supposed to call them 'prisoners.' The clients are bunched together according to things. That's how I remember it."

"What kind of things?" asked Johanna.

"Lots of things. Like, some of the really, really small ones are kept together. They are in T wing. I remember that, because 'T' is for 'tiny.'"

Clever, thought Eloise. Johanna was helping narrow down where they needed to look. Eloise joined in. "It must be the same with really, really big people. Clients—who are elephants, say, or giraffes or hippos are in B wing. For 'big?'"

"That's silly," laughed Këëërmïïït. "They're in E wing. 'E' is for 'enormous.'"

"Let me see if I can get some of the others," said Johanna. "The V wing is for the venal ones. R wing is for the recidivists. D wing is for the deranged. And X wing is for the fighters. Am I right?"

Këëërmïïït's look darkened. "Are you making fun of me?"

Johanna waved her free hand. "No, no, no. Gosh, no. Sorry. I was just thinking about how I might do it. How do you do it?"

"X wing is where the ones who were captured seeking treasure are kept. 'X' marks their spot. D wing is for dogs. We get a lot of dogs."

"Oh?"

"I'm not dog-ist or anything. I don't think dogs are inherently bad. But we have a whole wing for them."

"This is fascinating," said Eloise. "Where do you keep the condemned ones? In C wing?"

"H wing. 'H' is for 'haze.' The fog-bound go to H wing."

Johanna clapped her hands together and squeed with fake delight. "That's where we're going next. That is such an awesomely, excellent idea, Këëërmïïït. Imagine the drama. 'Dungeon Tours Presents the Wing of the Condemned.' It has everything. It's creepy, it's spooky, it's secret, and it's memorable. I can't wait."

"That's a super, super idea," said Eloise, trying to match her enthusiasm.

Këëërmïïït let his torch droop. "I don't know. H wing makes me sad."

"Kёёёrmïïït, our favorite dungeon guard, I really understand that." Johanna put an empathetic hand on his arm. "But you're a key part of this whole venture. We're relying on you."

"Really?"

"Imagine how disappointed our fans would be if they came on one of your Dungeon Tours—A Hole Lot of Fun tours, and missed out on H wing. You don't want to disappoint all of your fans, do you?"

"No. Of course not."

"No, you don't. And do you know why? Because you are a caring and thoughtful person, Kёёёrmïïït."

"I am?"

"And you understand. You know what disappointment feels like, don't you?"

Kёёёrmïïït sniffed. "I do. I know what it's like to feel disappointed. Look at these." He held out his hands. "Our mom and dad have seven fingers on each hand. Ёёëlmööö and I only have six. I used to cry myself to sleep at night wondering why Çalaht hadn't given me as many fingers as Mummy and Daddy. It always seemed so unfair." Tears dripped down his face, and he fought back sobs. "So yeah, I know disappointment. I know exactly what you mean. And I promise I will get our fans to H wing.

"Thank you, Kёёёrmïïït," said Johanna. "You are a good soul. And I think your hands are perfect the way they are."

The big man looked at Johanna like she was the first ray of sunshine he'd ever seen. "Really?"

"Really."

"Because I've always felt like such a freak only having six fingers."

"I understand. It's hard to be different to the ones you love."

Kёёёrmïïït squeegeed wetness from his face with his hand. "Let's go to H wing."

❧ 46 ☙

H WING

They followed Kёёёrmïïïït through one form of misery after another to get to H wing. The dungeon cells were packed full of hopeless people enduring boredom and uselessness, without the benefit of light, exercise, or hope. They cried out to them as they walked past, begging for help, mercy, or food. The mere existence of the place and the appalling conditions in which the inhabitants were kept made Eloise feel ill, but there was nothing she could do about it. At that moment, her biggest priority was to make sure she didn't end up in one of those cells.

The entrance to H wing was guarded by four humans, an elk, and a pangolin who seemed to be in charge. All wore serious armor and carried impressive weaponry. "Wait here," said Kёёёrmïïïït. "I'll need to speak with them." He walked to where the guards stood, leaving Eloise and Johanna out of earshot.

"This place is horrible," said Eloise. "Foul, squalid, disgusting."

"Yes. And that just describes the good bits."

"Have you ever been to the dungeons at home?"

"Once," Johanna confessed.

"Really? I was always too scared. Mother and Father were always very clear that going there was a very, very bad thing to do. I believed them. So, why?"

"It was 'very, very, very'—three times, and I went for fungi."

"What?"

"About three years ago. I was talking to Eldridge the Apothecary about fungi, and he mentioned one edible type that glowed in the dark. They give off a greenish or purplish hue, depending on if they are male or female. I was fascinated, and he said there were some in the dungeons. There was no way I wasn't going to see that for myself."

"So he took you?"

"Eldridge? No way. Too scared of Mother, although I spent a couple of weeks pestering him."

"How did you get in there?"

"Nesther de Duck."

"Nesther? Your handmaid got you into the dungeons?"

"She got sick of me talking about 'those Çalaht-forsaken blankety-blank-blank fungi.' There's evidence I might have been obsessed."

"I had no idea she knew such strong language."

"For her, that's as strong as it gets."

"I remember your fungus phase. You convinced Chef to put mushrooms in everything."

"So, yes, I talked about them for months. On and on. Finally, Nesther said, 'If I get you to see them, will you stop talking about them?' Of course I agreed. Her husband—did you know she had a husband?"

"No. Odmilla isn't married. I didn't know Nesther was."

"Her husband has a gruel business. He's got a contract to supply gruel for the prisoners. Nesther convinced him to have a word with the appropriate guard, who agreed to take me to see the fungi. She had me dress like a scullery maid, and her husband snuck me down to the dungeons posing as an apprentice grueller. He was fond of making jokes about it being grueling work."

"I can't imagine Nesther married to a punster."

"I assure you she is."

"And?"

"Oh, El. They were stunning. Nestled between murderers, swindlers, and arsonists were the most delicate little fungi you've ever seen. They had a soft purple and green glow you could only see if you waited for your eyes to adjust to total darkness. I sat down there for a whole afternoon, just looking. Looking, and then right at the end, tasting. I nibbled the tiniest bit of each color. The green ones have a fruity tartness, and the purple ones are nutty. But they were so pretty, so perfect, that I didn't want to disturb them more than just a little."

They were quiet for a few moments, listening to the small snatches of conversation that carried to them from the H wing door. In between wild gestures, Eloise picked out the words "permission," "fans," "tours," and "key part to the venture." Now and then, the conversation stopped, and Këëërmïïït and the guards all peered at them from their end of the hall, before resuming their discussion.

"What were they like?" asked Eloise. "The dungeons, I mean. Were they this kind of cesspool of misery?"

"Maybe," said Johanna. "I was pretty focused on the task at hand, and didn't really think about context. Certainly, it didn't smell this bad—I would have remembered that. It's going to take a week to get this stench out of my hair."

"I don't have that problem at the moment."

"No, you don't. Nesther's husband arranged for guards to protect me, and they kept the prisoners in check. I remember a lot of moaning—not pain moaning, more crazy moaning—and screams at one point. Screams and someone crying, 'No, no, no, no, no.' That was unnerving.

I don't remember them being this big, or having this many people in the cells. Dozens, but not hundreds, like here."

The pangolin strode up the tunnel toward them, his scales bristling. Kёёёrmїїїt lumbered behind him, saying, "Yes, I do trust them."

The jailer stopped two lengths from them, crossed his arms, and stared. Finally, he turned to Kёёёrmїїїt and barked, "Fine! But you owe me. And I want some of those fans for me, too."

The pangolin took out a set of keys and walked back to the H wing door. Kёёёrmїїїt waved for them to follow. The pangolin fiddled with the keys in the lock, which didn't want to cooperate. Finally, he jiggled them just right, and the door swung open.

"Awesomely excellent," muttered Eloise as she and Johanna stepped into the gloomy isolation of the fog-bound, followed by the armed clanking of the guards.

H wing was quiet with a hush you normally find in a scrollarium. Eloise imagined scholars scribbling away behind the dozens of locked cell doors. It was better than imagining what was actually in there.

The pangolin cleared his throat. "I'm Second Attending Corporal Bräääd, and if you or your fans have questions about the inner workings of H wing, I'd be more than happy to address them."

"That's super, super nice of you. I'm Gїїїllian and this is Fräääncine," said Eloise.

Johanna gave him a little wave. "Hi there. Awesomely excellent to meet you."

They both found it harder to fake enthusiasm when faced with the grim reality of H wing

"Let's start with an easy one: how many clients do you have here?" asked Eloise.

"One per cell, so that's around a hundred or so. It fluctuates, depending on the king's whim and the availability of foggers from the Foggers' Guild to carry out the ceremonies. There's a steady flow. But these are the worst of the worst, so it is an honor to serve the realm as their way station between their crimes and their fates."

Johanna tried to look fascinated. "And what sorts of crimes deserve that fate?"

The pangolin waved a hand to take in all of H wing, gesturing like he was rehearsing for an amateur theater production. "The range of depravity knows no bounds, I'm afraid. Crimes against society. Crimes against the crown. Crimes against neighbors. Crimes against strangers. They're all here, awaiting a final fate."

"Right," said Eloise. "That's super, super interesting. Are they from the Half Kingdom?"

"Mostly, yes, Mistress Giïïllian." Bräääd sighed, like this was a great personal disappointment to him. "But we do get them from all the realms. The Southies are the worst, coming here with their Çalaht-bothering ways. The king's, and now especially the regent's, limited patience often lands the Southies here in H wing. Such is the king's justice."

"Do you have any Westies?" asked Johanna. "I hear they can be pretty bad."

"Actually, we do. A couple of particularly bad ones. The king and the regent really threw the scroll at them."

"Ooh, that sounds exciting," said Eloise. "It would be awesomely excellent to see them."

"She's right. It would be super, super fabulous if we could tell our fans how awesomely excellent the depravers are that they might see on Dungeon Tours—A Hole Lot of Fun," said Johanna.

"I'm really not supposed to do that kind of thing," said the pangolin.

"Oh, please, please, please," begged Eloise. "What would a dungeon tour be without Westie marauders to gawk at?"

"'Westie marauders' does have a catchy ring to it," agreed Bräääd. "I really shouldn't." But he was already walking down the corridor, flipping through the keys on his keyring and whistling.

Everyone followed.

They walked several dozen lengths down the corridor until Bräääd stopped in front of a door that looked like every other. He inserted a key, turned it, then pointed to Kёёёrmїїїt, indicating that he should stand at the closed door. He then walked to the next door along and unlocked that one as well. The pangolin mouthed an exaggerated, "One, two, three..." and with a "Ta dah!," he and Kёёёrmїїїt swung open the doors at the same time.

Eloise stepped forward, letting her torchlight seep into the bleak cell. There was a rustle in the corner. It was Lorch—filthy, unshaven, gaunt, but it was him. His eyes blinked against the unaccustomed light, and he jerked upright when he saw who it was. Lorch rocked forward from the pallet he sat on, and in one swift motion, dropped to a knee. "Princess." His voice croaked, emotion forcing through his discipline and control.

The implications of what he said, calling her by name, zoomed through her head. Eloise hadn't thought this through, hadn't prepared for this moment. She tried to cover. "No, no, sorry, my name is Gїїїllian and I'm with Dungeon Tours—A Hole Lot..."

Something smacked into her leg, almost knocking her over. Claws dug in, piercing her breeks, the thing wrapping itself around her right thigh, and a wetness soaked through her breeks.

The thing was Jerome.

The wetness was tears.

"El!" he cried. "El, El, El! El, El, El, El, El, El, El, El, El, El, El, El, El, El, El, El! It's you, it's you, it's you, it's you, it's you, it's you, it's you, it's you, it's you!" His face was buried in her leg, but his voice was clear enough.

"Client! Restrain yourself," barked Kёёёrmiïït. "And her name is Giïïllian."

"It's OK," said Eloise. "He seems harmless."

"Wait. Wait, wait, wait," said Bräääd. "He called you 'Princess,' and he called you 'El.' You're not... You're the Westie princess!"

"No, I—"

"You're on the Arrest on Sight list!" The pangolin drew out a knife, and by reflex so did all the other guards. Everyone except Kёёёrmiïït. A dozen steel blades glinted in the pale torchlight. "Princess Eloise Hydra Gumball III, I hereby arrest you in the name of the crown and the regent."

"But her name's Giïïllian," argued Kёёёrmiïït. "And this is Fräääncine."

"They lied, you kapok head," snapped Bräääd.

"Lied?"

"It was a ruse, a trick, a de-cep-tion."

"You mean, there's no Dungeon Tours—A Hole Lot of Fun? No fans?" Kёёёrmiïït's face crumpled. "You lied to me? Both of you?"

"I'm super, super, awesomely sorry," said Eloise. "I really am."

ATTENTION

Guards pried Jerome from Eloise's leg and tossed him back into his cell. They slammed shut the doors on both Lorch and Jerome, leaving them as un-rescued as they had been before the sisters had arrived.

With their wrists tied in front of them and surrounded by guards, Eloise and Johanna followed Bräääd out of the dungeon and through the main entrance. He led them back toward the main part of the castle and, to Eloise's surprise, straight to the Throne Rome. It was easily three times the size of the one at Castle de Brague, and an interesting octagonal shape, with high windows that let in light at all times of the day and in all seasons.

There was the king, lying flaccid-faced, mouth agape, in an oversized bed. Why was he there and not in his chambers?

Johanna broke through the circle of guards. A couple of them moved to stop her, but the pangolin waved them off. She walked to the king's bedside. "Uncle Doncaster?" she whispered. "Uncle D?" Eloise came up and stood beside her. The monarch looked horrible. There was no other word for it. He'd lost ten, maybe twenty, weight's worth of weight, which made his sallow skin hang slack on his face and neck.

Platters of food sat untouched next to him. Worst was his snoring. It rang out from his open mouth, dominating the space around him like a novice bombard player honking out a strange four-beat monotone. The snore-snore-snore-pause ripped from the back of his throat and drowned out any possibility of conversation within half a dozen lengths.

"That snoring is so strange," whispered Eloise in one of the pauses.

"Why is he here?" asked Johanna. "Why is he not being tended?"

During another one of the pauses, Eloise noticed there was another sound. She looked across the room and saw Gouache. He was tucked into a bed a third the size of Doncaster's on the far side of the Throne Room. He, too, was slack-faced, and snored out the exact same pattern as Doncaster.

Johanna walked to Gouache's bed, and Eloise followed. "He was nice to me."

"Except for the part where he threw you into the fog."

"Yes, there was that. But he felt like he had to."

"You're making excuses for him?"

"Look at him. He's skin and bone. You know, I think he was sweet on me," said Johanna. Her voice warmed.

"Like anything would ever happen there."

Johanna ignored her and put a hand to his slack cheek. "Come on," she whispered. "Wake up. Who else is going to sing 'Three Bags of Groats for My Sweetheart' for me?"

No response. Just the irritating snoring.

Suddenly, guards snapped to attention and a handful of trumpets blew a fanfare. An old herald stood at the doorway. "His Jesterness and Affirmed Regent Turpentine Snotearrow McCcoonnch the First, known to all far and wide as Turpentine the Magnanimous."

Eloise looked at Johanna. "What the...?"

Turpy slouched into the room and headed for the dais. He'd not gone so far as to put on Doncaster's crown, but he held the royal scepter and wore the king's Declaiming Cape, which was close enough. He wore a version of his black and gray jester's harlequin, but it was newly sewn and brocaded with silver and gold. A sling for his injured hand had been made from a matching triangle of the same fabric.

Turpy sat down on the throne, but was clearly restless. He squirmed to find comfort and ended up with a leg over one of the throne's arms, leaning diagonally. It gave the impression that he could barely be bothered to right himself enough to rule.

Around him lay all kinds of goods—the rents and tributes due the crown. Eloise thought it crass that Turpy received them in the Throne Room instead of a counting house or warehouse. The items around Turpy had no clear method or reason. Eloise guessed they were simply the day's takings. Sitting on a trestle table were eight bolts of linen dyed royal blue, three bushels of broad beans, a crate of candles, sixteen pairs of shoes with orange sash ties, a basket with "Danger. Handle with Care" lettered on the side, which was filled with raw haggleberries, an open sack spilling out couscous, and several pots of vegetable stock for soup. On another were a block of marble suitable for sculpting, five score rolls of red tape for tying up royal decrees, and a stack of coins piled as high as Turpy's shoulders.

The dozen Throne Room guards stationed themselves along the walls and behind the throne. The show of force was as crass as the display of wealth, and the message was clear—look who has the power now.

The sisters were moved so that they were off the dais, but in front of Turpy.

He stared at them, eyes calculating. "Took you long enough," he said. "I was starting to think I would have to send someone out to arrest you. But here you are. Thanks for organizing the arrest yourselves. Saved me the effort."

"What's wrong with King Doncaster?" demanded Johanna.

"Same thing as my brother," he said. He stood up, wincing as he jostled his hand, and stepped off the dais. Turpy walked idly around the room, casually inspecting the goods stockpiled on the trestles, then walked to Doncaster's bedside, and with a half-kneel, said, "Your Highness." It was hard to tell if this was a genuine expression of respect, or mockery. Turpy raised himself and looked at the fruit platter next to the king's bed. He scrutinized his options, picked up an apple, and took a bite. Chewing, he gave a nod of appreciation, then tossed the rest to the ground. The apple bounced and rolled, stopping when it bumped into Eloise's foot.

Turpy moved to the trestle table. He rubbed the blue cloth between his fingers, seeming unimpressed by the quality. He dipped his finger in a pot of vegetable stock and tasted it, pocketed one of the rolls of red tape, then bit a coin to test it.

Then Turpy walked in front of Johanna, looking her up and down. His eyes were cloaked, the way Eloise remembered them, but there was an intensity that had replaced the insouciance he'd previously shown. She stared into those eyes when he came to stand in front of her. Squinting, he wrinkled his nose like he smelled something putrid, humphed, and turned his back on her as though he couldn't be bothered.

Without warning, he spun fast and hard on the balls of his feet and backhanded her across the face with all his strength.

Johanna gasped.

Eloise's head snapped to the side, and the force of the blow spun her around. Pain shot through her head and specks of blackness floated in her eyes. She'd been clunked in the head on the hockey sacking field more than once, but she'd never been hit before. Not like this. This was deliberate, aggressive, and intentional, designed to humiliate. And it worked. It was instantly devastating. Eloise felt embarrassment mingle with shock and stinging pain. What had she done to deserve that?

She righted herself, and turned to face him, determined not to let him see how rattled she was.

Turpy's arm was already swinging forward again. The slap to the other side of her face spun her in the other direction, its meaty "thwap" echoing off the walls.

"Stop it!" yelled Johanna.

Eloise felt dazed, rattled. Tears formed, snot streamed out, and she pressed the back of her bound hands against one cheek, then the other, trying to figure out how much damage had been done. Was one of her molars loose?

"The first one was for this," Turpy said, holding out the bandage around his hand with the fragmented thumb. He stepped up on the dais, towering over her. "The second was for my brother."

"What do you mean 'your brother'?" said Johanna.

"There's only one difference between His Highness's situation and my brother's. I know whose fault it is that Gouache is like this."

"How dare you blame me," snarled Eloise. "You had him try to kill my sister!"

"Details. And it was fog, not kill."

"I saved your brother, you idiot. Me!" Eloise had never felt fury like this

"What?"

"I rolled him out of the fog. Or did you not bother to stick around and see?"

"I—"

"Have you been in there? Of course not. It's death. Death! Death and bones and nothing else. Your brother was flailing around, dying on a pile of death, and I shoved him up the hill and out."

"Liar. You were the one who knocked him in there. The two of you disappeared. That he got out was a Çalaht-given miracle. Don't try to aggrandize yourself."

"The only reason he has skin on his bones is because of me."

A commotion in the entryway interrupted their argument. A dozen guards entered, led by Second Attending Corporal Bräääd, bringing Jerome and Lorch into the Throne Room. They were gagged and bound like they had been on Fogging Hill, but this time Lorch was tethered to six guards by ropes extending like spokes. Jerome dangled from a rope held by another. They moved to a far spot near Gouache's bed, where the pangolin forced them onto their knees. "Eyes down," he commanded.

Back at the entrance, a larger group of guards brought in Hector and the Nameless One. Both were hobbled, making their gaits awkwardly choppy, and a dozen ropes connected each to the soldiers who restrained them. They moved to the wall opposite Jerome and Lorch, where the guards forced them down onto the flagstone floor. "Bow your heads and show your respect to the regent," demanded the one in charge.

Next came Guild Master Frÿÿÿdenburg, his purple foggers robes swishing. Behind him trailed Fogger Abigail, and two others—large men whose robes did not conceal their huge arm muscles. Each wore a sword, and took a place next to one of the prisoners: Frÿÿÿdenburg by Lorch, Abigail by Jerome, and the others by the horses. At a sign from the Guild Master, they drew their swords and readied to raise. Abigail looked nervous, her sword unsteady above Jerome, sweat forming at her brow. It was one thing to send people into the uncertainty of the Purple Haze. It was another to be pressed into the role of direct executioner and ordered to slice their heads off.

Eloise looked from the prisoners back to Turpy. "What are you doing?"

"Trying to get your full attention. Do I have it?"

"Yes," said Eloise. "You have my attention."

"It could only have ever come to this. I have to be honest," Turpy said. "I expected to control the realms by other means, but our beloved King Doncaster is as incapable as he is arrogant, and he was never good at the long game. He wanted—or more accurately, I helped him understand that he wanted—to rule the Western Lands and All That Really Matters. How hard could that be? Simple, if you are playing the long game. Marry the sister. Fog the heir. Wait. Three simple steps. Eventually, the sister would inherit, and as you're married to the sister, you inherent. Simple." Turpy slouched back onto the throne. "But now all that's ruined. It's ruined because you, Eloise the Meddler, stopped the wedding, and you, the king's betrothed, got lucid and let her. Now the king is a snoring, useless hunk of meat one step away from being a corpse."

"But—" started Eloise.

"Silence. I really have had enough of you." He sat, thinking. "Maybe this is actually better. As regent, I can do on the throne what I've always had to do standing behind it. Much more efficient."

"You have no right to sit there," said Eloise.

"No right?" Turpy coughed a laugh and pointed at Doncaster. "What right did he have? He was born of a woman and a man. They happen to be a particular woman and a particular man, which seems to make a difference somehow. But I, too, was born of a woman and a man. It seems like our beloved king and I are equally qualified."

Eloise again rubbed one cheek then the other with the backs of her hands. The sting of the blows had passed, and her jaw was unbroken, although a molar had definitely loosened. "What is it you want?"

"So, I have your attention, and it appears you have finally asked the right question." He leaned forward and locked eyes with her. "I want the Star of Whatever."

"What?" said Eloise.

"What do you mean 'what'? Did I knock the hearing out of you? I said, I want the Star of Whatever."

"That's crazy. It's dangerous. How do you even know about it?"

"An associate of mine did me the kindness of listening to your conversation at the Splintered Dray. People pay little attention to cockroaches. Sometimes that's useful."

"No," said Eloise. "There is no way you're getting your hands on it." Eloise shifted her body so that the Star of Whatever's box on her hip faced away from Turpy.

"Apparently, I don't have your full attention." Turpy feigned disappointment. He waved at one of the larger guards nearby and pointed at Johanna. "Her." The guard grabbed Johanna from behind, lifted her up, and carried her kicking and squirming across the room. He forced her to kneel next to Jerome.

Guild Master Frÿÿÿdenburg called out, "Öööscar!" The apprentice fogger stepped into the Throne Room, looking even more nervous than Abigail. He wore borrowed guild robes that were much too tight, and, like the others, carried a sword. He took his place next to Johanna, and unsteadily unsheathed his sword, holding it like it was a leprous viper.

Eloise's mind raced. Everyone she truly cared for was mere weak lengths away from death at the hands of blade-wielding executioners. She couldn't let Turpy have the Star of Whatever. It was too powerful. If it could destroy half a realm for two centuries with a single spell, who knew what else it was capable of. His hands were definitely the wrong ones. But that seemed trivial next to the lives of Johanna, Jerome, Lorch, Hector and the Nameless One. At that moment, she would give anything to have them spared.

She looked at Turpy. "You will free them?"

"Yes."

"You will let us all go?"

"Don't do it, El!" called Johanna. "Don't!"

The pangolin grabbed her hair and shoved her head back down. "Quiet!"

"I promised Mother I would bring you home," Eloise told her. "I couldn't live with myself if I had to do that with your head in one sack and your body in another. I'm sorry, Jo, I love you too much." She nodded to the others. "All of you."

There was no real choice. Eloise would give him the Star of Whatever, but not give it unto him, as Melveeta had given it unto her. Maybe that would matter. She wondered if Turpy could discern the difference, or if he had any weak magic affinity at all. "Agreed."

"I thought you might," said Turpy. He stood, set the scepter across the arms of the throne. "Foggers, stand down." Abigail and the others sheathed their swords, each grateful not to have to use them.

Turpy slid over to Eloise. He leaned forward, and whispered, "You're not as stupid as you seem. Where is it?"

"You don't know?"

"Just give it.

Eloise held up her wrists. "You'll need to untie me."

"Certainly not."

Eloise used an elbow to swish her cloak away from her hip, revealing the box tied there.

"You have it here!" Turpy's greedy eyes glimmered.

"What else would I do?" asked Eloise. "Leave it under the pillow at the Splintered Dray?"

Turpy reached for it, but she twisted out of reach. "I'll do it."

Even though she was resigned to this outcome, Eloise could not help but feel anger building inside her. As heir to the throne, she'd been taught to control her emotions, even in the shadow of her habits, because public outbursts were unacceptable. But there it was anyway. It was anger at her powerlessness, and at how easy it had been for him to convince her to hand over this terrible thing. Her anger waxed as she picked at the knotted sash holding the Star of Whatever to her. The feeling gathered and eddied as the knot loosened, and swelled when the box dropped and dangled from the sash she held between her clasped hands. Saying nothing, and certainly without giving it *unto* him, she handed Turpy the most beautiful, most horrible thing she'd ever encountered.

Turvey snatched it away and tested the weight of the dangling box. "I thought it might be heavier." He seemed genuinely disappointed. He turned his back to her. "Stupid bitch," he muttered.

"What did you say?" Eloise wasn't sure she'd heard him right. She'd just given him what he wanted, and he'd called her a name?

Then Turpy stopped and looked around, as if something had slipped his mind. He glanced at the prisoners and foggers. "Oh, right. Proceed." Then he went back to looking at the box, holding it up to examine the clasp.

The foggers unsheathed their swords again, and chaos erupted. Lorch, who had been still and silent until then, somehow pulled the gag from his mouth and cried, "Princess, run!" He began bucking and jerking against his ropes, trying to escape. His six guards, caught unawares, yelled as hemp slipped through their grips, giving each a rope burn. One even dropped his line, and rushed to catch it back, the five others struggling to keep Lorch in check.

Hector and the Nameless One saw what Lorch was doing and, as if on cue, also heaved against their restraints. Their guards, however, had seen Lorch, and were ready. Hector tried standing, but it was near impossible—both the hobble and the ropes restricted his movement. The Nameless One, however, flung himself from side to side, rolling, trying to shake off his guards that way. This worked better, and despite his hobble, he managed to stand. Seeing this, Hector changed tactics and also began rolling.

Jerome, limp and passive until Lorch's outburst, gathered himself and jerked free of the one guard holding him. They had not bothered tying his feet, so Jerome shot away, running as hard as he could, two lengths of rope trailing behind him like a twisted tail. "Get him!" yelled the pangolin guard giving chase. Guard after guard lunged after him as Jerome circumnavigated the room. By the second time around, all the guards who were not struggling to contain Hector, Lorch or the Nameless One were after him. A cacophony of jangling armor and weapons pursued him from all directions, trying to hem him in.

Eloise was only vaguely aware of the commotion. She was still stunned by Turpy's "stupid bitch" comment, her welling anger boiling over. How dare he! She'd saved his brother, even though she thought the lout had just killed her sister, spent every weak weight of energy she had to find the Star of Whatever, disarmed a spell that had eaten half a realm, almost died coming back, then negotiated with him in good faith for the lives of her friends. But she was a stupid bitch?

She looked down, cheeks burning, mind raging, and saw the apple at her feet. He'd wasted a perfectly good apple after a single bite. Well, he could have it back. Without thinking any further, she bent down and picked it up between her bound hands. Drawing on every bit of weak magic she had, Eloise spun herself into her hammer thrower's circles. Long hours of practice made the complicated heel and toe foot movements perfect, despite the long time away from the Flinging Field. Once, twice, thrice she wheeled, her arms straight in front of her, imagining the trajectory the apple would need to take. On the fifth and last turn, she let it fly with the same grunt of effort she used when throwing a 7 1/4-weight hammer. The apple shot from her hands, compelled by her will, her anger, and her weak magic, and headed for the noggin of her nemesis.

❧ 49 ☙

RETURN OF THE MAID OF
HONOR

At the moment Eloise let loose the apple, Jerome found himself cornered on a high windowsill. He'd managed to scuttle up a trestle leg onto a table by a wall and then jump up onto the sill. He flicked the rope so it didn't hang down. Below him, it looked like an entire phalanx of extremely annoyed guards pressed in, determined to snatch him.

Jerome yanked the vial he wore from around his neck. It was the gift his mother had given him on the day of his Naming Ceremony, and contained the ear hair that Gordon the Noisome had plucked and given to his mother as a token of respect. Jerome gripped the wax-sealed stopper with his teeth and pulled it free, then dropped the open vial into the mass of soldiers and clamped his paws across his snout.

A stench like Çalaht's own halitosis wafted forth, mowing down everyone it reached. The smell was the stench of nightmares, a stink from the pits of depravity, a fetor so vile it deserved its own planet.

Cries of disgust and anguish filled the Throne Room. Swords and pikes clattered to the ground as the smell overcame everyone within five, then ten lengths. Stomach after stomach clenched, then emptied, adding to the evil assault on the nose. Those who could, ran from the hall. Those who couldn't, retched and prayed that Çalaht might take their souls then and there so they wouldn't have to endure such earthly torture.

Those outside the blast radius continued to struggle to hold prisoners, but there were a mere handful of people not preoccupied with revisiting their lunches. In a single action, Jerome had disabled the bulk of the palace's muscle.

Eloise, oblivious to the olfactory assault underway across the hall, watched the apple fly toward Turpy. It took less than two seconds to reach its target, smashing into the back of his head and splattering into pieces. An apple would never do much damage, but there was so much anger, weak magic, and sheer force in it that it knocked the jester over. Turpy flew forward, twisted to protect his shattered thumb, and fell sprawling across the edge of one of the trestle tables near the throne. The unattached tabletop flipped up under his weight, sending an arc of couscous, haggleberries and vegetable stock flying across the room.

Öööscar, the apprenticed fogger, looked at Princess Johanna and the guard who held her. His hands shook and his mouth went dry. He would rather have jumped into a volcano than be there among the chaos with a drawn executioner's sword.

Öööscar looked over to Abigail, hoping for guidance, she was lost to the pandemonium around her and didn't seem like she could spare any mentoring at that moment. He saw that Guild Master Frÿÿÿdenburg had his sword raised, but the Westie guard was struggling too much for the Guild Master to take a clean swipe at the prisoner's neck. The two foggers who were supposed to execute the horses lay flat on the ground, looking like something had rolled over them.

Öööscar looked back at Johanna. At least the guard holding the princess seemed able to keep her still enough for Öööscar to do what he was supposed to do. He didn't exactly like the idea, but his place in the Foggers' Guild was tenuous, and there was a lot riding on him doing a good job today. He didn't have anything against the princess. She didn't strike him as someone who needed to have her head cut off, but who was he to judge?

Öööscar sighed, then raised his sword.

❧

Johanna screamed and thrashed, struggling to get loose. "Somebody help me! Please, help! Help!"

Her plea was heard in a completely unexpected place—Gouache's dormant mind. Gouache stopped snoring with a loud, startling snort. Johanna, Öööscar—sword still poised in the air—and the guard all froze and looked at him.

Gouache sat up, blinking furiously. "What—? What's going on?" Then he saw Johanna. "Princess, are you OK?"

"Gouache, stop him! Don't let him hurt me!"

Gouache stood up, legs unsteady from disuse. He took a single wobbly step toward Öööscar. "Are you going to hurt the princess?"

Öööscar shrugged and looked chagrined. "Well, I am supposed to chop off her head."

"Why would you want to do that?" Gouache's expression mixed curiosity and confusion.

Öööscar slowly lowered the sword. "That's a really good question." He paused, thinking for a few moments. Then he turned to the guard and said, "Can you hold this?"

The guard took the sword, still holding Johanna firmly by one arm.

Öööscar pulled off the ill-fitting Foggers' Guild robe, dropped it on the floor, and wandered out of the Throne Room, muttering something about his uncle shoving something somewhere particularly unlikely.

"Thank you, Master Gouache," said Johanna. "Welcome back. As you can see, things are a bit of a mess."

⊛

Eloise was unprepared for the tumult that her apple throw caused. His Jesterness and Affirmed Regent Turpentine Snotearrow McCcoonnch lay sprawled in a mess of couscous, haggleberries and soup. He pushed himself to his hands and knees, shaking his head like he was clearing his ears of water., then looked around like he was missing something.

The Star of Whatever. She had to get it back.

Eloise saw it on the floor several lengths beyond Turpy. She jumped onto the dais, sprinting for it. Turpy must have heard her coming, because he lurched up just as she came near, planting a shoulder into her solar plexus, a perfect hockey sacking defensive girder move. Eloise went flying, bouncing into the pile of coins next to the throne. She wouldn't have picked him for a girder—more of a flutter, and a right flutter at that.

But Eloise, too, had played plenty of hockey sacking, and instinctively rolled like she was avoiding taking a down. She let forward momentum carry her through a full somersault, then landed on her feet, winded from being struck in the guts, but still moving. She reached the Star of Whatever seconds before Turpy, grabbing the sash and dancing out of the jester's reach.

Turpy grimaced, rage twitching his cheeks and eyes. He looked around and saw that Johanna was nearby. The jester stepped off the far end of the dais, snatched the executioner's sword from the guard, and stood where Öööscar had been. He wrapped his left arm around Johanna's forehead, shouldering the guard out of the way, and locked her against his chest. Turpy leaned back to stretch out her neck and positioned the blade a weak length from her jugular. "Silence!" he shouted. His command echoed through the room, and the turmoil subsided as the remaining guards and foggers not preoccupied with tossing their biscuits froze in place.

Turpy pressed the sword into Johanna's neck, hard enough to dimple her skin, but not enough to cut into it. Johanna whimpered, but didn't dare move.

"I will slit her clean through," he whispered, staring straight at Eloise. "I will take her life here and now. Do I make myself clear?"

Eloise nodded, slowly walking toward him.

"Give it back to me."

Eloise stopped. "No."

"No? Do you doubt my threat?"

"No, I'm pretty sure you'd kill her. I'm also pretty clear you'll do it anyway."

"El! Just give it to him!" Johanna's panicked breathing echoed across the room.

Eloise ignored her sister, but resumed walking slowly toward Turpy, dangling the Star of Whatever's box like she was enticing a kitten with yarn. "You lied before. Why should I believe you now?"

Turpy shook his head and added just enough pressure that a single drop of Johanna's blood dripped across the blade. "Last chance."

Eloise's manner was all bravado. She knew nothing was worth losing Johanna. Maybe she could try to hit him with the box, but if she knocked him backwards or sideways, the blade would certainly go with him and through Johanna's throat. If she didn't comply, she was certain he'd kill her sister. If she let him have it, well, maybe he wouldn't. "Move your blade away. I'll give it to you."

"Hand it to the guard."

Without another word, and keeping her eyes locked on Turpy, she handed over the box. The guard took it.

"Bring it to me," Turpy said.

The guard cautiously stepped toward Turpy.

"Tie it around me."

The guard's brow furrowed, but he stepped behind the jester.

Suddenly, Eloise saw Gouache there, stepping between the guard and his brother and taking the Star of Whatever from the guard. Gouache? When had he woken up? Last she saw, he was an inert, snoring blob.

Eloise assumed that he wanted to be the one to tie on the Star of Whatever. Maybe Gouache didn't trust the guard.

But something wasn't right. At first, Gouache looked like he was reaching around Turpy's waist with his left hand to position the sash. But that wasn't it at all. Slowly, unobtrusively, Gouache's right hand wrapped around Turpy's right wrist, preventing him from moving the sword, and his left arm hugged his brother in restraint.

"What? What are you doing?" Turpy turned his head and saw Gouache. "You! You're awake! When did you wake up?" Then he realized Gouache was restraining him. "What are you doing?" Turpy still had Johanna by the forehead, and the sword remained pressed against her throat, but there was no way he could break Gouache's grip, or move the blade even a weak length. "Let me go, you idiot! Let me go!"

"I don't want you to hurt the princess," said Gouache. "Let go of her."

Turpy gripped Johanna tighter and tried to kick free of his brother. Gouache, three times Turpy's size, ignored the stomps and flailing, silencing them by gently but inexorably increasing the pressure of his grip around both waist and wrist.

"You fool," Turpy cried. "You utter imbecile. Stop!" Turpy struggled as long as he could, but the pain in his wrist was too much. Face red, tears welling, he flailed to get free. When the first, then the second, carpal bones broke free of their tendons and cracked, Turpy screamed and released the executioner's sword. Metal clanked onto the flagstone. "You ruin everything! You always ruin everything! You always have and you always will!"

Johanna shoved Turpy's arm up off her forehead and dashed out of reach.

Turpy went limp, still caught in the vice of his brother's hug. "Why? Why didn't you do what I said?"

"I think what you did was wrong. She was nice to me," said Gouache. "You shouldn't have told me to throw her into the fog. I didn't want to hurt her, and you made me. I don't want you to hurt the princess anymore. She was going to let me be her maid of honor."

"There's no wedding!"

"That doesn't matter. I was going to be her maid of honor."

❧ 50 ❧

THE SALIENT PROPERTY OF RAW HAGGLEBERRIES

An awkward murmur fell over the Throne Room.

Eloise stepped toward Gouache, saying, "Keep holding him, please." She slid the executioner's sword away from the jester with her foot, positioned the handle between her ankles, and carefully sliced though the ropes binding her wrists. Not looking at Turpy, she moved behind him to retrieve the Star of Whatever. Eloise picked it up, sent it a mental "Hello, again," and retied it to her hip. Then she looked at the guard who had held Johanna, and pointed to Turpy. "Could you please restrain him? And perhaps call a healer to look at his wrist."

"Yes, mistress. I mean, yes, Princess."

"And get the sick ones seen to."

"Yes, Princess."

Still holding his nose, and with the stopper in his teeth, Jerome jumped down from the windowsill and found the glass vial. He made sure that Gordon the Noisome's ear hair was still in it and shoved the stopper back in. Around him, the dry heaves of guards were the loudest sounds in the room.

Lorch, Hector, and the Nameless One had all stopped struggling when Turpy silenced the room with his threats to Johanna. Neither prisoners nor jailers were sure what to do, so they all stood where they were, ropes limp, waiting for an order from someone in charge or for something to resolve.

Guild Master Frÿÿÿdenburg, Abigail Splintfinger, and the two remaining foggers awkwardly sheathed their swords. Their guild and its role in the realm remained uncertain, but at least they would not have to shed blood today. For that, Abigail was grateful.

It was Johanna who noticed that something was missing. "Shush, shush, shush," she said. "Shush, everyone!"

The hushed rustling around the room stopped, replaced by the silence of anticipation.

"King Doncaster isn't snoring anymore." Johanna ran to his bed. "Uncle D?"

Eloise went to the other side of the bed. Jerome and Lorch, still hobbled by ropes, moved to join them.

Doncaster lay on his bed, covered in couscous, splashed with vegetable stock, and his face and head adorned with haggleberries. His body had lost its gape-mouthed, slack flaccidness. Instead, his teeth clenched, his wide eyes oscillated, and he jigged with tremors.

"No!" cried Johanna. "No, no, no!"

Eloise reached past to push aside the mess, but Johanna shouted at her. "Don't touch the haggleberries! They're raw. That means they're full strength."

Eloise pulled back, unsure how to help. "What can I—" She grabbed the edge of her travel cloak and used it to wipe at Doncaster's face, careful not to let her skin touch the berries. Johanna ripped a pillow case from a pillow and did the same.

The intensity of Doncaster's shaking increased, and the twins stepped back. His rigid spine arched, pushing his torso upward. His neck stretched back, shoving his head back into the pillows. The stretching forced his mouth open. It was full of haggleberries. They dribbled out, a foamy ooze of berry juice, spit, and blood. An involuntary, guttural "Huuhuuhuuhuuh" forced its way from his throat, a ululating, haunting clamor for death to come claim him.

King Doncaster Worsted Halva de Chëëëkflïïïnt jerked wildly in his death dance, still arched up from the bed. His arms flailed, but Johanna managed to catch a hand and fold hers around it. Eloise grabbed the other. She had done this for Melveeta, so she knew she could do it for Doncaster. And this was her uncle, even if she'd never gotten along with him, even if he'd kidnapped her sister, even if he'd been complicit in what had happened in ways she didn't quite understand. Eloise pushed all those thoughts aside as she held his hand, trying to lend comfort.

"It's OK, Uncle D. It's OK," Johanna whispered. "Let it go. Let go. You're done now. Let go."

And then he was. There was a further arching of his back and neck, a final "Huuuuuuuuuuhhhhhh," this one sounding somehow of resignation, and a last, violent spasm.

And then stillness. The only sound was the whisper of air as the king's body eased back to rest on the mattress, forcing the remnants from his lungs.

"May you stand with Çalaht, Uncle D," whispered Johanna. She patted his hand and let it go, placing his arm across his chest so his hand lay over his now-still heart.

Eloise placed the hand she held on his other hand. "Yes, King Doncaster," she said. "May you stand at Her side."

Johanna stepped back and dropped to one knee. Eloise followed her lead. "The king is dead," Johanna said, loud enough that all could hear, her voice filled with genuine sadness.

Lorch and Jerome took a knee in respect. So did everyone else in the hall.

Everyone except Turpy, who lay on the flagstone floor, gagged and trussed up with ropes, cradling his broken wrist in his bandaged hand. His eyes radiated hatred.

<h2 style="text-align:center">❦ 51 ❦</h2>

<h1 style="text-align:center">OFFER OF BLOOD</h1>

The rest of the night and most of the next day went by in a blur. Neither Eloise nor Johanna had been anywhere near the death of a monarch before. There were obvious things to think about, like funeral arrangements for Doncaster, the declaration of a period of mourning, and the dispatch of notices to the other Courts. There were also less obvious things to work out, like how long it would be until Eloise and Johanna could travel home, how to keep the castle running in the face of disruption, what to do with Turpy and, broadly, who got to decide what and when in the face of the empty throne.

There was definitely a power vacuum, and it wouldn't be long before someone rushed to fill it. The business of succession would be tricky, since the king had left no direct heirs. The most obvious candidate would be Chafed, the dead king's younger brother, except he'd all but walked away from his claim to the throne when he took Queen Eloise's hand and name as a Gumball. Whether that would hold up to scrutiny was unclear. It would all be messy, and the whisper of negotiation and jockeying at the Half Kingdom's Court seemed to begin mere moments after Doncaster's body had exhaled its final breath.

Eloise found it all tedious and exhausting. She barely had time to process the facts in front of her, let alone the emotions she was feeling, and even less time for sleep, which she desperately craved. Several times, she found herself jerking awake, having dozed off during a discussion of what the *Livre de Protocol* said about funerals, regal or otherwise, or having nodded off during a meeting of guild heads. But there was duty to be done, and being close kin, the twins were treated with deference and included in the goings-on. Who they were was relevant, after all, and Eloise found people trying to be very, very, very nice to her. She just had trouble figuring out how she fit into it all. She really, really, just wanted to get a good night's sleep and start heading home.

That wasn't going to happen.

Johanna, on the other hand, quietly inserted herself into the middle of everything. First Advisor Kёёёvёёёn Läääctööösёёё Frühstück—decent, competent, and unambitious—guided the first hours of decisions and planning. He soon recognized that Johanna's knowledge of Protocol was profound, and began deferring to her expertise in matters where Protocol shaped a discussion or influenced a sequence of events. By lunch time the next day, the two of them had become an informal, interim steering committee.

It was not until the next afternoon that Eloise managed to extract herself long enough to go and find Jerome, Lorch, Hector and the Nameless One.

She found them in a side courtyard arguing about transportation.

"I'm telling you, I don't mind pulling a carriage," said Hector. "Normally, no. I find them restrictive. But I'll do it if the princess is within."

"It's inefficient," said Lorch. "Compared to a cart, or even a travois—"

"A travois? Am I a Central Ranges savage? Should I get some tattoos while I'm at it? Maybe they have an old chariot lying around somewhere."

Lorch ignored that. "With a carriage, you'll be hauling weight that serves no purpose. It would just slow us down."

"It serves the purpose of comfort," said Jerome. "Surely there's value in that."

"Are you referring to the princess's comfort, or your own?" asked Lorch.

"Winter is almost on us. Comfort equates to safety."

"G'mid-morning," Eloise interrupted. "If it's all the same, I don't want to ride in a carriage."

"Princess!" said Lorch and Hector.

"El!" Jerome launched himself at her thigh in a very unchampionlike way. He broke into sobs, which made it hard to understand him, but eventually Eloise worked out that what he was gasping through the sobs was, "I'm sorry. I'm sorry. I'm sorry."

It wasn't the reception she'd expected.

Eloise patted the chipmunk's back. "Hey. Hey, there." She looked to Lorch for an explanation, but the guard shook his head, also baffled. "Hey, Jerrific. It's OK. What do you have to be sorry about?"

It took a full five minutes for Jerome to compose himself enough, then he slid off her leg, took two steps back, wiped his eyes, and knelt in front of her. "I have failed you, Princess Eloise Hydra Gumball III. I failed to protect you. I failed to stay by your side or in your stead. I failed to defend your honor. I failed to lift burdens from your shoulders. I failed to keep you safe. I have failed as your champion." He put down his other knee and put his forehead to the ground. "I, Jerome Abernatheen de Chipmunk do hereby formally offer to stand down from the role of champion, and free you to pick another. And I beg your forgiveness."

"Oh, Jerome, don't be so dramatic."

He didn't move. Neither did Lorch nor the horses.

"You're not being serious?" He still didn't move. "You are being serious."

Lorch moved to kneel next to Jerome. He, too, put his forehead to the ground. "I, Lorch Lacksneck of Lower Glenth, have also failed you, Princess Eloise. I ask your forgiveness."

"That's enough, you two."

As one, Hector and the Nameless One also bent to the ground. As horses, they could not kneel so well, so they sat, stretched their front legs forward, and placed their foreheads as low between them as they could—their posture of supplication. "We, Hector de Pferd and the one known as the Nameless One also ask forgiveness for having failed you."

"Fine. This is giving me the pip, but fine." Eloise straightened herself into a formal posture, and raised her right hand so her palm faced them. "I, Eloise Hydra Gumball III, Future Ruler and Heir to the Western Lands and All That Really Matters, do hereby acknowledge these offers of supplication and requests for forgiveness. It is my opinion that these are inappropriate requests, for I do not accept that anything has been done that requires forgiveness, nor do I accept that any of you have failed me in any way, with the possible exception of certain persons sometimes humming 'Three Bags of Groats for My Sweetheart' to the point that one might want to address said person with a blunt instrument. Having said that, I formally thank you for these requests. I reject all notions of you standing down from your roles and ask that you please continue serving me in the same stellar manner you have until now. I also offer heartfelt and fulsome forgiveness on all matters and covering all concerns, except the aforementioned humming."

"Thank you, Princess Eloise," they all said.

"Please arise."

The four of them stood. Their smiles reflected a sense of atonement received and mild amusement. Good. She'd hit the right tone. Her turn.

Eloise bent down on both knees and put her forehead on the ground. "I, Eloise Hydra Gumball III, have failed you. I ask your forgiveness."

The others were scandalized.

"Princess Eloise, please," said Lorch. "This is inappropriate. You are a royal."

She didn't move.

"Come on, El. This is inappropriate, period. You didn't do anything."

She stayed where she was.

Hector caught the eyes of the others, who nodded. He could not put a palm forward, but stood straight. "I, Hector de Pferd of the Horse Guards of Castle de Brague, speaking on behalf of the four of us, do hereby acknowledge your offer of supplication and request for forgiveness. It is our opinion that asking our forgiveness does not befit your station, nor have you asked anything of us that requires forgiveness, or that we did not willingly do, or would do again. Having said that, we formally thank you for this request, and offer our complete forgiveness on all matters and covering all concerns."

"Thank you," said Eloise.

When she didn't stand up, Jerome added, "Please arise."

She stood, and said, "So, if we're going all formal like this, then there's one other thing." She reached into a pocket in her cloak and pulled out the small knife she'd most recently used to hack off her hair. "I offer you my blood," she said, and sliced a shallow cut across her palm.

The others gasped.

"Princess, no," said Lorch. "Please don't do this."

"You won't accept?"

"I did not say that, Princess. I do not require an offer of blood to want to continue to serve. And I am uncomfortable with the obligation that puts on you toward me."

"I don't care."

"I have to agree with Lorch, Princess," said Hector. "I serve you will-ingly. An offer of blood would obligate you to make decisions that might not be in your best interest or those of the kingdom, favoring me instead. It might force you to render aid to me, no matter the other factors or consequences you face."

"I'm making an offer of blood, and you're discussing circumstances with me? What are you, a bibliotecarian? A philosopher?" Eloise waved her cut hand in a circle, encompassing the others, as well as the world around them. "What about the circumstances that have brought us here, to where we stand right now? I say, an offer of blood and the obligations of aid and favor it imposes are completely appropriate."

"They're right, El," said Jerome. "It might put you in difficult circum-stances in the future. Who knows what you might have to do or not do because of a blood offer. As queen—and you *will* be queen one day—it's wrong for you to be bound to people like us in that way."

"'People like you?' 'People like you?' Really?" Eloise extended her hand. "Stuff 'people like you.' I *love* 'people like you.' And I offer you my blood and all the commitment that entails."

"By Çalaht's punctured eardrums, you can be stubborn," said Jerome.

"My blood's dripping on the ground here, guys. Make a decision."

There was a long moment of quiet. Then the Nameless One stepped forward and bowed his head. He whispered so only Eloise could hear him. "I accept."

"Thank you." She dipped a finger in her blood and put a dot on his forehead between his eyes. "With this blood I am bound." They bowed to each other, and the Nameless One stepped back.

Hector was next, then Jerome. Each said, "I accept," and received a dot of blood on the forehead and her promise to be bound.

Lorch was last. Eloise could tell it went deeply against the grain for him. His obligation, and the obligation of his family for generations, flowed toward the Gumball line. To have flow in the other direction felt wrong to him. But to refuse also seemed wrong. "I am honored, Princess Eloise. I, too, accept the offer of blood."

She daubed his head and made her promise.

The five of them stood quietly, acknowledging the seriousness of what they had just entered into.

"Now, can we return to the matter of travel arrangements?" said Eloise, lightening the moment. "I really don't want to ride in a carriage."

"Why not?" asked Jerome. "It's not like you're not entitled to do so. And winter grows with every day."

"I've grown used to riding. I like the exposure to the elements, and I like experiencing the world directly, not through a window." Eloise put a fond hand on Hector's side. "And I like the connection. Plus, there's no way I'm going to spend days and weeks cooped up with him in a carriage. I'm sure Johanna feels the same."

"Him" meant Turpy. Johanna, Eloise, the First Advisor, and everyone who cared to express an opinion (which was everyone at Court and everyone not at Court) all agreed that some form of justice had to be administered. The problem was that that no one in the Half Kingdom had sufficient stature to administer it yet, and wouldn't until the succession issue was resolved, which might take months. That meant months of languishing in the dungeon for Turpy, with no clear judicial path forward. Johanna and Eloise agreed that was cruel, so some other approach had to be found.

Eloise had been the one to suggest that Turpy go back with them, so their mother could administer the queen's justice.

"I still say we tie him to a travois," suggested Lorch.

They settled on a cart. Eloise would ride Hector, and Lorch would ride the Nameless One.

"I'll look into procuring the services of a horse and cart, as well as a horse for Princess Johanna," said Lorch.

52

I THINK I MIGHT

Johanna sat on a padded stool looking at her reflection in the vanity mirror. Eloise brushed out her sister's hair, which looked and felt much better now that it had been washed and nurtured with restorative oils. She separated the white strands into three bunches, ready to plait it, something she hadn't done since before the Thorning Ceremony, when things had become strained between them.

"Can you do a Southie braid?" asked Johanna. "Or a sand-dweller's plait?"

"Are you making fun of me?"

"It's a fair question. I don't know what hair skills you've picked up."

"You can get Nesther to do that kind of thing for you when you get home. Or Odmilla. Odmilla's clever that way. With me, you're stuck with a standard old three-bunch over and under. I could weave in some ribbon, if you like. That might fancy it up a little."

"Only if you live in the boondocks. No, a simple plait is fine, thanks. The mourner's veil will cover a lot of it."

Johanna picked up a hand mirror so she could look at her hair from different angles without disturbing Eloise's work.

"I'm still a little surprised you volunteered to lead the mourning," said Eloise. "But I guess it makes sense."

"There isn't anything in the *Livre de Protocol* about what to do in this kind of situation, but the commentaries give it a few pages. There are no children or spouses. Father is next of kin, but isn't here, nor could he arrive in a reasonable amount of time. We're kin enough, and frankly, I don't mind the fasting or the rending of cloth. And the long stretches in the castle's devotional house will be respite, really, given everything that's happened. Despite it all, I remember Uncle Doncaster fondly. Mostly fondly. Fondly enough to lead the mourning."

"I think it's generous of you. It wasn't your problem, but you're fixing it, anyway."

"That's kind of you to say."

Eloise picked up a comb and ran it through each of the three bunches a few times to make sure no knots remained. It was nice feeling this comfortable with Johanna again. She hadn't realized how much she'd missed their conversations and confidences, the sense of closeness. She felt like they could actually talk again.

"I killed him, you know."

"Who?"

"Uncle Doncaster."

"Don't be ridiculous."

"How can I face Mother and Father?"

Johanna turned in her seat and looked her. "Really, now."

"Eyes forward." She tugged the hair gently to get her sister to turn back around. "And don't pander. I threw the apple. I lost my temper, drew on my weak magic, and threw the apple. The apple hit Turpy.

Turpy fell onto the table. The tabletop flipped, sending everything flying. The haggleberries landed in his mouth. Uncle Doncaster died. Ergo, I killed King Doncaster."

"That's not how I see it."

"No? How do you see it?"

Johanna met Eloise's gaze in the vanity mirror. "How do I see it? Turpy threatened everyone you loved in the room, putting you in a lose-lose position. Despite your better judgment, you gave him the most terrible object in all the realms to save us. Turns out, he lied about his intentions and negotiated in bad faith. Wackiness ensued."

"I wouldn't call Doncaster's death 'wackiness.'"

"No, sorry. Poor word choice," said Johanna. "But you get what I'm saying."

"I guess."

Johanna picked up a teacup from the vanity and took a careful sip, keeping her head still. Eloise thought it strange they'd been served tea from the same berries that had killed their uncle the day before. Johanna set the cup down again. "I have a question for you."

"Sure. Go ahead."

"When we planted that acorn near Melveeta, you told me to use my weak magic. How did you know to say that?"

Eloise's face flushed crimson. "I'd rather not say."

"Go on. Now you have to."

"Hand me the ribbon so I can tie this off." She took the length of black ribbon and wrapped it tight around the bottom of the braid, tying it in a square knot so it would hold, then finished it with a bow to make it look nice.

"I'm waiting."

"Oh, OK. Several years ago, Jerome and I broke into your garden."

"You what?"

"I'm going to start by saying I'm sorry, and I'm not proud of what we did. I got it in my head you were being horrible to me, and it's possible you actually were. Jerome and I decided we would prank you somehow. We picked the lock of the wrought-iron gate and snuck in with the intention of mischief. Your garden, by the way, is beautiful. Even back then, I could see that."

"What does that have to do with weak magic? I might just have a green thumb."

"Your notes. I read your notes."

"What? Those are private!"

"I'm really sorry. I thought it might be a diary, and that I might find out something embarrassing. When I saw the scrolls hidden away like that, I couldn't help myself."

"Did Jerome read them as well?"

"Gosh, no. I swear on Çalaht's blessed nose hairs he didn't even peek over my shoulder. Just me. I admit, I told him a little of what I found there. Your little experiment with pukeweed. Pretty clever, the way you worked out a test to see if you have weak magic. It gave me confidence to think about trying some tests myself. You have no idea how many things I've thrown at the back of your head. Secretly, of course. And all in the name of experimentation."

"Do you think Mother and Father know?"

"I don't know. I've never spoken to them about it—neither yours nor mine."

Eloise picked up a mourner's veil and placed it on Johanna's head. Once upon a time, mourner's veils fully hid the face and gave a measure of privacy. These days, they were symbolic, and subject to fashion. This one was delicately woven lace that came down to just below the eyes. It had been procured by the First Advisor's wife, and its stark black was a striking contrast to Johanna's white hair. "There," said Eloise. "Suitably funereal."

Johanna set down the hand mirror and swiveled on the stool. "Thank you for doing my hair. You've done a lovely job. Maybe in a year or two, I'll be able to return the favor."

Eloise ran her hand over the white stubble, which wouldn't need brushing for months. "I look forward to it. Although, I have to admit, this is a lot easier to take care of."

"I bet it is." Johanna patted the seat of a nearby chair. "Sit down, El. I have to tell you something."

"Oh?" Eloise pulled the chair around in front of Johanna and sat.

Johanna reached out and took Eloise's hand. "I think I might stay."

"What? What do you mean?"

"I mean, I'm not going to go home."

Eloise pulled back her hand. "You can't be serious. You have to come back with me. I promised Mother I would bring you home. I'm going to bring you home."

"What you promised Mother is not my problem. El, think about it. If I go home, I go back to being second born, the half-eaten crumpet on the high tea setting of Court life. You have to to go back. You have to continue getting ready to someday take over Mother's place. You have a full and interesting life ahead of you. What do I have to look forward to? Getting flogged off—if not auctioned off—to a noble somewhere."

"No, that's not true."

"Of course it is. But look at what's going on here. Uncle Doncaster's death leaves a political vacuum. Someone has to stabilize the realm. They're going to need a monarch. I reckon I'm not a bad candidate."

"That's absurd."

"How very kind of you."

Eloise stood and paced. "I don't mean you wouldn't be a good queen. I mean there's a whole court here, and Protocol and mechanisms for deciding this sort of thing."

"I know all that. I do know a thing or two about Protocol. And it may not always look like it, but I do know how to deal with Court. But there's more to it than that." Johanna reached out for Eloise's hand again. "El, this realm, this land, needs healing. It needs pride. It needs plants to thrive and people to care again. We don't know what will happen inside the Purple Haze. But you and I know that you broke the spell that kept it in place. People will start going in there now. That land needs healing, and I can help with that. It's what I was born to do."

"We need you at home." Eloise felt tears filling her eyes. Darn it, she was about to cry again. This really was becoming a habit. But she and her sister felt like sisters again. Twins again. She didn't want to go home and leave that behind.

"I don't know if there's a case for making me queen or not. But someone has to sit on that throne. And even if I do it just for a little while to help right the listing ship that is the Half Kingdom, then, well, that's something. The rest can take care of itself."

It made sense. Johanna always made sense.

Eloise stood and drew Johanna up. Then she gave her twin a Western Lands kiss—right cheek, left cheek, forehead. "'Queen Johanna.' It has a nice ring to it."

A knock on the door interrupted them, and Gouache looked in. "Princess, excuse me. The funeral procession is ready for you." He pronounced the words deliberately, like he'd practiced them.

"Thank you, Gouache." Johanna gave Eloise's hand a final squeeze. "Shall we?"

Eloise followed her from the room, and as she watched her sister's white hair bob along in front of her, she suddenly realized that Seer Maybelle's prophecy had been right. Sort of. Johanna did look old before her time. She would sit with an empty throne next to her. But, as always, there was another way to look at the prognostication. Johanna was happy to be here, helping guide a land emerging from centuries of sleep.

It suited her.

53

LEAVE-TAKING

Eloise stood in the main courtyard at Castle Blotch rugged up for winter travel, her travel cloak flapping in a chill wind that held the promise of plenty more cold to come. Jerome and Hector waited a few lengths to her right, and beyond them, Lorch and the Nameless One. They were packed and ready to go.

To the far right, Kïïït stood tall, proud, and harnessed to a cart that held supplies and a shackled prisoner who had been also roped, gagged, shoved into a bag to minimize movement, and then tucked under blankets so he wouldn't freeze to death.

Eloise smiled at the memory of the scullery mare's "job interview." Hector asked her if she knew anyone who might help them out with some cart pulling to get Turpy to Castle de Brague. "Oh!" said Kïïït. "I would be so perfect for going with you to the Western Lands and All That Really Matters. I've never been more than five strong lengths from Stained Rock really—I've lived here all my life—but I would love to see a bit of the world, and the thought of going with you and Sweetie Pie, being two such wonderful gentlemen, and the princess and the chipmunk sounds so exciting, and I don't mind pulling a cart— I'm strong and I'm used to pulling carts since I have to do it for Cook, and I'm sure Cook would let me be away for a few days since His Highness King Doncaster no longer needs attending, which I'm sorry to say but it is the truth, and His Jesterness Master Turpentine isn't very heavy, maybe four sacks of potatoes worth, so I wouldn't have any problem pulling him along with supplies and maybe some souvenirs you might like to take home with you. I have a cousin I could visit while I'm there in the Western Lands. and I'll be very quiet when we're traveling, you'll hardly know I'm there and I can come home on my own, there's no need to worry about that either because I'll just trot all the way home and be back before anyone even notices..."

It went on like that for a full ten minutes. Ultimately, Eloise chose her because she liked and trusted her, and Hector, the Nameless One, and Jerome had all nodded silent assent during the mare's excited verbal onslaught. Plus, all they were doing was the two-ish week trek down the main road to the Adequate Wall and then on to home, staying at inns along the way. No big deal.

Johanna and First Advisor Këëëvëëën Läääctööösëëë Frühstück emerged from the front door to give them a formal farewell. The First Advisor said a few quick words, then stood back to let Johanna say goodbye. She had a small private word with each of them. Kïïït did an awkward horse curtsy at whatever she said, the Nameless One nodded, Lorch touched his hand to his heart, Hector smiled, and Jerome blushed.

Johanna walked over to Eloise and took her hands. "So, here we are."

"Yes. Here we are."

"It's odd doing a leave taking without Mother and Father around to lead it."

"Yes. Like something's missing."

"I know I gave you a note for them, but you'll explain for me? They'll get it if it comes from you."

"I'm sure they'll have plenty to say about it all. Everyone will. Such is Court."

"Yes, such is Court. Are you going to be OK traveling with that thing?" Johanna pointed to the bump that the Star of Whatever made under Eloise's cloak.

"I'm going to have to be. I'm sure we'll be fine. Mother will know what to do with it, or at least will know who I should ask. There'll be scrolls in the Bibliotheca de Records and Regrets, or something. I'll let you know what I find."

"I'd like that."

They stood holding hands for a few more moments.

"Well. That's it, then," said Johanna.

"Yes, that's it."

"Boring travels to you, El." Johanna gave her a Western Lands kiss.

"Thank you." Eloise returned the Western Lands kiss, then gave her twin a hug. "I'm sure they will be."

EPILOGUE

T hey weren't.

Thank you for reading *The Star of Whatever*!

Next up is *The Light Bearer*. You'll definitely want to find out what happens to Eloise now that she's heading home without her sister and with the felon jester, Turpy. She's far from home, and her story is far from over.

※

Want to read more about Eloise and Jerome? Six months before the start of *The Purple Haze*, they
played hooky from Court and headed out for a stolen adventure. It goes well. And then it really doesn't.
Claim your copy of The Wombanditos today to find out what happened!

※

And if you're wondering just what exactly happened at their Thorning Ceremony that caused Eloise and Johanna to go from being as close as twins can be to as estranged, then you'll definitely want to check out the standalone prequel novel, *The Thorning Ceremony*. I promise you, you'll never guess what caused the rift.

THANK YOU

Thank you for reading *The Star of Whatever*. Reviews are crucial for helping other readers discover new books to enjoy. If you want to share your love for Eloise, Jerome, and all the gang, please leave a review. I'd appreciate it.

Recommending my work to others is also a huge help. Feel free to give this book and the whole series a shout-out in your favourite book recommendation group to spread the word.

This clown must face the penalty for his murderous treason. Except he always seems to be two giant steps ahead of them...

The Light Bearer is the wickedly witty third book in The Western Lands and All That Really Matters humorous fantasy series. If you like endearing casts, dastardly villains, and pun-filled wordplay, then you'll love this ripping yarn. (Get it using the QR code below.)